PRAISE FOR NAIMA SIMONE

"Passion, heat, and deep emotion—Naima Simone is a gem!"

—Maisey Yates, *New York Times* bestselling author

"Simone balances crackling, electric love scenes with exquisitely rendered characters."

—*Entertainment Weekly*

heated

The Sweetest Taboo

Sin and Ink
Passion and Ink

Blackout Billionaires

The Billionaire's Bargain
Black Tie Billionaire
Blame It on the Billionaire
Ruthless Pride
Trust Fund Fiancé

Billionaires of Boston

Vows in Name Only
Secrets of a One Night Stand
The Perfect Fake Date
The Black Sheep Bargain
Back in the Texan's Bed
Broody Brit

Rose Bend

Slow Dance at Rose Bend
The Road to Rose Bend
A Kiss to Remember
Christmas in Rose Bend
The Love List
With Love from Rose Bend

Fairy Tales Unleashed

heated

BURNED Inc.

NAIMA SIMONE

 Montlake

Published by Montlake, Seattle

www.apub.com

Amazon, the Amazon logo, and Montlake are trademarks of Amazon.com, Inc., or its affiliates.

ISBN-13: 9781542038294
ISBN-10: 1542038294

Cover design by Elizabeth Turner Stokes
Cover image © Michelle Lancaster, @lanefotograf

Printed in the United States of America

To Gary. 143.
To Connie Marie Butts. I will miss you forever and will love you even longer.

CHAPTER ONE

ZORA

"Well, aren't you the brave soul today."

I glance up from my study of the ad layout for my company's latest planned social media blitz to look at my brother. As usual my older twin by two minutes is impeccably dressed in one of his gorgeous, immaculate three-piece suits. I don't know. Tom Ford, maybe? Honestly? I can't tell a Tom Ford from a Tim Gunn, but Leviticus—Levi, for short—Nelson makes it work.

Oooh. See what I did there?

"I'm brave every day. I work with family, don't I?" I switch my attention back to my monitor.

Hmm. The colors are vivid and eye catching, but the image of the couple standing back to back, arms crossed, doesn't exactly fit the brand and mission statement of our company.

Yes, Breaking Up, Reversing Nuptials & Evading Disasters—BURNED Inc., for short—is a full-service breakup company, but we're all about aiding people in a hopefully peaceful, drama-free termination of their relationships. Whether it's with a text or video. Or a quiet dinner. Or even a singing telegram—yes, a singing telegram. We've done it all. Don't judge. At BURNED, we're about what the client needs, and we want to prevent them ending up in a relationship that resembles the Battle of Antietam.

Look. I might not recognize a Tom Ford suit, but when you have a high school social studies teacher who's obsessed with the Civil War for a mother, you tend to pick up a few facts. Such as the Anaconda Plan, Mary Lincoln was a swindler, the North got its ass kicked at Bull Run, and Abraham Lincoln was *not* a vampire hunter.

And when you have a Civil War–obsessed social studies teacher mother and a Bible-thumping sports-apparel-store-owner father who spent your entire child- and adulthood fighting over everything from the power bill to whether pork is *really* the other white meat, you and your siblings open up your own breakup-service company.

Some might say Levi, Miriam, and I have mommy and daddy issues. And there's probably some truth to that. But if so, we've constructively addressed them by taking the war zone we grew up in and turning it into someone else's Switzerland.

Much more lucrative than therapy.

"Brave or insane," he mutters, sliding his hands into his pants pockets and exposing his pinstripe dark-blue vest and flat abs. I try not to glare at them. But seriously, we're twins. Not even one small belly roll to even things up? So unfair. "Even after three years I'm still trying to figure that one out."

"You're still here." I stop wishing a glazed-donut curse on him long enough to drag my attention back up to meet the long-lashed dark-brown eyes I greet every time I glance into the mirror. "Why? What's this about?" I fall back in my chair and draw a figure eight in the air, encompassing his tall frame. "You never make casual visits."

My brother, God love him, doesn't . . . people. The story goes he came out my mom's vajayjay giving the doctor his ass. And that attitude hasn't changed at all in our thirty years.

I, on the other hand, emerged headfirst, following the birth rules, offering the doc and Mom no trouble. Again, setting the stage for our lifelong roles.

Levi glances over his shoulder, frowning at my closed office door. "I know, and believe me—I don't want to be here. I have more important things waiting on my desk." Ah. My brother, the charmer. How a real, breathing woman let this curmudgeon's penis anywhere near her vagina will forever be a mystery to me. "But on my way to drop off an outgoing package to Deanna, I passed by Dani's cubicle . . . and saw Miriam there."

"Oh shit."

A dark eyebrow climbs halfway up his forehead, and if Levi wasn't the human equivalent of *Star Trek*'s Data, I'd say that one gesture contains a whole lot of smug "I told your ass so." But that can't be so because this is Levi, the emotional mushroom.

"Exactly. Especially since I overheard alarming phrases such as 'Not dirty enough,' 'Start from scratch,' and my personal favorite, 'Money is no object.'"

For the love of . . .

He's the chief financial officer of BURNED and a man who makes ol' tightwad Scrooge look like Jimmy and Rosalynn Carter, so those last four words probably have him breaking out in vicious hives beneath his three-thousand-dollar suit. But hell, I'm not even in need of a late-night visitation by three spirits in order to save my immortal soul like Levi—that situation's not looking too good, by the way—and I'm cringing.

Our younger sister, Miriam, is—in a word—brilliant. And I'm not just casually throwing that word out there. It's true. She graduated from high school at fifteen, entered college at sixteen, and graduated five years later with a BA in graphic design with a double minor in marketing and contemporary women's rights and also a master's in graphic illustration. So yes, brilliant. But what's the saying? There's a fine line between genius and madness? I'm not saying my sister's crazy, but . . . let me put it this way. If the CIA raids our building and uncovers a secret laboratory in the basement where a mastermind has invented a chip for a global hive mind, well . . . I'm not going down for my sister. Natural curls like mine don't fare well in prison.

"It's your day to babysit her," I accuse, stopping just short of jabbing a finger at him. I do narrow my eyes on him, and he'd better thank God, Allah, Buddha, and Zeus 'n' 'em that I don't have heat vision, or he would be an unrecognizable lump right now.

"No." Levi raises an eyebrow. "It's Tuesday. It's *your* day."

"Shit." It *is* my day.

Again, no verbal "I told your ass so," but the room rings with it like the Ebenezer First Baptist Church's choir on Easter Sunday.

"Right now, Miriam's with our marketing department, single-handedly dismembering our ad campaign so it looks less 'How can we be of service to you at this vulnerable and difficult period in your life?' and more 'Reverse cowgirl is my favorite hashtag on Pornhub.'"

"One." I pop up a finger. "Never in life say *reverse cowgirl* or *Pornhub* to me again. Two." I add another finger. "Since Dani is the only marketing personnel we have, technically, I don't think she can be considered a department. And three." Yet another finger. "Why in the world didn't you stop her right then? God knows what havoc she's wreaked in the"—I turn over my wrist, glancing down at my watch—"ten minutes you've been in here lollygagging."

His chin snaps back toward his neck. "Excuse you. I've never *lollygagged* a day in my life." Wow. That's what he took away from all three very valid points. "And like I said, it's *your* day. So I came to you. Handle her."

Another quirk of Levi's. An almost obsessive dedication to schedules, and woe to anyone who dares to try and interfere with his.

God knows I love him. I mean, we shared a womb together for thirty-seven weeks. And despite his reserve that makes the guys on Mount Rushmore look like a group of zany court jesters, he's . . . mine.

But damn, sometimes I just want to set that stick in his ass on fire with diesel fuel and a blowtorch.

"Okay, how about this?" I narrow my eyes on him. "Since I have a client that should be arriving in the next five minutes, and I don't have time to wrestle Miriam to the ground, could you at least talk with Dani and remind her that any changes—marketing or financialwise—must be okayed by me first?"

Levi cocks his head, studying me, as if trying to figure out my angle. Suspicious, that one. Finally, he gives me a sharp nod.

"Yes, I can do that."

"Thanks. 'Preciate it." I swear I try and keep the sarcasm out of my voice. But hell, I'm only human. And it's fifty-fifty whether he catches it anyway. "If you'll—"

A knock reverberates on the door, and a moment later, Deanna Lynn, our office manager, opens it and slants her upper body inside.

"Hi, Levi." She smiles at my brother, and I mentally shake my head at the slight gleam in her eyes as she scans his tall frame. Oh, woman. If *lost cause* had a face. "Hey, Zora," she says, switching her attention to me. "Your eleven o'clock appointment just arrived."

"Great. I'll be right out to meet her. Thanks, Deanna."

"No problem."

She backs out of the office as I rise from my chair, closing out the files and programs I have open, and quickly pull up the intake form we have all new clients fill out before arranging a meeting with them. When someone requests any of our services—whether it's a text or a dinner in a Michelin-starred restaurant—we require an initial appointment. Most of our customers are sincere in their intentions to end their relationships with zero mess or acrimony. But occasionally, we have those—well, let's just call them what they are—assholes who either want to waste our time with ridiculous requests or the bitter ones who seek to humiliate and shame their soon-to-be exes. And that's not what we're here for. Hell, Levi, Miriam, and I lived that bullshit—still do when we can't avoid going home for family dinners or holidays—and

I'll be damned if someone uses my company to intentionally inflict that kind of damage on someone else.

So yes, we require a meeting as a weeding-out process as well as to determine our clients' needs.

Some people might find our company silly or even laughable, but we take what we do seriously. And laugh all they want; in the three years we've been in business, BURNED Inc. has enjoyed growth, and we're firmly in the black. Not many new businesses can claim that. I'm damn proud.

"Okay, you return to your bridge or office or whatever. And don't forget to speak with Dani." I round my desk, striding past him toward my office door.

"I won't. And don't think I didn't catch that reference to the troll under the bridge." He snorts. "You're attempting to insult me, but you're not. Frankly, that troll got a bad rap. That was his damn bridge, and he had a right to eat anyone who tried to tread their happy asses all over his territory. It has stand-your-ground law all over it."

Christ. Some of the shit that comes out of his mouth. Miriam came by her crazy honestly.

"Yeah, Leviticus, I don't think that's how that works. Not to mention *Three Billy Goats Gruff* didn't take place in Colorado, much less the United States, so again. Not sure how that applies."

And yes, I am arguing about a fairy tale with my brother as if it's a legal case study.

After exiting before he can launch his comeback—because there's *always* a comeback with Levi—I move down the corridor toward Deanna's desk and the lobby. Mentally and physically, I shed the roles of sister and peacemaker and assume the mantle of president of a successful Black-owned business.

I'd like to claim that I'm that confident, self-assured, take-no-shit businesswoman twenty-four seven. But as my father would say, "The devil is a lie, and the truth ain't in it." Despite our differences in personalities, I love working with my family. But sometimes the pitfall is being dragged back to feeling like that twelve-year-old girl who would tremble and cradle her stomach against the ache that bloomed there at just the thought of contention or raised voices or arguments. And that twelve-year-old girl has self-esteem the size of a pea. Like the pea that delicate princess slept on. Small as hell.

"You're a queen. And if you don't feel it today, fake the hell out of it until you do."

I smirk as I round the corner that leads into the lobby. If my mother ever retires from teaching, she might have a poetry gig waiting on her.

Shoving my parents and the circus of crazy that was my childhood to the back of my mind, I move forward to where a woman with a shining, thick sheet of long dark-brown hair sits on a tastefully upholstered couch. She flips through one of the magazines we leave fanned out on the cedar coffee table, and from the short distance that separates us, I note the flawless french manicure and flash of gems that circle her wrists and a couple of fingers.

Rich.

If the hair, nails, and jewelry didn't tip me off, the red soles of her glossy pink patent leather pointy-toe pumps would've been a blinking neon-red sign. Louboutin. A classic So Kate with its almost five-inch stiletto heel. One hundred twenty millimeters, to be exact.

I know my shoes.

Remembering the name on the intake file, I curve my lips into my polite yet with-the-perfect-degree-of-warmth smile—and yes, I've practiced it in the mirror.

"Ms. Summers?" I say, pausing next to the end of the couch.

The woman turns her head toward me and stands. All that's missing is the slow-motion panning and a backwash of golden light as she flips her light fall of hair over her shoulder. Because she is *that* beautiful. Only one other woman has made me question my devotion to dick. Now, Valerie Summers can be added to that short list right under Jennifer Lopez.

I'm not a small woman at five feet nine in my bare feet and six feet in my heels. Throw in my full D cups, round hips, and thick thighs, and I'm what a romantic soul would call Rubenesque. Some men—including exes—have called me fat ass or chubby. And they can go fuck themselves, thank you very much.

But my client, catwalk ready in her slim-fitting royal-blue pantsuit, towers over me by several inches. With her flawless features, at least size 4 figure, and excellent taste in shoes, no one would dare call her anything but perfect. If I hadn't fought hard to be comfortable in my own space and body, I might be in the corner right under the black-and-white print of the Rossonian, sucking my thumb and rocking back and forth.

As it is, I *might* be holding in my stomach.

Judge not lest ye be judged, as my dad would say.

Smiling, I extend my hand toward her. "Welcome to BURNED Inc. I'm Zora Nelson, president."

"It's nice to meet you, Ms. Nelson."

She accepts my hand, her palm cool, her grip brief before she loosens it and lowers her arm back to her side. Clasping her matching pink clutch to her waist, she scans the waiting area with an impeccably arched dark brow. Through her gaze, I take in the spacious lobby and the large smoked picture window that offers a view of busy Welton Street. Levi, Miriam, and I chose each piece of furniture and painting together, right down to the magazines and knickknacks that decorate the coffee and end tables.

It's the first impression our clients receive of BURNED, and we wanted it to reflect a place they could have the utmost confidence in. We also wanted it to reflect *us*. The practicality of the tall reading lamps with their energy-saving light bulbs for Levi. The high-back couches and love seat upholstered in a beautiful but chaotic pattern of flowers and stripes with a pine frame, accompanied by matching pine coffee and end tables, are Miriam's fingerprints. This business is truly a family affair. The black-and-white photographic prints of various historical Denver landmarks, especially African American landmarks, are all me. It's truly ours.

Which is why when a faint wrinkle appears above her nose, my chest pinches, and I battle back a frown of my own.

"I was surprised to discover your offices were located in the Five Points neighborhood." Valerie Summers pairs the wrinkle with a small sniff, as if smelling something faintly ripe. "But this is a quaint little place. Especially given the location."

I grit my teeth and physically restrain the barbed comeback clawing its way up my throat. True, Five Points used to be pretty rough, but now it and RiNo are very nice, vibrant, and just cool areas. I barely restrain myself from channeling my mother and checking her about the neighborhood once known as the "Harlem of the West," where jazz greats like Louis Armstrong, Billie Holiday, and Miles Davis played clubs like the Rossonian and the Rainbow Room. Today, the district is a beautiful conglomeration of modern and historic. Museums, hotels, and music venues mix with coffeehouses, craft breweries, restaurants, and art galleries.

Five Points is proud, eclectic, and brimming with my culture.

And I'm five seconds from telling her to watch her mouth.

Client, Zora Neale Nelson. Client.

Right. But don't think for a second I'm not about to upsell her ass.

"Well, thank you. We like it." Smiling, I wave a hand in the direction of the hall. "Why don't you follow me to my office?"

Turning, I catch Deanna's eye, and in a voice that's just a shade too saccharine, she asks, "Should I bring in coffee or tea?"

I hope I'm the only one who catches the unspoken offer of wolfsbane. She's a paranormal romance lover, our Deanna is. And wolves are a particular favorite. Hence, that particular poison.

Just to be on the safe side, I should probably sniff any beverage we give Valerie Summers . . .

"None for me, Deanna, but thank you. Ms. Summers?" I pause and glance over my shoulder at the tall blonde. And silently will her to refuse.

"No, thank you."

Silently, I breathe a sigh of relief. Don't get me wrong. Deanna is a wonderful office manager, is an even better friend, and usually isn't homicidal. But she's just as protective of our business as we are and takes any slight against it personally.

Just another reason I want to warn her against crushing on my twin brother. I'd hate to lose her when she realizes that unlike the Tin Man, Levi has no desire for a heart.

Turning toward the corridor, I lead Valerie toward my office. When we reach it, I enter and gesture toward the large comfortable armchair in front of my desk before rounding it and sinking into my own desk chair.

"Can I be honest, Ms. Nelson?"

Valerie scans my office, taking in the large mahogany curved desk, the small caramel leather sofa tucked against the far wall, and the coffee table in front of it. Her gaze flits over the armoire that functions as a file cabinet as well as my prized Thomas Kinkade paintings. When her scrutiny meets mine once more, the same surprise that lit her blue eyes in the lobby is joined by a narrowed-eye speculation.

"Please do, Ms. Summers," I invite, spreading my hands wide, palms up, in the age-old sign of welcome.

Better be careful what you wish for, a small voice whispers in my head.

That voice is not wrong.

"A friend of mine recommended you."

I nod. "Charlotte Reynolds, if I remember correctly from your intake form."

"Yes. Charlotte and I were college suitemates, and when I confided in her about my . . . situation, she told me how your company helped her end her last relationship without drama or her having to deal with the messy aftermath."

I nod again, a warm glow of pleasure and satisfaction at not just the praise but a job well done blooming behind my sternum.

"That's BURNED's goal, Ms. Summers. To make your breakup as smooth and painless as possible for not just you but the other person as well."

"That's admirable." She once again surveys my office, almost as if expecting a camera crew and the host of *Cheaters* to pop out from behind my bookcase. "But I must admit I had my reservations, and I still do. While Charlotte speaks highly of you, it all seems a little . . . unseemly."

Clasping my hands on top of my desk, I slightly lean forward. This isn't unexpected, and it's not even the first time I've heard these words. Not from clients, not from other businessmen and women, not from my parents. Hell, it's the only thing in recent memory that they've agreed on. But some people find the idea of a company whose sole purpose is to break up with someone on the behalf of their significant other as ludicrous at best, exploitive at worst.

But me, Levi, and Miriam? We see it as Kevorkian-ing a terminal situation—assisting a person in terminating a relationship before it goes from bad to downright nuclear.

It's mercy, not ridiculous.

So while irritation spasms in my belly like a cramp after power walking too hard, I shove it aside. If I had a dollar for every sneer, smirk, or derisive comment aimed toward BURNED, I'd be able to afford weekly deliveries of her Louboutins.

"I understand your concerns. Why don't you tell me your reservations and concerns, and hopefully I can ease them."

"Well, it's really one. At the risk of being blunt, what do you get out of this? How can I trust that footage of this meeting or the actual breakup won't end up on a tabloid or trash gossip website? A person of my . . . social status can never be too careful. Or skeptical, I'm afraid."

"That's a fair question." I tilt my head to the side and pause, letting her know I'm giving her concern consideration. "We are a business, so our reasons aren't completely altruistic. But it's because we are a business that we ensure we protect our clients and provide them the best service possible. Our goal is to facilitate a respectful and civil resolution of a relationship for both partners. Yes, we want to honor our clients' wishes, but we will not humiliate or steal anyone's dignity. That is *not* what we are about. So to answer your question about what we get out of this? The satisfaction of helping two people peacefully go their separate ways so they may find the person they're meant to find happiness with or even joy with themselves. Plus, our not-insubstantial fee, depending on which package you purchase."

I lean back in my chair, meeting her gaze, mine steady, unwavering. "As far as any of our meetings being recorded, we have an ironclad contract that ensures confidentiality and protects your privacy. Like I said, our intention isn't to exploit you or your soon-to-be ex-partner. And if at any time during our meeting you feel uncomfortable, please feel free to end it."

Valerie studies me for several long moments, then slowly dips her chin.

"Okay, Ms. Nelson. You've sold me. Let's talk."

"Wonderful." Leaning forward again, I tap my keyboard and bring up her file. "Now, from the few details you entered on your form, I understand you and your boyfriend have been together for six months. I'm sorry that you're parting ways, by the way."

"Thank you." She sighs. "This isn't an easy decision for me. On paper, we're perfect for each other. Both Ivy League educated, successful, wealthy, and ambitious. We have similar goals as far as where we see ourselves five years from now with our careers, social affiliations, and family."

Sounds more like the perfect applicants for a business partnership, but what do I know? I'm single. By choice.

But hey, maybe if I'd selected my exes on such exacting criteria, I wouldn't have ended up with such raging assholes.

"Still," she continues, "for the last couple of months or so, he's been different. When we first started dating, he courted me. Took me to the finest restaurants, escorted me to gallery openings and galas. We were a supercouple—*the* supercouple. But now, it's all work, work, work with him, and he has no time for me. He's not the same man from six months ago. It's forced me to . . ." She sinks her teeth into her bottom lip and turns her head away. But when she returns her gaze to me, the flint in her blue eyes belies the regret or sorrow of her actions. "It's forced me to seek that attention elsewhere. I've found someone else who gives me what I need. What I deserve. So I need to end this with Cyrus as soon as possible. It's dragged on too long."

I'd like to say I'm surprised that she's cheating—or that she's admitting it to me—but I'm not. People's reasons for breaking up with someone ceased shocking me around the middle of week two after we opened. And more than a few involved finding someone new. Like I'm a counselor or bartender, they tend to spill their relationship woes in this office, and my job isn't to judge.

"Ms. Summers, we're here for you. Tell me what you need from us," I say gently. "On your form, you didn't check which package you preferred. And that's fine. We're also able to customize a bundle for you. Just let me know what I can do to make this easier for you."

She flicks her long sheet of hair over her shoulder, and a small wrinkle appears above the bridge of her nose.

"We were special to one another, so I'd prefer something more personal than a text or a phone call. But I also want him to fully understand why I'm ending our relationship . . ."

"You mentioned your partner is a workaholic, so our dinner package will most likely not be ideal. But we do have what we call our 'Dear John' option. This entails writing a letter to him, and we'll handle locating him, and when he's home, we'll deliver and read it to him."

Valerie looses a small hum, tapping a fingertip against her bottom lip. Finally nodding, she says, "Let's go with that. I'll email a letter to you no later than tomorrow. When can you have this done?"

"Today is Tuesday. If you'll have the letter to me tomorrow along with his schedule, we can arrange for everything to be taken care of no later than Thursday. We'll notify you as soon as our services are complete."

"Thank you." She sighs heavily. "I just want this to be over with so I can start fresh."

"Understood." I smile, hoping it reassures her that she's safe here and in a judgment-free zone. But damn. Inside? I'm wondering, *Who is this guy that she's so desperate to scrape off?* "I'll need his full name and a picture to ensure we approach the correct person."

"Of course." She reaches into her clutch and removes her phone. A moment later, she presses her screen and stands, stretching forward to hand me the cell. "His name is Cyrus Hart. Here's a picture. I can email it to you."

Good. God.

That can't be right.

I asked her for an image of her soon-to-be-ex, so why is she showing me a picture of Apollo in a suit? Maybe she accidentally scrolled to a shot from some Greek-god-retelling movie casting instead of to her boyfriend. She never did tell me her profession. With her flawless features and tall slender figure, it makes sense she would be a model.

Yes, that explains it.

Why relief trickles through me at my conjured justification, I don't know. Can't explain. And don't even try.

"This is Cyrus?" I ask, my voice somehow void of the "What tom-foolery is this?" swirling in my head and chest. But even I catch the waver of hope in my question. The hope that she's mistaken. That she'll glance at her phone's screen, give me a little *my bad* shrug, and then skim to the correct picture.

But no.

Impatience flickers across her face, there and gone before she does tip the phone back toward herself. And as she turns the screen back to me, my paradoxical duet of relief and hope dances off into the dark wings of a stage, gleefully waving their middle fingers at me.

"Yes, this is him," she confirms, the irritation missing from her expression now tinting her voice.

Duly noted. Valerie Summers doesn't appreciate being questioned.

I cling to that information, file it away, and even peer at her for a few additional moments longer than necessary. Even after she arches an eyebrow.

Shit.

I should be embarrassed. Should apologize. But I can't do either. Because this is what desperation does to a woman. Turns her into a grasping-at-straws-and-whatever-else-kindling-happens-to-be-nearby kind of person.

All because I would give up my prized pair of Chloé baroque pearl drop earrings to *not* look at that picture again.

But my brain, as if flooded by dopamine by just that one glance, refuses to acknowledge any sense of self-preservation. The purely prim-itive, pleasure-driven side takes over and orders my eyes to feast, to gorge.

And that's what I do.

I slide my hands to my lap, underneath my desk, and curl my fin-gers into my palms, the short, no-nonsense nails biting into the softer flesh. Deliberately, I trap my breath in my lungs, doling out small flat sips of air that still whistle through my head like whips of wind.

Yet . . . I stare. And stare.

At a face that once upon a time would've been carved into marble and worshipped in a temple. Or pressed into a bronze coin. Or extolled in a tale that would be passed down from generation to generation to become myth.

A high, clean brow that speaks of intelligence and a hint of severity. Thick slashes of eyebrows that hide the shade of his eyes but not the intensity that seems to fairly burn from them. Cheekbones honed to such sharpness that just a mere brush across them would be capable of drawing a thin line of blood. Beneath my desk, I rub my thumb and forefinger together, already feeling the slight burn of that phantom slice.

An arrogant blade of a nose. Lean, sculpted cheeks. An indomitable, chiseled jaw that fairly screams a ruthless strength of will and stubbornness. And . . .

A heated shiver undulates in my belly, attempting to work its way up through my body, but I stifle it. Totally inappropriate for a client to witness me shudder in unacceptable and—*dammit*—untimely lust over her man. True, soon-to-be ex-man. Still . . . unacceptable.

But, God, there's nothing I can do about what the lust is doing below my navel, though. Twisting into something snarled and tangled. Invisible fingers pluck at it, only further knotting the dirty, hot mess.

Because that mouth . . .

To claim it's the only soft feature about his face would be a fallacy. There's nothing soft about those almost too-lush curves. No, that wide mouth carries a dark shade of cruelty around the edges, a twisted hint of sin that abolishes any romantic ideas of tenderness.

And goddamn, if that doesn't turn the screw of need in my belly tighter, harder . . .

Somehow, I tear my way-too-enraptured gaze away from the phone. Wow. It seems I've discovered my new superpower.

He's a beautiful man. So what? Jamie Dornan is too. And if I remember correctly, I experienced the same "Ovaries, thou art loosed" reaction the first time his luscious ladder of abs flashed across Regal's movie screen.

No big deal. A chemical response to a pretty face. That just happens to belong to the man who will soon be dumped by our company.

Reality pours over me colder and faster than any ice-bucket challenge.

This is business. And I have a job to get done. Valerie Summers came to BURNED—to me—for help in ending one phase of her life so she could start another, and that should be my only focus. Not the inner workings of her relationship and definitely not the man in it.

I resist the urge to give my head a good, hard, wake-the-fuck-up-buttercup shake. If anyone knows the pitfalls of becoming besotted by attractive packaging.

"Thank you." I lean back in my chair, away from the phone. Away from that image. "If you'll include the picture with your letter, that would be perfect. We'll confirm the date and time with you first before we proceed. This is to just make sure you haven't decided to go in a different direction or changed your mind about ending the relationship altogether."

"I won't," Valerie says, a vein of steel running through her tone and reflecting in her eyes as she sinks back in her chair.

I nod, but it's happened.

And this is with a couple so beautiful they look as if they fit more perfectly than puzzle pieces.

So no, wouldn't be surprised.

But again, judgment-free zone. And this is business.

Tugging my keyboard toward me, I smile.

"Let's get you broken up, then."

CHAPTER TWO

CYRUS

I'm not a superstitious man.

When I was a kid, if I walked under a ladder, my mom would yell at me using all three of my names—that's when you knew she wasn't playing—and order me to cross in front. As if that somehow canceled out the bad luck. Still, even with an eye roll, I obeyed.

Despite my mother's attempts at indoctrination, though, I've never given in to those old wives' tales. There's no such thing as luck—good or bad. Life is a fuck. And it's your choice whether you lie down and take it up the ass or take control and make it the best goddamn screw possible.

And since my parents' deaths and a transient, hellish childhood, I've become a master fucker.

So no, not a superstitious man.

Yet as I step out of my black Audi A6 into the two-car garage of my Washington Park home, an irritating and persistent itch prickles the back of my neck. Persistent because it's been pestering me all day. Like an omen. If I believed in that.

Still, feeling like an ass, I glance over my shoulder and immediately reach back in, press the garage remote control button on my visor, and watch the door lower.

"Damn. What're you waiting on? Black cats to slide underneath? Mirrors to break?" I growl, opening the back door with a harder-than-necessary yank and removing my briefcase.

Yes, I'm giving myself shit, but hell, I deserve it.

Shaking my head, I enter the house, going through the utility room and into the spacious, open kitchen. I exhale a deep, cleansing breath as I lay my briefcase on the wide island, my shoulders already relaxing, my muscles loosening. As usual, just the sight of the state-of-the-art gas range stove and double oven, custom-made steel hood, glass-front Sub-Zero refrigerator, and beautiful marble countertops and island sends a soothing calm flowing through me like the iced tea my mom used to brew and sweeten every summer. It's not because I can cook—because God knows I can't. Bake, yes. Cook, no.

It's the sense of walking into something that's mine. No, that's not correct. Something that's *ours*. Mine, my mother's, my father's. Even though they're gone—been gone for twenty-one years now—this kitchen with its huge picture windows and view into the corner lot, where she would've planted a gorgeous garden full of flowers and vegetables, would've been her dream. And the glass-encased wine closet connecting the living room and the kitchen would've had my wine-collecting father damn near weeping in joy.

The rest of the house—the five bedrooms and baths, floating staircase, fireplaces, home office, game room, and gym—is all the epitome of luxury and comfort, but it's those two features that sold me on the house. Those two features are like tiny greetings from wherever they are—heaven, beyond the veil, "out there"—welcoming me home. Making this place home.

Yeah, I know how it sounds.

Crazy as fuck.

But it's my crazy, and damn if anyone deserves an explanation. Even Val when she asked why I, a thirty-three-year-old successful attorney with one of the most prestigious law firms in Denver, choose to live in a single-family home rather than a high-rise Riverfront Park condominium with all the amenities.

We've been dating for six months, and if my plans continue on their present trajectory, I'll propose in another six. Still, I can't confide the truth to her. Being a cherished and spoiled daughter from one of Denver's wealthiest and most-connected families, having every need and want supplied, and never going one day wondering if the place she'd woken up that morning would be the same place she'd fall asleep means Val has led a charmed life. No, she couldn't possibly understand my particular brand of neurosis.

Not that it matters since I'm not dating or one day proposing to her for her capacity to empathize. Just the opposite. I originally pursued her because she's the antithesis of who I was and the mirror reflection of who I've scrapped, hustled, and, yeah, even lied to be.

She's my reward.

And yes, I know how sexist and objectifying that sounds.

But it's true.

I earned her. Busted my ass for her. Still am.

With Val by my side, the future I not only imagined but carved out for myself is so close.

Success. Wealth. Respect.

Security.

Glancing at the clock over the range hood, I jerk at my tie, loosening it. Six o'clock. Early for me. Val hasn't called all day. I reach into the inner pocket of my suit jacket, pull out my cell phone, and check the screen for any missed-call notifications.

Nope. Nothing.

It's not like Val usually bombards me with calls throughout the day; we're both very busy people with packed schedules that demand our time and attention. But it's odd that not even one voice mail, text, or notification reminding me about some new restaurant opening or dinner party or benefit is claiming space on my cell.

22

If I'm honest, over the last few weeks, the fewer and fewer calls have become more of the norm instead of the aberration lately . . .

I frown, and a curl of disquiet unfurls inside my chest. Yeah, not superstitious, I remind myself. Even as I rub the heel of my hand to the middle of my sternum, directly over that quietly expanding sense of foreboding that has stalked me all day.

"Bullshit," I mutter, shaking my head and deliberately dropping my hand to the marble island.

Everything is fine. So what if she hasn't called? This is Val. She probably got caught up in one of her charity foundation meetings or lunch with her mother or shopping. Because damn, does the woman love to shop. It's not like our relationship is one where we live in each other's back pockets and keep each other abreast of the other's every move or itinerary.

So why the fuck am I still staring at this phone like I can Houdini her number to flash across the screen?

It's official. I need a drink.

I cross to the refrigerator, jerk open the right-side door, and pull out a beer. Another thing Val sneers at—my plebeian choice in alcohol. As hot of a fuck as she finds me and as acceptable as my career and spendable my money are, I'm still a fixer-upper for her. Doesn't bother me. That's part of the reason I chose her. But no way in hell am I giving up my IPAs.

Just as I twist the cap off, the peal of the doorbell echoes through the house. I pause, narrowing my eyes on the kitchen entrance, that unease ballooning in my chest, clawing up my throat until it coats my tongue like an acrid, thick grime. For a moment, my feet remain glued to the floor, as if they sprouted roots and plowed deep into the hardwood.

My mind drawls that I'm being a damn idiot, to go answer the door. But every primal, self-protective instinct that shielded and warned me when I was a kid roars that I avoid that door at all costs.

But I'm no longer that small, vulnerable, twelve-year-old boy dependent on his instincts and desperation to read the mood of the room to determine whether he would eat that night or if he would need to dodge a smack.

I'm a grown man who relies only on himself—and has for longer than he should've. A man who owns this fucking house and doesn't need to be afraid of anyone or anything in it. Or on the other side of it.

After setting the beer bottle on the island with a sharp rap, I stalk out of the kitchen, down the short hallway that flows into an open, airy expanse of breakfast nook, living room, and dining room. At this moment, the oatmeal, slate grays, forest greens, and wood accents fail to exert their usual soothing effect. Not when every bit of my focus is centered on the front door.

Because a sliver of me still cringes at the thought of approaching the entrance, of my fingers curling around that knob, I charge forward the last few feet like I'm headed to battle instead of just crossing my foyer.

Not bothering to check the small video camera mounted on the wall to my right, I twist the lock and yank the door open.

And stare down at a young Black woman I've never seen before.

I blink, my grip on the door and the doorframe still tight enough to have wood biting into my fingers. It's on the tip of my tongue to tell her I have a **No solicitors** sign—I don't, but now I plan on buying one first thing tomorrow—but the relief pouring through me is so damn thick, so powerful, my throat temporarily closes around the words.

"Mr. Hart?" she asks, and her voice is all wrong.

Even before entering the law field, I was a master at reading people. I had to be in order to navigate my childhood. Discerning moods and personalities determined the difference between remaining in a house a few weeks longer or being shipped off to another aunt. The difference between new school clothes or borrowing your older cousin's shirt and hoping he only busted your lip when he found out instead of delivering a beatdown that made you "think twice about touching his shit."

So yeah, I'm good at reading people. And looking at this woman in her perfectly tailored but conservative blue-and-gray pinstripe pantsuit with matching light-gray stilettoes, I find the smoky contralto, reminiscent of long-ago speakeasies with crooning blues singers, liberally flowing alcohol, and zero inhibitions, doesn't fit.

My gaze drifts upward, scans over thick dark hair with its mass of tight curls that billow around her face and shoulders. It's not unruly or untamed. It's . . . free. Fuck, that hair.

I swallow.

Yeah, her voice matches that hair.

As do her earrings.

I cock my head to the side, studying the incongruity of those large swinging silver-and-red chandelier earrings with the reserve of her clothes.

"Mr. Hart?" she says again, and I jerk my attention from her earrings to meet the dark brown of her eyes.

"Yes."

Wait. The hell? I shake my head. How does she know my name? And what is she doing on my doorstep after six in the evening? Isn't that too late to be out selling magazine subscriptions, vacuums, or whatever the hell people go door to door peddling these days?

Lowering my arms, I shift forward, sliding my hands into my suit pockets, the relief that had streamed through me shutting down, as if someone reached inside me and twisted it off.

"What can I do for you?"

I don't ask her name or ask her to come inside. Something . . . ominous knocks inside my chest that warns me against doing either. That I don't want any part of either. And as she reaches into a dark-red satchel slung over her shoulder, pulls out a sheet of paper, and begins reading, that knocking grows louder.

"Dear Cyrus, for six months you have meant the world to me. When we first met, I believed you were the man I hoped to marry one

day. Handsome, smart, ambitious, driven, a fantastic lover. You're everything I wanted in a man. But now things have changed."

Ice creeps through my veins, and my muscles stiffen with the uttering of each word, each syllable, in that whiskey-and-blues voice.

What in the *fuck* is going on here?

"Over the course of the last couple of months, I've discovered that
while I admire your work ethic, I cannot continue in a relationship
where I am second to a man's job. More and more I find myself alone
when that's not how relationships are supposed to work. I need to feel
loved, admired, valued. I need attention and catering to. I deserve it."

Is this shit really happening?

I blink slow. Blink again.

But no. The stranger with the gorgeous hair and boring pantsuit is
still standing on my doorstep breaking up with me via a goddamn Dear
John letter from my girlfriend.

I should scrape together the steadily disintegrating scraps of my
pride and close the door on this . . . this . . . God, I don't even have a
name for *this*. But I'm frozen, stuck in one of those nightmares where
my brain is screaming to move, run, get the fuck out of there, but my
body is locked into place, a prisoner of skin and bone, shock and fear.

"I'd like to say it's not you, that it's me. But that would be a lie. It
is you. You changed; I didn't. You knew who I was and what I needed
when you met me. I feel like there was a bit of a bait and switch. You led
me to believe I would be a priority, and I clearly am not. So I'm ending
our relationship. It's better this way. There's no need to drag this out any
longer, as it will only be more painful for both of us. I will always reflect
on our time together fondly, but it's in the past now. I'm looking toward
the future, and I hope you will as well. All my best, Val."

All my best?

I'd been balls deep in her and had planned to propose in another
six months and *all my best*?

That's it. I'm in the fucking twilight zone.

"Here. This is for you." The woman (I still don't know her name. Shouldn't I at least have a name for the woman who just detonated my world into pieces?) who not only has witnessed my humiliation but read it folds the letter in half and extends it toward me. My arm moves without express permission from my mind, and I take the paper. "I'm truly sorry, Mr. Hart."

I believe her.

And isn't that a kick in the nuts?

Glimpsing the softness in her dark eyes, I believe her, and it doesn't mean a damn thing. For some reason known only to her and Val, my girlfriend—no, *ex*-girlfriend as of five seconds ago—sent another person to break up with me. If it wasn't so fucking mind boggling, it would be hilarious.

If it was happening to someone else.

Not me.

Not when I'm seeing my carefully designed plans for my immediate future starting to unravel thread by thread. And if life has taught me anything, it's that all it takes is that one weak strand to initiate the loosening. One slip of the foot to cause an avalanche.

One neglected pocket of air in a tire. One "I'll get the tire changed next week."

One blowout on I-70.

I briefly close my eyes, and my fingers curl around the letter, crushing it. The crinkle of the paper is the only sound in the early-evening silence.

And this is why you don't trust people. Don't depend on them, and God forbid, don't let them close.

They'll abandon you every. Single. Time.

Me. Myself. And I.

That's the only holy trinity I believe in.

"Mr. Hart?"

Why is she still standing here? Hell, why am *I*?

I've given her enough of my dignity for consumption today.

Opening my eyes, I step back until I'm on the other side of the doorframe and somehow blindly locate the knob and curl my fingers around it.

"Thank you."

I'm certain the appropriate reaction in this bizarre situation should be anger or, at the very least, frustration. I mean, this is the kind of shit that happens in quirky rom-coms featuring the latest fresh-faced, girl-next-door star, not in real life.

But I'm not angry. I'm not frustrated.

No, as I deliberately close the door and stare at it, only one emotion creeps through me.

Fear.

For the first time since reaching fifteen and six feet and becoming too tall and big to be "handled," I'm scared as hell.

And I don't know what to do with that.

CHAPTER THREE

ZORA

Oh, this is not going well.

That way-too-familiar churning cranks up in my stomach, but I force my soft, sympathetic smile to remain in place. Even though the sauvignon blanc I paired with my grilled scallops and mushroom risotto is in imminent danger of making an encore performance. Even though a dark-red stain continues to mottle the face of the gym-rat large man seated across the dinner table from me.

This is the third time in the last week that I've had to step in and cover a contract. A perfect storm of a stomach bug, a honeymoon, and a family emergency has left us shorthanded, and both Miriam and I have had to pinch-hit during an inordinately busy last few days. Not that I'm complaining about the amount of business. Not at all.

But I haven't had to take part in this side of it in the last two years. I hate confrontation. And understanding this, Miriam and Levi have done everything they can to shield me from it. Which always paints my belly in a slick coat of shame. I detest being weak. Being seen as weak. Still, this is our company, and I can't hide in my office while Miriam carries the load. Because she would. Besides being a little on the "eccentric" side, my sister is surprisingly good at breaking up with people. And she enjoys it. Which is either a good thing . . . or a very scary thing.

I choose not to overanalyze it.

Either way, pride won't allow me to be a coward.

Which leads me to my current predicament.

One Richard Henley and a dinner for two at one of the best steak-houses in Denver since a nice medium-rare rib eye is his favorite meal. That's one of the pluses of ending a relationship at a restaurant. Ply the person with great food they love and just the right amount of alcohol to mellow them but not have them belligerent.

Apparently, I'm out of practice. Because even with only one glass of cabernet, Richard is definitely *belligerent.*

"So let me get this straight. Not only did Sheila lure me here under false pretenses of meeting a 'friend'"—Richard lifts his hands in air quotes, a sneer riding his mouth—"but she isn't even showing up? She doesn't even have the balls to break up with me face to face but has to send her 'friend'"—more finger air quotes—"to do it? Is that what you're really telling me right now?"

Technically, she doesn't have balls at all, but it doesn't seem prudent to point that out to him when a vein is starting to pound along his temple.

"Richard, I understand you're upset at the moment. I do," I calmly say, hoping my low even tone will influence his. Hoping. But again. That vein. "And Sheila truly cares about your feelings, which is why she asked me to speak with you—because this is so difficult for her. And for you as well, obviously."

"I don't mean to be rude . . ."

Which means you're about to be rude as hell, but go ahead, sir.

"But I don't know you, and you're not in our relationship. I refuse to believe she would send a . . . a proxy to break us up . . . for what? Some bullshit reason like she's a different woman from the one I started dating? Hell, it's only been four months!"

He has a point. The excuse is weak. But "You're a controlling, belittling, loudmouth bully whom she's smart enough to get away from now before she does something damaging like marrying your abusive ass" seems like a nonstarter. So I went with "different woman."

Smile. Keep smiling.

I've practiced this in the mirror, so I know it appears halfway between "I sympathize with you" and "I have a Taser in my purse and am not afraid to use it. Don't let the knockoff Manolo Blahniks fool you." It's a careful but effective balance.

Still keeping my smile fixed and my voice low and calm, I lean forward. "She regrets if you believe she wasted your time and wants you to know that she values the months you two spent together." Mainly because next time my client becomes involved with another person, she will recognize the signs of an asshole earlier and not remain in an abusive relationship a moment longer than the first veiled insult or ridiculous demand. Lesson learned. "Sheila wishes you well and wants nothing but the best for you."

"I'm not listening to any more of this bullshit," he growls, digging in his suit jacket for his cell phone. After tapping the screen, he holds the phone up to his ear. "Yeah, Sheila, what is go—" His head jerks back, and he holds the phone away from him, gaping as if it hissed and spit at him before swinging a venomous glare my way. "She's blocked me. She's actually *blocked* me!"

Alarm shoots out jagged spikes, embedding them in my belly, my chest.

Of course, this is one of the hazards of the job—potentially facing irate exes. Which is why, though we seek to protect the other person's dignity and pride, we always arrange the meets in public places . . . or at homes, but we never enter them. And we employ a one-person security detail as added protection. But as I slide a glance over my shoulder toward the bar, where Doug, my backup for the evening, is supposed to be sitting and keeping watch, a tight coil tautens, then unfurls inside me, spilling a slick, oily dread through me. Because unlike when he accompanied me to Cyrus Hart's house, he's not maintaining a careful eye on me. Instead, Doug's careful eye is focused on the cleavage of the redhead he's chatting up at the bar.

Dammit.

My heart slams against my rib cage, a sledgehammer wielded by panic. I stare at the narrowing of his eyes, the blotching of his pale skin, and the curling of his mouth, and sweat prickles on my skin; a white noise crackles in my ears.

Deliberately, I draw in a deep heavy breath and imagine circulating it around my lungs, then push it out my nose. In my head, I carefully and quickly erect a white padded wall around the razor-sharp, jagged edges of the anxiety threatening to jerk me out of this chair and have me racing for the restaurant door.

I won't give in to it. I refuse to surrender to it.

"Like I said, Sheila thought a clean break would be best for both of you. Make it easier for you to move forward. If you have a message you'd like me to—"

"Is this fun for you?" He slams his cell on the table, leaning forward and jabbing a finger toward my face. "Do you get a little sick thrill out of sticking your nose where it doesn't—"

"Is everything okay over here?"

Relief washes through me like a swollen river. Thank God I'm sitting down, because even though I've managed to clutch on to my composure with a clawlike grasp, my knees have given up the ghost.

Oh, Doug. Earlier flirtation with the redhead's breasts forgotten. And I see a huge tip in your future for this timely save.

I am a woman who's perfectly capable of rescuing myself, but screw it, I'm not above grabbing hold of this life raft.

I turn, looking over my shoulder. "Thanks, I—"

Holy shit.

Blue. The color of his eyes.

I hadn't been able to see them in the photograph that day in my office, but the moment he opened the door at his home, I couldn't help but notice. They're not your run-of-the-mill blue. His eyes are the deepest, hottest heart of a flame. The brilliant blaze of a sky when the sun is at its highest. Those eyes are dazzling in their intensity, damn near blinding, and difficult to look at. There's no way I can forget them. Forget *him*.

Cyrus Hart. The Cyrus Hart I broke up with on behalf of his girl-friend. Beauty-in-hard-golden-flesh-and-harder-muscles Cyrus Hart, who nearly had me tossing professionality to the wind on his doorstep.

A shallow breath shudders free from my parted lips.

Definitely *not* Doug.

"Is this the night for people not minding their business?" Richard snaps. "There's no problem. You can leave."

"I'm not talking to you."

A shiver that isn't altogether unpleasant trips down my spine at his flat tone. But then again, I'm not on the receiving end of it. Dick—I mean, Richard is.

Cyrus's gaze remains pinned on Richard for another taut, silent second; then it shifts to me. And for an insane moment, I have to bite the inside of my cheek to prevent myself from begging him to turn that piercing bright stare back to Dick.

"Everything okay?"

I nod. "Yes." With a quick glance at my dinner companion, I add, "Now that dinner is just about over."

"The hell it is," Dick argues, and damn. When I call my client with an update on the evening, it's going to really cost me not to be able to congratulate her on being rid of this guy. She dodged an asshole-shaped bullet. "We're not fin—"

"Yes, you are."

Again with that flat tone. And this time, Richard pauses, his thin lips snapping shut and his spine hitting the back of his chair. Maybe he's finally shut up long enough to notice what I did the moment Cyrus spoke in that voice with the faint thread of menace weaving through it. Maybe Richard finally noticed the stark power and animal magnetism that Cyrus's obviously expensive black slim-fitting suit couldn't hide. No, if anything, its impeccable . . . civility emphasized the perfectly contained male beast underneath.

It's an intimidating sight.

It's breathtaking.

And my fingers itch with the need to grab my Canon 90D and snap picture after picture of him, just trying to capture that almost visceral quality of his on film.

I jerk my way-too-fascinated and probably too-revealing gaze away from him. A snort stops just short of escaping. I can stop looking at him, but there's not a damn thing I can do about the rave happening between my legs—lust thumping and throbbing so loud, so hot, it's become its own soundtrack.

"Your dinner's finished," Cyrus says, that hooded unblinking stare fixed on Richard in a way that has *my* heart pounding. "Don't bother asking for the check. I have it covered."

"I can pay for my own meal," Dick sputters . . . even as he throws his cloth napkin to the table and shoves his chair back.

Smart man.

Or one with a strong sense of self-preservation.

After shooting to his feet, Richard fires one last glare in my direction, then stalks off, not stopping until he pushes through the restaurant doors. Only after he disappears through the double door does the tension leave my shoulders, and the tight, thorny knot in my belly slowly loosens, unfurling until I can breathe without drawing tiny painful pricks.

"Is this a habit for you?" Cyrus murmurs, and as he settles his tall wide-shouldered body into the seat Richard just vacated, a new tension infiltrates me.

One that has nothing to do with conflict and panic and everything to do with the intensity of those flame-blue eyes, that rudely carnal mouth, the power of his six-foot-plus frame . . . and the oily guilt swirling inside me like week-old brown liquor.

If I possessed any doubts before now that he recognized me as the woman who delivered that Dear John letter on behalf of his girlfriend, then his question has torpedoed them. But nothing in his eyes or his voice betrays how he feels about my actions—about me.

And doesn't that just have the tension drawing tighter?

If I didn't already know he was an attorney, his ability to have me fighting not to fidget in the face of his inscrutability would be a flashing neon clue.

"Is what a habit for me?" I pick up my wineglass, buying time to . . . to . . . hell, I don't know. Prevaricate? Apologize? Thank him? *D*, all of the above? "Disastrous dinners or getting told off by men over excellent steaks? The latter, no, not a habit of mine. The former? Well, that unfortunately happens more than I'd care to admit."

"I think we both know that's not what I'm referring to." He cocks his head. "But now I'm all kinds of intrigued by the former. We can discuss that first, if you'd prefer."

If I prefer? Uh, yes, let's talk about Craig, my very first breakup over dinner, who wouldn't stop weeping into his glazed salmon. I ended up having to go into his phone and call his mom to come pick him up. Explaining who I was had been fun. Or we could discuss the time Miriam crashed a local matchmaking event at a sushi bar to hand out our cards along with the dragon rolls. Rushing down there to talk the organizers out of having my sister arrested was a blast.

A pity I can't disclose any of those occasions without betraying our clients' confidentiality.

Yep. A real pity.

"No, I'm good." Smiling, I pick up my wineglass again and down another gulp. His dark eyebrow arches, and the question in it is fair.

I, too, am wondering if I'm about to become an alcoholic. At least for tonight. Sighing, I set the glass back down next to my plate with my half-eaten entrée. "Just so you know, I intend to pay for tonight's dinner, so his whole outrage over you covering the check was fake."

"I would ask what kind of fuckers you've been dating, but he wasn't your date." Any trace of amusement evaporates from his demeanor, and though his expression never changes, there is a palpable shift in him. In the atmosphere over our table. As if he's capable of charging the particles in the air with just the force of his personality, his presence. "Which leads me to ask the same question he posed. Is this fun for you? Do you get a thrill out of delivering painful news just to get off on people's reactions? Or are you the doormat friend who can't say no, so friends use you to do their dirty work?"

"Neither," I breathe.

Pain flares inside me, a flash fire that sears my chest. I don't know why I'm surprised—or hurt—that he assumes the worst of me. He's not the first—damn sure won't be the last. And his opinion of me, of my company, shouldn't matter—he doesn't know me. Doesn't understand why I do what I do. Hasn't lived my life or traversed the loud, embattled footsteps of my childhood that have brought me here. So I don't give a fuck if he judges me.

Only I do.

The soreness directly under my rib cage that I'm fighting not to rub my fist against declares I do.

I part my lips to give him my pat answer; he can either accept the company line or, frankly, suck it.

But then his words strike me.

"Or are you the doormat friend who can't say no, so friends use you to do their dirty work?"

Wait. He doesn't . . . I replay the words again. Oh shit, he *does*.

He believes I'm a friend his ex asked to do her "dirty work" of breaking up with him. Cyrus has no idea that I break up with people for a living.

Here's where I tell him the truth, that "No, no, you have it all wrong. I don't personally know Valerie Summers or the guy you just ran out of the restaurant. This is my job. What I do for a living."

Only . . . the words remain stuck somewhere between my brain and mouth.

Because past experience has taught me what I will see in his gaze, his face. The sky in those eyes will become overcast with storm clouds, dark with disdain. The chiseled bones will sharpen, appear even more stark under the disapproval that tautens his golden skin. That beautiful, sinful mouth with a capacity for cruelty will curl into a sneer that I somehow know will follow me out of this restaurant. Follow me into my dreams.

Is it horrible of me that I don't want to see that familiar esteem-stripping tableau play out in front of me? That just for tonight, maybe I'd rather be that friend? Rather be anyone but Zora Nelson, owner of BURNED Inc., who has to defend her choices? Maybe I just want to be simply Zora, a woman sitting across from a criminally beautiful man for a few short hours before returning home and forgetting he ever exists for me.

It's not just selfish; it's a lie. By my silence, yes. But a lie just the same.

And yet my silence isn't golden. It's damning.

"Neither?" A faint quirk at the corner of his mouth. "Then please explain to me how Val got you to show up at my house and end a relationship that, as far as I'm aware of, you weren't involved in. Same with this one here." He dips his chin toward the table. "Because you claim not to get a kick out of this kind of thing, but here we are."

Shit. I'm walking a very thin line here. My own desire aside, Valerie Summers is still my client, even though the job is done. And I have a personal conviction and a contract that demands my circumspection and discretion.

"She asked me," I say, and even that's edging so close to the line that an uncomfortable sensation skitters across the nape of my neck. "And sometimes it's . . . kinder to hear it from someone who isn't as close, as emotionally involved. Chances are they will be gentler, more careful with your feelings."

"Even while they're reading a letter intended to rip your heart from your chest?"

"Did it?"

I don't know where that question came from. Don't know where the nerve to ask it originated. One, his feelings—or lack of them—aren't my business.

Two, not my business.

But I don't rescind my question. And I can't deny that the air in my lungs stalls; hell, every necessary function in my body seems to halt in anticipation of his answer.

"No."

The breath expels from my chest in a deep, hopefully silent *whoosh*. Disbelief pours through me. Not because I think he's lying and trying to save face. No, the exact opposite. It's because I believe him.

But that doesn't make sense. I remember the bleak devastation on his face while I read that letter from Valerie before he concealed the stark emotion behind a stone-cold mask. That couldn't be faked.

This man. He's a labyrinth of contradictions. And I want to navigate every meandering, twisty path to figure him out.

A movement behind Cyrus catches my attention. Doug heads in the direction of the bathroom, and the redhead is nowhere in sight.

Oh, you're so fucking fired, Doug.

Giving him a tiny shake of my head, which I hope he reads as "Your services are no longer needed," I return my attention to Cyrus. As if it's a choice. His presence *demands* my full focus as his due. And I willingly surrender it.

Before I can unwisely but irresistibly dive into that enigmatic and blunt "No," Cyrus—thankfully—interrupts me.

"How did you meet Val?"

I'm not in a law-office conference room or a courtroom, but that fact doesn't stop me from feeling like I'm being interrogated. Doesn't prevent sweat from popping under my arms or along my palms.

Don't even think about picking up that wineglass, my subconscious hisses.

"Through a mutual friend." Friend. Client. I'm kind of horrified with myself at how easily that white lie slides off my tongue.

Once more his dark eyebrow wings high, and a reclusive mole could spot his skepticism.

"Excuse me, sir, ma'am. Is there anything else I can get you? Dessert? Another glass of wine?" The waiter appears at the side of the table and doesn't even bat an eye at the exchange of my dinner partners. Talk about professionalism.

"The check, please," Cyrus says, reaching into his suit jacket, withdrawing a thin black leather wallet, and removing a credit card. It, too, is black. "And a double Glenlivet neat." That knowing gaze alights on my nearly empty drink. "And another glass of whatever she's having."

"Very good." With a nod, the waiter discreetly accepts the credit card and disappears.

She. He calls me *she.* Probably because he doesn't know my name—kind of difficult to introduce yourself when you're narrating a Dear John letter—and he hasn't asked me for it since he sat down. And I don't offer it. Maybe it's wishful or even desperate thinking, but the omission of my name keeps this from becoming too personal. Too . . . intimate.

Like I said, wishful *and* desperate.

"Do you feel like you're going to need whiskey for this conversation?" I ask, only half teasing.

"If I needed it, I wouldn't have ordered it," he replies, and God, isn't he the king of enigmatic answers tonight? I wish it didn't make him even more fascinating. Or impossible to glance away from. "You and Val don't seem to be the type of women who have anything in common."

My chin jerks toward my chest, as if his words delivered a verbal blow. *That* comment succeeds in making him a little less fascinating.

"Why? Because she's a white woman from Cherry Hills who can trace her family tree back to the original settlers and I'm . . . not?"

"Do you mean because you're a Black woman not from Cherry Hills whose ancestors probably have more to do with actually building this country than hers? No, that's not what I'm referring to. I'm not going to lie and claim Val is color blind, but your race wouldn't be as much of a factor as your social connections, financial portfolio, and career growth. I'm proof of that."

As I'm digesting that bit of information—not about Valerie but the taunting and tantalizing *I'm proof of that*—our server appears again with the check folder as well as a tray bearing our drinks. He sets the dark-red billfold in front of Cyrus, then carefully delivers our drinks.

Once Cyrus signs the bill and hands it back to the waiter, he picks up his whiskey and sips it. To avoid staring at those beautiful lips wrapping around the edge of his glass, I echo his movements and gratefully sip my sauvignon blanc.

Let it go. I should let it go. *Don't ask.* Dammit, I shouldn't ask. *Don't you ask . . .*

"So why am I not the type of woman who Val would be friends with?"

I stifle a groan. And then another one when he swipes the pad of his thumb over his full bottom lip. I've already crossed the line of professionalism, so why shouldn't I wonder if the flavor of his skin adds a complementary or sharp contrast to the smoothness of the Glenlivet? Why can't I admit that my stomach twists in hunger pangs to find out for myself? It's not like I'll ever see this man again after tonight.

Well, if one doesn't count dreams.

I don't.

"Your dress tonight and the pantsuit from the other evening. A little boring, still fine. But they're off the rack and not designs offered by stylists or the designers themselves. Same with your shoes." He dips his chin toward the table, as if he can see my gray stilettoes with the asymmetric branch of crystals across the front underneath. "Knockoff Manolo Blahniks. Beautiful. But still knockoffs. Your earrings are obviously real, but they're too flashy, too loud. Not understated or considered 'elegant' enough. Everything I've mentioned is fine for most people. But most people aren't Valerie Summers."

My breath shimmers in my throat, and it's rimmed in shards of glass. Humiliation razes a path through me. Not just because everything he's listed is true. It's the matter-of-fact tone. The cold measurement of his gaze. Screw giving him my name. He didn't need it to make this personal. I've been stripped, picked over, and catalogued and categorized under *lacking*.

Fuck him.

"Now who's getting off on being an asshole?" I allow the corner of my mouth to kick up in a small smirk when, really, I want to tell him where he can shove that tumbler of whiskey and how hard.

"You're offended," he states without the tiniest inflection of apology in his voice. Something tells me this man doesn't even understand the concept. He raises his glass for another sip, his gaze narrowed on me over the rim. But then he sets the drink down hard enough for the crack of glass meeting wood to echo between us. "I'm not an asshole; I'm stating facts. Facts that don't reflect negatively on you. If anything, they speak more about Val and her values."

"And yours," I point out, not willing to let him off the hook. He, after all, spent months in a relationship with the woman. Might still be in one if she hadn't ended it.

"And mine," he easily agrees.

Surprise bolts through me, and I blink.

"I notice things like brands and originals versus a reproduction because of my clientele. Also, as an entertainment attorney, I can't walk in with a knockoff Brooks Brothers suit because they will spot it right away, as will my colleagues. On the other hand, I grew up with a mother who didn't give a fuck about labels. Why spend her hard-earned money on something as foolish as a name when she could buy a similar piece of clothing for less and put the rest toward far more important things like bills, her family, or even something simple like a damn ice cream cone that would put a smile on her son's face?" His sky-blue gaze flicks over my chandelier gold-filigree-and-ruby earrings. "And she would've adored your earrings."

His lips flatten into a firm line, and for the first time since sitting down at the table, he glances away from me, a tiny muscle flexing along his hard jaw. As if regretting his admission to me. But that doesn't really make sense to me. Because, like apologies, regret doesn't seem like a thing Cyrus Hart indulges in either.

Then it hits me.

"She would've adored your earrings."

Would *have*. Not *would*.

Pain, hot and blindingly bright, flares inside me, and I slip my hands to my lap so he can't witness me curling my fingers into my palm. The bite of nails into skin grounds me, warns me to keep my sympathy to myself, to not stretch an arm across the table and cover the hand gripping the glass of whiskey.

Again, I don't know him well—as in *at all*—but I sense offering any condolences to Cyrus would be akin to sticking my steak-wrapped hand into a starving lion's cage.

Stupid as fuck and begging to come back in pieces.

"Your mother had excellent taste," I say, uncurling my fingers to casually grab my wine for a sip. His gaze swings back to me, and the urge to fidget is so powerful I deliberately stiffen my muscles. But I meet those too-shrewd eyes and refuse to look away. "And I can't speak for Val, but we do have an acquaintance in common, and that's how we met."

"And her 'acquaintance'?" he presses. "She use you to dump the dick?"

Snorting, I shake my head. "That wasn't a favor. That was a mercy killing. And one I was glad to do."

Truth. No matter how much conflict has me yearning for a dark room and a darker corner, I wanted to take this job and end Sheila's relationship. She deserves a fresh start away from that controlling dick.

His lips curve into an almost smile, humor flickering in his eyes. And it's that flash of amusement that sends guilt careening through me. Even though, logically, I recognize it's misplaced—this is my business, the company I'm very proud of and have worked hard for these last few years. I have nothing to be ashamed of. Yet . . . that knowledge doesn't stop the guilt.

Here I am joking about breaking up, and he's just suffered one . . . at my hands.

It's insensitive. And made worse by my deception.

"I'm sorry," I whisper. "About the end of your relationship."

He studies me for a long moment, his gaze roaming over my face. And though it's evening and we're indoors with muted lighting, every feature—my forehead, cheeks, nose, mouth—feels touched, *burned* by the blue flames of his eyes.

Liquid heat pumps through me, lighting my veins up as if fluorescent gas is flowing along their thin pathways. It requires every bit of restraint I possess—and some I had no idea I did—not to lift my hand to each detail of my face and trace it. Try to brand his visual touch into the pads of my fingers until it's like a second set of prints.

"Yes," he murmurs. "Me too."

Beestings of . . . of . . . dammit, no. I refuse to label the prickles of heat in my chest. But whatever they are, they're inappropriate. Have no business there. But as sore as my sternum is, I'm thankful for the unidentified hurt. Those pinpricks are just the reminders I need. Reminders that the only connection he and I share is Valerie Summers, his ex. The same ex who hired me to break up with him.

This dinner . . . it was a mistake. I shouldn't have allowed him to sit down. Shouldn't have indulged in a conversation with him. Shouldn't have been selfish and stolen his time from him for my own personal gain. My desires.

Mouth dry, I reach for my glass and take one last sip of wine. But the fruity flavor can't drown out the grimy grit of shame. Or wash down the lump of guilt.

Cyrus Hart is a client's ex.

And though I didn't have a hand in the downward spiral of their relationship—lack of communication, inattention, and cheating contributed to that—I did aid in the actual dissolution of it. Was paid to end them as a couple.

Being here with him is a conflict of interest and a violation of Val's trust.

Cyrus's too.

I need to end this. Now.

"Well, thank you for paying for a dinner that you didn't even get to enjoy." I summon up a smile and, after picking up my clutch from next to my hip, rise to my feet. "It was nice officially meeting you. Have a good evening, Cyrus. And I wish you all the best."

Not risking the chance of saying anything more or giving him the opportunity to—because part of me isn't 100 percent certain I won't sit my ass right back down regardless of my resolve—I walk from the restaurant without a backward glance.

Not that I need one.

Cyrus Hart is not a man you forget.

Ever.

Doesn't mean I'm not going to give it one hell of a try.

CHAPTER FOUR

CYRUS

"So word on the street is you got dumped."

My hand freezes while crossing out a ridiculously restrictive exclusivity obligations clause in this endorsement contract. A cold snap crackles inside me, spidering out through my gut and chest and climbing up my throat so that for a long moment, I can't do anything but lift my head and mutely stare at Jordan Ransom.

And as my best friend jabs a forkful of gravy-covered waffle at me, I mentally run through the list of about five Denny Crane–esque attorneys who can easily get me off for first-degree murder. Never lost a case.

"Well, it's about time, bruh. Ding-dong, the bitch is dead," he continues, waving the fork, sending gravy to the left and right of his plate before stabbing the food in his mouth. "And don't look at me like that. I said what I said."

Not uttering a word, I swipe my napkin from my lap and dot wayward gravy from the top of the contract. Irritation flares, but like a comet sweeping across a dark night, it's there, bright and hot, then gone. There's no point being angry with Jordan. The man makes Honest Abe look like a pathological liar in need of meds. And if anyone takes issue with it, there's a fallow field somewhere south of the city where he daily buries all the fucks he has to give.

There's also the fact that he's a professional basketball player, a three-time NBA champion, and, at thirty, one of an elite few to win NBA MVP, All-Star Game MVP, and Finals MVP awards in the same year. Those facts make a lot of the shit he does and says forgivable in people's eyes.

Not for me.

There is the not-so-small detail that under the mohawk, miles of tattoos, piercings, and blunt-to-the-point-of-pain honesty, Jordan possesses an unbreakable, stubborn loyalty for those he calls friends. And I'm one of those people.

For me, that's as precious as the gold settlers once mined these hills for.

Even more so.

Still . . .

"Don't call her a bitch."

Jordan arches a brow, cutting into his fried chicken breast. "Oh, so you saying she's not? That one's so cold I had shrinkage just from being in the same room with her. Which wasn't often since she saw me as the riffraff."

He's not wrong. Val couldn't stand that I was friends with a man she considered a foulmouthed, ignorant thug, millionaire or not. Her words. And I defended him then just like I did her with him. Neither Jordan nor I had it easy growing up. Both of us had to fend for ourselves, damn near raise ourselves, and forge our own paths and futures. I did it with a college education. He did it with basketball. We both did it with sheer will and by any means necessary.

She could never understand why we bonded so quickly. Resented that I didn't acquiesce to her demands to relegate our relationship to just attorney and client. But Jordan and I had been friends before she'd come along. And surprise, surprise, he's here after she's gone.

Not so surprising, really.

"So what, bruh? Is it true? She dump you? You two done?" He cocks his head, squinting at me. "Cause I gotta tell you. My boy was at this fashion show and charity fundraiser this past weekend and saw your girl—well, your *ex*-girl—there with another man. And according to him, they looked five minutes from fucking. That tells me either she moved on pretty damn quickly or she was already smashing homeboy when you were still together. Both shady as fuck. And I don't care what zip code her daddy lives in, so is she."

I should be shocked by this news. Shocked and enraged.

But I'm not.

Hell yeah, my pride is stung, and that chafes like a motherfucker. Because I should've seen the cheating coming, should've recognized that she had someone else as her plan B so, one, I could've stopped fucking her and having an unwilling ménage à trois with some guy I didn't know. And two, I could've ended the relationship before she did. At least then I wouldn't have had a stranger show up on my doorstep, robbing me of the satisfaction of facing Val.

That's what stings most out of this, even more than my battered and bruised dignity.

She stole my control.

And for a man who has tasted, fucking feasted on the bitterness of powerlessness for too many years to count, that's hard to stomach. It's unforgivable.

"You don't seem the least bit shocked by what I'm telling you." Jordan sets his fork down and leans back in his chair, crossing his inked arms over his chest. "You don't care, do you?"

Sighing, I set my pen down and pick up my own fork. After pressing it down into a corner of my garden omelet, I scoop up the egg and bring it to my mouth. The flavors of the spinach, mushrooms, and goat cheese explode on my tongue, and I take another bite. Jordan always chooses the Bacon Social House to meet for the chicken and waffles and boozy french toast, and I grudgingly agree. Still, I have to confess their food is on point—

"You're stalling, and that doesn't work on me."

Yeah, I am, and no, it doesn't.

But why he's suddenly expecting me to be a "sharer" when I've never been one is confusing as hell.

Didn't seem to mind oversharing last Thursday night.

My grip on the fork tightens before I deliberately loosen it. I've purposefully avoided thinking on that dinner. On what drove me to intervene in the first place. On why I sat down at that table across from the woman who not just witnessed my humiliation but was an active participant in it. Hell, she played postman and hand delivered it.

Even now, nearly two weeks later, I still can't answer the whys and whats.

Can't explain what the hell possessed me to mention my past, my mother.

"She would've adored your earrings."

Damn. I give my head a mental shake. It's the truth, but why the fuck I found the need to share that with *her*, a nameless woman I should resent, I have no goddamn idea.

And it bothers me that I don't. Bothers me that I confided in her of all people *and* that I still don't know her name.

I don't like unknowns. Too much of that shit in a lifetime will spoil your appetite for it. And this woman falls into that category.

My cock takes this moment to jerk in complaint against my thigh. Translation: *I don't give a fuck. Who needs a name with a mouth and ass like that?*

My dick. Such a gentleman. But it doesn't rule me. Never has. Not even with Val.

"Yes, I care," I say, breaking off another piece of egg.

Jordan snorts. "Liar."

"I care because this breakup could potentially damage the connections I've made through her. Not the least of those connections being with her father. I can only hope he has gotten to where he is today by being able to separate his personal life from business."

Calvin Summers is CEO of one of the largest media groups in the western United States. Cable, telecommunications, production companies—some of the most well-known names in the industry fall under Columbine Media. As an entertainment lawyer, I would be an idiot not to be concerned about losing the influence and references he can throw my way as he's done in the past months while I dated his daughter.

So yes, I care.

"Also, I'm on the short list being considered for partner. I've been busting my ass for this, and it would make me the youngest associate to make partner in the firm's thirty-year history. I want this. What I *don't* want is my personal life interfering and fucking it up."

Jordan, again, arches a pierced eyebrow. "So you only give a damn about how this affects your career. Wow. That's cold." He shakes his head. "What the hell kind of relationship did you two have, anyway?"

One where we understood each other and what we wanted. No, we weren't some couple out of a ridiculous romance movie—thank God. We were better. No messy, inconvenient feelings involved to distract me or, worse, have me dependent on her. Just straightforward logic, plans, and reason. That she didn't inspire anything more than admiration, respect, and lust made her the ideal future corporate and social wife. It's what made her perfect for me.

"We had one based on common goals and mutual respect."

Jordan stares at me, blinks. Then he throws his head back and roars with laughter, drawing more than a few curious glances our way. And phone cameras.

Shit.

He might be used to ending up on Facebook and Instagram from fans' videos, but I'm not, and I have no desire to do so now.

"Can you keep it down, dammit?" I snap, leaning across the table. "You're making a spectacle of yourself."

"So? Jesus, Cyrus, I swear—sometimes you act like you're fucking seventy-three instead of thirty-three. Although . . ." He narrows his eyes, tapping a black-painted nail against his bottom lip. "Coach Fowler must be pushing his midsixties, and last time I stayed with him and Miss Pam, I promise you I heard them getting it in one night—"

"Stop right there." I throw up a hand, palm out, shaking my head. Hard. "No way in hell I want to hear about the sexual proclivities of your old college basketball coach and his wife."

"You sure?" Jordan grins. "The sounds those two were making gave me hope for when I hit that age."

"Stop. Talking."

He shrugs. "The point is you just described a business associate or a partner in a goddamn escape room, not a girlfriend or a lover." He resumes eating, shoving more chicken and waffles into his mouth. "Where's the mention of passion, affection, love, for Christ's sake?"

Now it's my turn to stare.

"You don't really believe that shit, do you? I've seen you juggle more women than a Venice Beach mime."

His hand freezes over his plate; then he slowly straightens in his chair, a serious expression that I rarely glimpse on him crossing his face.

"First, I don't 'juggle' women. Do I date and fuck my fair share? Yeah. But never at the same time. I'm not that guy. I'm always straight up about who I am and what I'm looking for and how it ain't them. Second, hell yeah, I believe in *that shit*. I may not have seen much of it growing up—as in not at fucking all—but it exists. And not just in fucking fairy tales. I see it with Coach and Pam. Just from the little bit you've told me about your parents, you saw it with them. So yeah, I believe in it, and what's more, I want it. And I'm not settling until I have it."

"I'm . . . not really sure what to do with that."

Because of all the things I expected to come out of this inked, bad-boy ballplayer's mouth, it wasn't some romantic shit like *that*.

Jordan flashes his trademark "I don't give a damn" smile, then dives back into his food.

"Not yours to do anything with. But for you, I predict one of three things." He looks up from sawing into his fried chicken to deliver his prophecy. I choose to ignore the shiver of foreboding that ripples down my spine. "You're going to end up in a miserable, loveless marriage that you'll stay in out of pure stubbornness and some misguided sense of loyalty. Or you're going to end up a lonely old man with your job as your everything. Or you're going to eventually fall in love, and if you don't pull your head out of your ass, you're in for a world of hurt. Which is fine if it'd only be you. But you're going to take her down with you."

"The hell, Jordan?" I bark out a hard crack of laughter. "You would be shit as a fortune-teller. That was macabre as hell. Do I get any good news?"

He lifts a shoulder in a half shrug. "You're not giving me a lot to work with. I only call it as I see it. 'I look like Miss fucking Cleo to you?"

What the fuck?

But apparently, he's done grilling me about my relationship status and the grim future of my love life.

"So what's this endorsement contract looking like? Is it as shitty as I think?"

For the next forty minutes, we finish reviewing the contract, and I cross out the exclusivity obligations clause; advise him on negotiating compensation and the trademark and intellectual property rights; and, because this is Jordan, fine-tune and specify the morality clause. There are a few other items we discuss, but by the time we step out in the early-afternoon sunshine, Jordan has given me the go-ahead to open dialogue with the athletic-compression-clothing company.

"I'll give their attorneys a call as soon as I return to the office," I say, striding toward my car. "I can't see this dragging on since they seem to wa—you've *got* to be kidding me."

"What?" Jordan draws to an abrupt halt next to me, his gaze scanning the parking lot. Within seconds he spots what—or rather *who*—had me scowling and staring. "Who's that?"

"No one."

"No one, huh?" The corners of his mouth kick up, and a gleam I recognize only too damn well enters his eyes. "So you don't mind if I head on over and introduce myself to *no one* . . ."

"Don't even fucking think about it."

His low chuckle grates against my ears. Yeah, I've been played, but I'm still not rescinding that order.

"Which one?" he muses, cocking his head to the side and scratching his dark-blond scruff. "The blonde with the hips and ass? Or the dark-haired one with tits and ass? Hmm . . ." A moment later, he shifts his attention from the women carrying bags with the Bacon Social House logo on them to me. "I'm going with the dark-haired one. Just 'cause she's the exact opposite of Val. And because I saw that muscle jump in your jaw when I mentioned her tits and ass."

Another of those diabolical laughs rolls out of him. Probably because of the involuntary growl that just escaped me.

Goddammit. And him.

"So are we going to say hi to no one or not?" he presses, that gleam back in his eyes.

It's on the tip of my tongue to order him to get in his fucking Range Rover and drive away, but that would be like waving chum in front of a starving shark. And assigning more importance to this woman than she warrants.

Why can't I just say hi and then move on?

To avoid her means I'm running scared. Or there's something about her that stirs fear in me.

And that's untrue. She's like any other woman. If anything, she'll probably lose her mind and her panties at the sight of Jordan.

Yeah, not feeling any irritation at that thought. At all.

"Let's go," I grind out.

Grinning, Jordan falls into step beside me as I stalk across the parking lot. She notices us first, and she pauses at the bumper of the dark-blue Acura.

Goddamn.

Still as stunning as she was the other night. I catch myself just before I shake my head in disbelief. I sat in that restaurant chair, nailed to the seat and chairback by shock. The hair, the earrings, even the eyes, I remembered from when she'd shown up on my doorstep. But all of her facial features? No, those had escaped me. But they didn't at that table, and they don't now.

Those dark, tight curls that I want to grip a handful of and hold up to the light and determine for myself if they're black, brown, or a gorgeous sensual blend of both. Yeah, that's not all I'd want to do with those curls while I had them. Beautiful, oval-shaped chocolate-brown eyes endowed with a thick fringe of lashes. High, sweeping cheekbones that would be wasted on a supermodel—only a queen would do. An elegant nose with wide, flaring nostrils and a mouth. A mouth that would make a teenage boy blush and a grown man groan. It's a work of erotic art, a sinful masterpiece.

Yeah, I don't know how I missed that face.

The slam of the back door shutting yanks my gaze from her, and I glance at the blonde, who rounds the car, her eyes widening as she catches sight of us.

"I think that's for me, not you," Jordan stage-whispers to me.

He's enjoying this way too damn much.

"Jordan Ransom," the blonde breathes. "Are you finally here to sweep me away from the drudgery of my everyday life and carry me to your magnificent mansion for an easy, carefree life of domestic bliss, Jimmy Choos, and orgasmic lovemaking?"

I choke while Jordan releases a loud crack of laughter that echoes across the parking lot. His whole huge bod shakes with hilarity.

"Oh. My. *God*, Miriam," the woman I've come to see half snaps, half groans.

"What?" The blonde—Miriam—shrugs. "It's a fair question."

"It is." Jordan crosses his arms and purses his lips, as if actually giving this ridiculousness thought. "I can give you the domestic bliss—if by that you mean people cleaning up after your shit—shoes, and orgasms. Definitely the orgasms. But for how long, sweetheart? Basketball season is about to start, so this isn't going to have a long shelf life. You up for a week?"

"Two."

"A week and a half and courtside tickets to our first game."

"Meh." Miriam waves a hand, flicking off his counteroffer. "I don't really care that much about basketball. Too many rules to follow. How about a week, those tickets so I can sell them on eBay, I get to keep all the shoes, and you throw in a shopping trip at the Cherry Creek Mall?"

"You drive a hard bargain, Marilyn. But counteroffer accepted."

"Awesome." She beams, and oddly mystified, I gawk at them like they're an Olympic table tennis match. "And it's Miriam, not Marilyn."

"Not with that hair."

Miriam snorts. "Men. Next thing you know you'll be asking if the carpet matches the drapes."

This time, my Dear John dumper chokes, and one quick look reveals she appears about three seconds away from committing at least a second-degree felony against the blonde.

Jordan tilts his head back. "Does it?"

Oh *shit*.

Miriam pauses. Blinks. "Yes."

Holy . . .

"Miriam, dammit," my dumper growls, and though her murderous glare is directed at the totally unrepentant blonde, that low rumble vibrates down my spine . . . my cock.

Hell, I shouldn't have come over here. Should've got my ass in my car, headed home, and fucked my fist before returning to the office. Because if I'm getting hard at a goddamn *growl*, then this no-sex situation is more dire than I assumed. I need to get fucked sooner rather than later.

"Please excuse my sister," she continues through gritted teeth. "It's wonderful to meet you, Mr. Ransom." She shifts her deep-brown gaze to me, and though we've been in each other's presence two times now—three counting today—it's still a visceral punch in the gut. "It's nice to see you again, Cyrus."

I nod, pretending that the husky melody of her voice isn't sweeping over my skin in its own personal, seductive song. Goddamn, that voice. It's a singer's instrument, a siren's weapon.

"You too."

"Oh, you and Zora know each other?" Miriam tilts her head, her gaze switching from me to her sister. Sister. I should've known. Besides the different hair color and the difference in height, they both share the same wealth of gorgeous curls, the same gleaming teak skin, and the same pretty brown eyes. "Where and how did you two meet?"

I stiffen and resist glancing in Jordan's direction. Yes, he knows or heard a rumor that Val dumped me, but he obviously doesn't know the details surrounding our breakup. If he did, there's no way in hell he would've let that conversation go. And I'm not in the mood to enlighten him.

Maybe she—*Zora*, that's her name—senses this because she turns to her sister and pops up a finger.

"One, none of your business. Two, unlike you, my motto is not 'Sharing is caring.' And three, please refer back to one."

"Fine, fine." Miriam holds up her hands, palms out, eyes comically wide. "No need to be so aggressive. If you want to be all cagey and squirrelly about your relationship, then cool by me." She lowers a hand and props it on her hip. "But you know that's only going to leave me to speculate, right?"

"Miriam, don't you—"

"Hmm." Her sister wheels around toward me, nose scrunched, bare-and-bitten-down nail tapping her full top lip. "Saving her from a long drop out of an office building is out, since I can't see you wrinkling your suit even to strip out of it for a cape and tights underneath. So copycat Superman is out."

"Good God."

"She's not wrong," Jordan comments at the same time Zora tips her head back toward the sky on a whispered prayer.

Me? I'm caught somewhere between horror, annoyance, and a morbid amusement that has me frozen and curious about what crazy-as-fuck thing will emerge from her mouth.

"That leaves one-night stand that my loving but follow-all-the-rules big sister is too embarrassed to admit to. Which would explain why she appears so determined to keep her eyes above your neck because she has biblical knowledge of what you can do when that suit comes off and she's imagining it riiiight now—"

"Okay, that's enough," Zora interrupts, and if I'm correct, a faintly hysterical note threads through her voice. "Cyrus, can I speak with you for a moment? Privately?"

She's marching off toward the other end of the parking lot before I can agree, so I follow, Jordan's chuckle echoing in my ear. I don't even break stride as I throw up my finger. Of course, he laughs harder. The man is impossible to offend.

As I trail behind her, I order my gaze to behave, to remain on the back of her head, the other parked cars, the ground . . . anywhere but the gentle yet utterly sensual sway of her hips and the plump, dick-defying curves of her ass in her purple pencil skirt. Like the other clothes she's worn every time we've encountered each other, there's nothing overtly eye catching about the skirt, the white long-sleeved shirt with the ruffle down the front, or the black stiletto heels with the ankle straps.

But unlike those other times, I'm realizing now that I was completely, criminally wrong.

I can only blame the circumstances of our initial meeting and her sitting down most of the time at the restaurant, but I was a blind idiot.

Yeah, her clothes might still be off the rack and her shoes knockoffs, but there's nothing boring about them. There's no way in hell they could be anything but sexy and stunning when they're wrapped around that wonder of a body.

Good God, she is that unveiled art piece that brings a man to his knees, his palms and fingers tingling with the desire to touch, to stroke . . . to possess. Staring at that almost prim white shirt, that skirt that conceals as well as reveals, I strain at invisible restraints, hungry to strip away each piece of cloth that hides silken brown flesh, traces shadowed dips, protects secret, hot places . . .

Fuck.

I wrench my gaze away from her ass, from those thick thighs that press against the seams of cloth with each long stride.

I'd been joking about taking a detour home and jerking one off to alleviate the pressure in my cock, my balls. But now . . . yeah, maybe that's not such a bad idea.

"I'm sorry about that," Zora says, turning around and scanning the parking lot, as if ensuring no one is close by to overhear our conversation. "Miriam can be . . ."

I do the same. I might not be as famous or well recognized as Jordan, but I have appeared several times on those blog sites dedicated to Denver society news and gossip simply because Val and I were dating. I haven't gone searching to discover if our breakup has made the columns.

"A handful?" I supply since she paused.

Her ripe, just-a-shade-too-wide mouth twists. "Crazy as hell. But thank you for being much more diplomatic." She sighs, her hands lifting between us and fluttering, and the gesture strikes me as vulnerable. And endearing in a way I don't want to associate with her. "I assume your friend doesn't know how we met?"

"No. And I prefer to keep it that way. Dammit." I drag a hand through my hair, blowing out a breath. I hadn't intended for my voice to come out so sharp. Why it's sharp is another subject altogether. Especially when I just convinced Jordan—and myself—that I didn't care about the relationship with Val ending. "I'm sorry. I didn't mean to snap at you. But yes, there are some details about my breakup I'd like to keep to myself. And explaining how we met means going into that."

"I understand." She nods. "And I'm sorry. Again."

A faint smile touches her lips, and it draws my attention to her mouth once more. To the almost indecent fullness that incites thoughts of illicit acts and filthy groans. A mouth like that could take its fair share of abuse and beg for more, take more . . .

I release a hard deliberate breath and slide my suddenly too-sensitive hands into the front pockets of my suit pants. To be on the safe side, I shift backward a step, inserting space between us. Because I don't trust myself at this moment. Not when I'm envisioning those lips, swollen and damp from my lips and tongue, parting for my dick . . .

What the hell is *wrong* with me?

"Sorry for what?" I rasp. Clear my throat. But how do I get rid of the unexpected—and unwelcome—lust abrading me raw?

"That we seem to be bumping into each other every time you turn around. I'm a reminder of the loss of your relationship, and the last thing you want or need is for me to constantly be in your face. I must be like salt in a wound. So I'm sorry."

Don't apologize. It's not your fault that fate seems damned determined to keep us bumping into one another.

The words sit heavy on my tongue, but I don't say them. Even though that's exactly what she should be—salt in an open wound.

So why isn't she?

Except for that initial meeting, I haven't experienced pain around her. Curiosity, amusement, bemusement, resentment . . . lust. Those I've known in her presence.

Pain would be so much easier, simpler.

"Zora. So that's your name." I taste it, savor it. The name fits her. Unique. Strong. Beautiful. Powerful. *Her.*

One, I don't believe in fate, karma, or any of that other bullshit that people use as excuses to alleviate themselves of ownership of their own choices and accountability. Two, part of me wants to blame her. That part wants to unjustly assign fault for my pulse jumping at my throat, my dick jerking in my pants at the sight of her, at the anticipation of hearing that throaty voice.

I've turned into *that* guy—the one who blames a woman for his uncontrollable reaction—and it sickens me. Even as I want her to do something about it. To make it stop.

I take another step back and futilely hope she doesn't notice.

But, of course, she does. The slight tightening of her wide mouth and the almost imperceptible narrowing of her eyes telegraph that she misses nothing.

"Yes. I guess you wouldn't have had time to catch it. Or even care to know it."

That's where she's wrong. I want to forget she existed, want to put her in my rearview mirror, but apparently, I'd like to know her name too.

"Look, Cyrus, I'm not going to hold you up. I'm sure you're busy, so I'll make this quick. It occurred to me that considering who you hang around"—she hikes her chin in the direction of Jordan—"and your reaction to protecting your privacy, maybe you might feel more comfortable if I sign an NDA about my part in your breakup with Val. If it's reasonable, I have no problem signing it."

"Fine."

My reply is automatic; I'm an entertainment lawyer. NDAs are as normal and necessary to me as breathing. So that flash of . . . something in her eyes before her lashes lower, hiding that . . . something from me shouldn't have my fingers itching to grasp her chin. Tingling to tilt her head back while I wait until she looks at me so I can decipher what she's hiding in the depths of those dark-chocolate eyes.

She has secrets. And I want to unearth them.

No, that's not exactly right.

I want her to tell me.

Shit.

Stop this.

Remember the plan. Focus on the plan. Val already altered it, and I'm scrambling to adjust, to get it back on the correct track. I can't afford to deviate from it any further. More importantly, I have no desire to.

This woman—with her fantasy-inspiring explosion of curls, wet dream of a mouth, and eighth wonder of the world of a body—is a deviation.

"Great." She nods, and her thick dark strands graze her shoulders. After reaching into the purse at her wrist, she pulls free her cell phone, taps on the screen, and then passes it to me. "If you'll enter your phone number, I'll text you my email address."

I accept her phone and do as she requests. And moments after she takes it back, my cell vibrates against my chest.

"There." She tucks the phone back in her purse, and a small tight smile stretches her mouth. "I hope that helps you feel more comfortable or at least secure. If I talk, you can sue me for everything I own."

I still, studying her. And she rolls her lips in, attempting to flatten them. I want to advise her on the futility of that impossible feat but doubt it will go over well.

"You're offended that I agreed to the NDA." She is. I don't know how I do, but that testy note in her voice, the flexing of her jaw, and the shift of her eyes away from mine . . . "You offered it," I remind her. "Did you expect me not to accept?"

"No." She returns her gaze to me, and this time a more natural smile graces her mouth. It's warmer, more real and inviting. It's also utter bullshit. "You have to protect yourself, which is why I suggested it. I'll keep an eye out for the document." Giving me another flash of that too-polite smile, she steps forward and around me. "It was nice seeing you again. I hope for your well-being it's the last time."

She strides across the parking lot, back toward her sister and Jordan.

I hope for your well-being it's the last time.

It's on the tip of my tongue to say, "Me too."

But it remains there, heavy and silent.

Because it's a lie.

CHAPTER FIVE

ZORA

Damn straight, I'm offended.

I pull out of the parking lot at a deliberately sedate pace, when all I want to do is smash my foot to the accelerator and tear out of there.

Away from that beautiful, aloof mask that managed to be both inscrutable and disapproving. Away from those crystalline, cold eyes that saw too much and offered nothing in return. Away from the living temptation in taut, golden flesh.

Good Lord.

I'm crazy. I'm losing it.

Lust for the most wrong, inappropriate man in the world is making me lose my mind.

"Spill it, Zora. And don't try to tell me *nothing*. Otherwise, you wouldn't have a chokehold on the steering wheel like it's a Karen who tried to touch your hair in the grocery store."

Okay. Miriam does have a point. I let up on the steering wheel, slightly wincing at the low-grade ache in my fingers. Straightening and flexing them, I sigh and shake my head, throwing a sidelong glance at my sister.

Both of her dark eyebrows jack high.

"Oooh. That good, huh? C'mon, Nelson. Get it off your chest. It'll make you feel better," she says in a singsong voice.

I snort. Doubtful. Still, my sister might be crazier than a bedbug, but since we were younger, we've been the keeper of each other's secrets. In a house like ours, where a failing test grade or a secret boyfriend or a chore gone undone could be the excuse used to set off the Wars of the Roses, we learned early on to be the other's confidante. Old habits die hard.

"It's Cyrus Hart."

"I *knew* you were going to say that," she crows, wagging a finger at me.

But not satisfied with that, she pokes it in my side, and with an undignified squeal, I just manage not to jerk the wheel into the next lane.

"Miriam! Dammit, I'm driving!"

"Sorry." Her wide grin says differently. "But I *knew it*," she sings again. "I was joking about you seeing him in all his naked glory but not about the attraction between you. Seriously, when you guys walked off, I thought I was going to have to cover some tender-aged youth's eyes. Hot, Zora. And I ain't mad at you. At all. What was it? Don't tell me a one-night stand? Oh shit! Was I right about that? Tell me his di—"

After removing one hand from the steering wheel, I stretch an arm out and clap my hand over her running mouth.

"Breathe."

She glares at me over the top of my hand, but she stops talking. I lower my hand and return it to the steering wheel.

"Cyrus Hart is a client's ex. She hired us a couple of weeks ago to end their relationship, and since we were short staffed at the time, I had to take the job."

"Sooo you broke up with him . . . and then you fucked him?"

"What? No! God, no," I practically yell.

Miriam shifts, the rustle of her harem pants sliding over skin filling the interior. A glance to the side reveals her shoulders squared against the window.

"Start from the beginning," she says, for once with no hint of humor shading her voice.

So I do.

And by the time I wrap up the story, Miriam is uncharacteristically silent.

"Why are you offended that he agreed to the NDA?" she quietly asks, voicing the question that has been bouncing around my head like a paintball, splattering me with my guilt, my doubts, my misplaced desires.

"I don't know." I stare straight ahead at the road, unable to meet her gaze even for a few seconds. I'm her big sister. The responsible sister. The one who avoided any hint of trouble or conflict. And yet here I am. "It's hypocritical of me, right? I'm insulted and maybe even a little hurt that he would believe I'd tell anyone. I think . . . I think I wanted him to trust me."

"But he doesn't know you. Not really. And what he does believe he knows is a lie. A lie you didn't originate but perpetuated."

Frustration, hot and blinding, flashes inside me, but just as fast, it fades.

"I know," I whisper. "I guess I wanted him to *see* me. Past who he thinks I am—who I allowed him to think I am. I wanted him to, to . . ." I huff out a short dry laugh. "God, I don't know."

"You wanted to be different for him."

The truth of that, no matter how unnerving, rattles in my mind and my bones and then settles in for a restless nap.

"You did right to offer the NDA," Miriam says, reaching over and squeezing my hand. "It redraws a line that you crossed. Because he might not be a client, but you becoming involved with him in any way is definitely a conflict of interest. You do know you can't see him again, Zora?"

"Yes, I do. Another reason I'm crazy to be annoyed that he accepted the NDA. Besides . . ."

The words stick in my throat, as if caught in a pit of quicksand. But it doesn't matter that I can't utter them. They swirl in my head and have been since the moment I first laid eyes on his picture.

"Besides what?" Miriam growls. Another poke with that finger that should be registered as a deadly weapon. This time in the thigh. "You better not be thinking what I think you're thinking. Because if you're thinking that, I'll be forced to think of new and creative ways to beat your ass without leaving bruises. And we *all* know what happens when I start thinking."

I snort. "Yeah, please. Don't do that. One global infrastructure collapse a decade is enough."

"Good. Then you can cease and desist any comparisons to other women where all of your gorgeous qualities end up in the deficit column."

It doesn't always suck having a sister who knows you well. This isn't one of those times . . . but it is. *Get out of my head* tramples my tongue, but so does *Thank you. I needed that.*

Too bad I don't believe her. And her words, though kind and unconditionally loving and supportive, don't silence the ones in my head. In my soul.

Even if Cyrus and I had met under different circumstances other than a third-party dumping on his doorstep, I still wouldn't be the type of woman he'd glimpse across a crowded gala ballroom, causing him to say to himself, "Now there's a woman I must have" and then pursue me.

Valerie Summers is that woman.

Slender. Flawless. Rich. Connected.

White.

I'm none of those things.

I boast curves that I long ago accepted and now embrace. I'm far from perfect. But fuck it. That's why they invented makeup, Spanx, and edibles. Even labeling myself *middle class* is incredibly optimistic, but I'm comfortable. The only connections I have are the ones I pay my cable company for.

And well, I'm definitely not white.

While I've had to fight the good fight regarding my body and hair with not only employers, exes, and society but also myself about conforming to a socially acceptable ideal of beauty, I've never entertained those insecurities about being a Black woman.

So Cyrus Hart might prefer thin, wealthy, blonde, and a B cup. But if that preference includes a particular race, too, I'd rather not know he would've rejected me out of hand simply because of the amount of melanin in my skin.

Ignorance is not only bliss, but in my case, it's a crutch. It allows me to walk away believing that beauty doesn't conceal a rotten center.

"What're you going to do?" Miriam asks, breaking into my thoughts. "Are you going to let the client know about Cyrus? That you've had contact with him outside of the contracted meeting?"

I'm already shaking my head before she finishes the last question. "No. There's no need. The client has moved on to another relationship, and just from comments Cyrus has made, I doubt they're in contact any longer. And since today will be the last time Cyrus and I will need to communicate, I don't see why I should disturb her with this."

"You just justified the hell out of why you shouldn't come clean with her."

I loose an abrupt, humorless chuckle. "How'd I do?"

She stretches out an arm and wags her hand back and forth. "Meh. Seven for the content but five for the delivery. You didn't make me *believe* it."

I snicker. "You're crazy; you know that?"

She sighs. "That's the rumor."

A beat of silence passes between us.

"Thanks, Miriam," I murmur. "I really appreciate it."

"Enough to let me take over the advertising campaign?"

"Hell no."

"Damn." Then she says, "You're welcome."

Smiling, I twist the volume knob, and Lizzo singing about haters doing what they do carries us on into the office.

CHAPTER SIX

CYRUS

"Sooo seriously, you're just friends with her?" Jordan presses, his skepticism clear in my ear. "Because if that's the story we're going with, I'll pretend to agree, but from my perspective, there was nothing *friendly* about the way you looked at her. Or that conversation, for that matter."

I lean back in my office chair, tossing my pen to the desk. As long as he's on the phone, work is a pipe dream. And when he's on a roll, it's best to let him get whatever is on his mind out or this could go on and on . . . and on. It's been only a day since our meeting in the parking lot of the Bacon Social House, and I've been waiting on this phone call. Frankly, I'm surprised it's taken Jordan this long.

"Yes, we're friends," I grind out for the fifteenth time in the last eight minutes, skimming my email to ensure nothing pressing has come through.

"Cool. So you should have no problem with me being friends with Miriam too."

"What the hell?" I scowl at my monitor as if it's Jordan. "Is that why you're bugging me for her phone number?"

If so, I'm kind of outraged on her behalf, even though I've met Zora's sister only once. Although, part of me is a little worried for

Jordan if he plans on treating Miriam like one of those nameless women he fucks, then never bothers calling or seeing again. Again, met Miriam only once, but something tells me she's not the type to go quietly into the good night. Fuck boiling a bunny. She looks like she'd go straight for his nuts.

A heavy sigh echoes in my ear. "No, goddammit. Haven't you been listening to a word I've been saying? I can't explain it, but she's different. I'd be lying if I said I didn't want to hit it, but she's cool as fuck. I want her as a friend. She's funny, crazy smart, and just plain crazy. But I still want to hit it." Another sigh. "That's why I'm calling your ass. I need advice."

"What about me says I would be good with relationship advice?"

No, I really want to know.

"You the only motherfucker I know who's been in one that's lasted longer than three months or who isn't cheating on his wife. I don't need advice from those assholes."

I snort. "And yet you're the one who claims to believe in love." I shake my head, even though he can't see it. "I don't know what to tell you, Jordan. You see how my relationship with Val turned out. Ours wasn't based on a friendship and damn sure not love. And sex isn't enough to make it survive."

"You are absolutely no help and a fucking killjoy to boot," he snaps. Then he says, "What are you doing tonight?"

"I—" I look up from my monitor at a knock on my office door. "Hey, let me call you back. Someone's at my door."

"Yeah, do that. Later."

Setting my cell on my desk, I call out to the person on the other side of the door to come in. And as soon as it opens, regret for my haste fills me like bad moonshine. The law firm of Ryson, Dare, and Gregerson LLC boasts a stable of thirty associates and then partners, including junior and senior. Since I joined right out of law school, my goal has been to become the youngest junior partner in the firm's history. I've billed no fewer than two thousand hours a year and not only brought in new business but also retained existing clients. The partners have counted on me to do the legal heavy lifting, as I don't depend on my paralegals or colleagues. My work ethic is above reproach. But that's what happens when you've been fighting for scraps since you were twelve. You're no longer satisfied with crumbs; only the biggest, most satisfying smorgasbord of a meal will do. And you don't stop until it's set in front of you.

Now, that goal is within my grasp. Gossip runs through this office faster than an STD in a frat house. I'm on a short list of names being considered for junior partner. And one of those people standing between me and that partnership is the man lowering his ass into the chair across from me. Without an invitation.

Derrick Warren.

I can't stand the asshole.

And he's not an asshole because he's my competition. No, he's an asshole because he'll use anyone, do anything, and *won't* do anything to get what I want. And smile the shark's smile the whole time. Derrick Warren is an entitled prick who cheats, lies, steals, and sabotages to get ahead. Growing up, I've lied and sometimes stolen to survive, but Derrick and his family hail from the same circles as Val. He doesn't need to—he just gets a kick out of it.

So yeah. Asshole.

"What?" I don't do pleasantries with assholes.

"Cyrus," Derrick says, crossing one knee over the other and straightening a nonexistent wrinkle from his pants leg. "Good morning to you too."

"Is that what you're in my office for? You could've called to do that. Or sent an email. Right now, we're wasting billable hours."

The corners of his mouth tighten, and his jaw flexes. Good. If I'm irritated because he brought his ass in here, then we both should be annoyed. It's only fair.

"Actually, I wanted to extend my congratulations. By now you've heard we're both on the list of senior associates being considered for partnership. Of course, they're only choosing two. And Lloyd Taylor is a shoo-in since he's the oldest senior associate and is Donald's golfing buddy."

Derrick wasn't wrong. Lloyd and Donald Ryson were friends and, as of a couple of years ago, related by marriage. The only reason the other man hadn't made partner before now was due to the smaller amount of business Donald had brought in. But in this business, who you knew counted as much as how hard you worked.

"Thanks for the congratulations and the update."

"That leaves one selection left," Derrick continues. "The competition's going to be tough. And you know the firm's reputation. Solid, grounded, family-oriented men with a firm foundation in the community. Lloyd has been married for twenty-two years, has a daughter in college and one about to graduate high school. His family has a street named after them and sits on boards of libraries, charity foundations, and museums. And of course, Jill and I have been together for five years with a son of our own. And Dad is the top cardiologist in the state, while Mom is from one of the oldest families. And you." The smile is back, and it's wider, glittering . . . delighted. "Well, you. We're all aware of your . . . unfortunate past. And present. So sorry to hear about you and Val."

You can't put your hands on him. An arrest would look really bad to the partners. Not to mention it's hell getting blood out of wool.

I heed my conscience but barely. I'll be damned if I ruin my chances at a partnership I deserve and give him the satisfaction of knowing he dug under my skin. Fuck him.

"Thanks."

The smile dips a fraction, and confusion flickers in his gaze. Probably wondering why I'm not going for his throat. Because contrary to what his elitist ass believes, I'm not one step above an animal just because I wasn't born in a certain zip code.

"Sure." He lowers his leg to the floor and straightens his tie. "It's such a shame. Valerie Summers by your side added to your credibility and integrity here. So now you not only don't have a partner but no prospects of being a family man." He tsks. "That partnership is not looking good for you, my friend."

"Thank you for taking time out of your busy day and coming in and sharing that with me." I keep my voice flat, void of emotion, and my unblinking gaze leveled on his face.

On one hand, Derrick isn't as confident in my loss of this partnership race as he seems, if he's sitting here. Otherwise, he wouldn't be trying to pull this psyching-me-out bullshit. He's here because he still sees me as competition, and he wants me to take my own self out.

Yet . . . I'm worried. As much of an arrogant motherfucker Derrick may be, he's not wrong. The partners do have certain criteria for the associates they choose to make partner. Yes, they hired me knowing my background, but Val had been a strategic choice for me. She provided me entrance into upper-echelon social circles to which not even my clients have been able to grant access. Now she's no longer by my side; I no longer have those connections. I'm also not family-man potential, which is important to some of the partners. My billing hours, work ethic, new business record, and client retention can take me only so far in their eyes.

Panic scales my gut, crawling on sharp talons for my throat. Ice-cold sweat rolls down my spine, and a dull roar moans low in my head. But I refuse to reveal the dread threatening to strangle me.

Not to him.

Not to anyone.

Another knock on the door interrupts whatever he's about to say next.

"Come in," I call out.

The door opens, and Donald Ryson enters. Both Derrick and I rise from our chairs to greet the silver-haired, distinguished founding partner of the firm. Tall, wide shouldered, and fit, he is one of the few men I respect and admire. And as his clear, shrewd green eyes scan the room, taking in me and Derrick and undoubtedly the temperature, he proves why he's a brilliant, astute attorney.

"Good, I'm glad I found you two together. Saves me from having to hunt you down individually. You know I'm an old man."

We both laugh as expected, but truthfully, the older man plays racquetball three times a week, golfs two times a week, and runs every morning. He's more fit than a man half his age. Including me.

"I'm planning a small weekend retreat a month from now, and I'm inviting the both of you. Your wife and significant other are welcome. We'll be flying up on the corporate jet on a Friday afternoon and returning on that Sunday." Donald smiles and claps his hands once. "It's going to be wonderful to get away from the office for a few days and spend time with each other. I'm counting on you to rearrange your schedules to make it."

In other words, *You have no choice. You're going.*

"A getaway sounds perfect, Donald," Derrick says, his ingratiating voice grating on my nerves. "Jill and I will definitely be attending."

"Great. Cyrus? I hope you can make it." He arches an eyebrow, waiting for my answer.

There's only one to give.

"Absolutely."

Donald smiles and inclines his head. "Wonderful. Well, I'll leave you to get back to work. Be on the lookout for an email with more details."

"I'll walk out with you, Donald. I wanted to speak with you regarding Gerard Clifton. He's coming in later this afternoon and . . ."

They exit, and as soon as the door closes behind them, I sink to my chair, staring blankly at the computer monitor. Donald's and Derrick's words rewind and play on constant repeat in my head.

Your wife and significant other are welcome.

So now you not only don't have a partner but no prospects of being a family man. That partnership is not looking good for you . . .

Fuck.

As in, that's what I am.

Totally and royally.

ZORA

Unknown: I received the NDA. Thank you.

Unknown. I don't need a name at the top of the screen to identify the messenger.

I stare at my phone, thumbs hovering over the keyboard to reply. Or not to reply. My goal in signing and returning the damn thing was eliminating further contact. And now he's reaching out.

Why?

Cyrus Hart doesn't strike me as the kind of man who does anything without a purpose.

My pulse pounds at my throat, my wrists. The throb of it reverberates in my head. Part of me is yelling, demanding I don't answer the text. But the other half . . .

That half has already wrenched control, and my thumbs are flying across the keyboard.

Me: You're welcome.

That's it. Nothing else is warranted. After closing out of the app, I go to toss the phone on my bedside table when . . .

Unknown: Do you need a signed copy? I can email it or have the document couriered.

Have it couriered? As in give him my address?
Uh, no.
Well, damn. He already has my address from the NDA, doesn't he?
Doesn't matter. Still no.

Me: Email is fine, thank you.

Now *that* should be the end of this. Miriam's cautionary words echo in my head. But she just reiterated what I already knew. Maintaining any contact with Cyrus would be detrimental to BURNED if anyone, mainly Valerie Summers, found out.

It'd also be harmful to me.

After my last relationship fell apart, I promised I'd never set myself up for failure again. Never inflict that kind of pain, the kind of damage that falling in love, that being rejected and abandoned can bring. And Cyrus—with his brilliant eyes, fallen angel's face, and Greek-god body—and the memory of that quiet devastation on his face as I read that Dear John letter has my rejection and pain scrawled all over him in permanent marker.

Unknown: Jordan asked me if I could get Miriam's number for him.

I literally gasp. Aside from the road map of tattoos, that naughty grin, and the bad-boy reputation, he seems like a nice guy. I can't do that to him!

Oh, right. I also can't just hand out my little sister's number to random professional basketball players. That too.

Me: I'll need to check with her to see if it's okay.

The reply pops up mere seconds later.

Unknown: That's fine.

Unknown: Should I be worried about my friend?

Me: Very.

I grin down at the phone.
Oh fuck. I'm grinning.
My stomach sinks toward my feet as they carry me the several steps backward to the bed. What the hell am I doing? I sit, barely feeling my ass hit the mattress. Not a minute ago I repeated why I had to keep my distance from Cyrus Hart—physical, mental, and I'm sure that includes digital. So why am I smiling down at my phone screen, staring at those little bubbles like they're a BOGO 80 percent off sale at Claire's?
Why does it feel like champagne bubbles are fizzing through my veins? Why am I giddy when the only thing to pass my lips today has been coffee and water?
Oh God. This is bad. Very bad.

Unknown: He also asked more questions about you & how we met.

Me: What did you tell him?

Unknown: Through work.

So we're both lying.

Tipping my head back, I close my eyes. Those bubbles transform to leaden balls and plummet to the bottom of my belly and settle there.

I'm already his dirty little secret, and all we've done is bump into each other a couple of times.

And him? Well, he's my secret, my fantasy, my downfall all wrapped in one beautiful package.

In some twisted way, I guess that makes us perfect for each other in a destined-to-end-in-scorched-earth-failure sort of way.

Unknown: Can I call you?

I blink. Slowly. But no, I didn't misread the message. Terror spikes sharp and hard, and my fingers fly across my screen.

Me: No.

Bubbles.

Unknown: Then call me.

A chuckle with a slightly hysterical edge escapes me, and I clap a hand over my mouth although I'm alone in my house.

Me: No.

What game is he playing? Irritation stirs in my chest, low in my belly, heating those leaden weights there until they glow. At this point, what do we have to say to each other? An image of his dramatic, hero-in-a-Netflix-historical-period-series face flickers before my mind's eye. What could he possibly want with me?

That annoyance sparks, as if dry kindling was tossed on its low burning embers, and it flares brighter, hotter. But even then, a tiny hateful voice whispers it's not him I'm angry with but myself. I'm angry for wanting to say yes. For hungering to hear that midnight-and-fevered-dreams voice in my ear and know it's all for me. I'm angry and hating myself for imagining what that voice will utter to me. What I so desperately desire it to utter . . .

I loose a long shuddering breath.

That's the thing I can hide from others but not from myself. That's my shameful secret.

The rule follower, the peacemaker of the Nelson clan, delights in hedonistic chaos.

And if I allow him, Cyrus could leave me in a wrung-out, carnal wreck without even touching me.

The phone vibrates in my hand, and for a second, I consider not reading the message. Just skipping the text, deleting the entire thread, and then blocking him. That would eliminate temptation. That would place him beyond my wayward fingers if not thoughts . . .

I read the message.

Unknown: Then meet me.

Me: If I won't call you, why would I meet you?

Unknown: I don't know. Why won't you?

I'm not answering that. Not in this lifetime, and that's how long he'll have to wait for my reply. Maybe he senses my spirit of stubbornness, because the bubbles reappear.

Unknown: I'm at Tattered Cover Bookstore on Colfax & will be here until 8.

Tattered Cover Bookstore? What is he doing there? Does he go there often? Why?

Oh for fuck's sake, I don't care. *You don't care,* I scold my unruly mind.

No more bubbles pop up, but I don't need another text to add the "I'll wait for you until then." It's implied. And if I don't show up? Will he assume I'm not interested in . . . whatever this is and stop contacting me? Will he go away?

Do you want him to go away?

Oh, shut up, and get some business.

That moment when you're snapping on your own self and realize you may have crossed the city limits of Crazytown. I'm there.

I toss the phone to the bed and stare at the Thomas Kinkade painting on the far wall. I bet in that world with stone bridges and skaters skimming over ice-covered ponds and a quaint village in the background that people meet at church socials and after a few low-angst dates of picnics and Sunday dinners with the families, they marry and live happily ever after.

Those women never have to agonize over what lines, what boundaries they're willing to cross just to . . .

Hell, I don't even want to touch on where that "to" leads. One, because I don't know, and two, because I fear where it goes. How far it goes.

"This is ridiculous. I'm not leaving this house. I have work to do. New clients' forms to go over. Ad to review. A couple of *90 Day Fiancé* episodes to catch up on. My ass is staying right here."

That's right. And saying it aloud, hearing it, renews my resolve. Reminds me of my priorities . . .

"Shit."

I wheel around, snatch up the cell, and march from my bedroom and house. But not before I pause and change *Unknown* to *MNBM*.

My Next Big Mistake.

CHAPTER SEVEN

CYRUS

The door to the entrance opens for what seems to be the twentieth time since I hit send on that text to Zora inviting her to meet me here at Tattered Cover Bookstore. And for what seems like the twentieth time, it's not her entering the building. My vantage point on the second level grants me a perfect view, and though I'm feeling a bit of an ass for scoping out the bookstore's customers like a creeper, I don't move.

Not until eight o'clock.

At 8:01 I'll leave and bask in all my what-the-fuck-am-I-thinking.

Flipping through my recent purchase, Harlan Coben's latest, I try to ignore the steadily twisting and tightening screw in my gut. The one that if I were dealing with opposing council, I would excuse myself and go figure out what I'd missed. It's not an itch as much as a warning that I'm about to fuck up.

And standing here, waiting on Zora Nelson—thank you, NDA, for solving the mystery of her full name—I have zero doubts that I'm about to fuck up.

I glance down at my cell and pull up our text thread—the one I initiated. I issued the invite at 6:46. It's now 7:32. From her place, it would take about twenty minutes to get here. She's not coming. And I can't blame her.

That text . . . I'd debated sending it. From the time the nebulous idea had coalesced in my head several hours after Donald and Derrick left my office, I'd gone back and forth on reaching out to Zora about this plan that alternately strikes me as harebrained and desperate. Still, none of that stopped my fingers from typing the words out. But in the time that followed, even after her outright refusal and then silence, I never messaged rescinding the invite. Just as I haven't left this store even though I've made my purchase. And I won't for another twenty-eight— now twenty-six minutes.

Because I need her.

And I want to see her.

Fuck it, I do.

As soon as she walked away from me in the Bacon Social House parking lot, I wanted to pursue her, cup that perfectly rounded hip, press my chest to her spine, my cock to the delicious curve of her ass, my lips to the curls covering her ear and . . . and . . .

And ask her not to leave.

Yeah, there. I said it.

I damn near vibrated with the need to beg her to be the very thing I can't afford with a potential partnership in my sights, with the goals I promised myself, promised my parents I'd obtain, within my grasp.

A distraction.

Distract me. Tease me. Disturb me. Make me feel something other than . . . me.

Use me.

God, I want her to use me.

But now, more than ever, I can't afford distractions.

Before this afternoon—before Donald dangled my future in front of my face like a golden carrot—would I have asked her to this book-store to proposition her? To beg her to let me taste her sweet flesh, find out for myself if it will melt on my tongue? To let me between those pretty thick thighs and lose myself in a body created for beauty, for pleasure, to offer a safe haven from the shit in my head, even if only for a little while?

No. Because I'm not that guy. And she's damn sure not that woman.

But . . . maybe. Maybe we could've been that guy and that woman for each other.

Still, that was before.

The door below opens again, and even before my eyes transmit the image of a mass of dark curls to my brain, my cock hardens, throbs, recognizing her. For a moment, I still, unable to tear my gaze away from her. From the cream long-sleeved thermal shirt and open navy puffy vest that can't conceal the thrust of her much-more-than-a-handful breasts to the toned and thick thighs encased in dark-blue denim to the brown lace-up knee-high boots. And back up again. Because she's a delightful terrain that has to be traveled more than once.

After setting my book down on the arm of a sofa, I quickly tap out a message to her.

Me: Look up.

She starts, pulls her phone out of the back pocket of her jeans—fucking lucky phone—and, seconds later, tips her head back.

I can't clearly see her eyes from this distance, but that doesn't make a damn bit of difference. The impact of her visual touch is both a soothing balm and a fist-tight stroke down my dick.

Goddammit. Everything in me craves to be that guy.

I don't move, struck motionless by her and my almost resigned need.

My feet moving before I grant them permission, I walk over to the landing, meeting her as she crests the top of the staircase.

For a moment, we stare at each other. I study each feature, separately and together. And those brown eyes take my inventory too. I haven't cared too much in the past about whether a particular woman found me attractive; since I hit high school, it was just a fact. I've never had to work too hard for female attention. But her? Suddenly, I understand the lure of a beautiful predator. If Zora finds my face pretty, my body tempting, then I'll unashamedly use them both to get what I want—her acquiescence.

Her, my greedy subconscious growls.

I ignore it. She's not on the table.

Then for precious seconds I battle back the lascivious images of her spread out before me on a table, those gorgeous thighs caging my head, those slim, capable, demanding fingers gripping my hair, dragging me closer . . .

Shit.

"Regret already?" I ask, smothering the vision in my head before it ignites into a conflagration. Tilting my head, I catch the flicker of emotion in her gaze before she lowers her lashes.

"Yes."

The dark fringe lifts, and her unwavering stare is a switch, setting the roar inside me to a higher volume. My thighs clench, and if I wasn't 110 percent sure she'd send me plummeting ass over head to the first floor, I'd shred every last one of the restraints binding my control and common sense to ribbons and crowd her against the railing behind her, grind my dick against the softness of her stomach, and show her just what that bald honesty does for me.

Honesty.

A shiver rips through me, and I fight like hell to restrain it. I move and excel in a world where deception and half truths are tools and necessities. I employ them myself. It's business. In my life, honesty is a rarity. I didn't know it in my childhood; my aunts and uncles said whatever they needed to get me for a check. I didn't know it through college or law school. Everyone lies to get ahead, to get the next big client.

Truth is a turn-on. Whether it's in a best friend or in the woman tipping her head back and staring at me with a wariness that bothers and arouses me.

"You buying, or are we leaving?"

"I came all the way to a bookstore. I'm not leaving empty handed."

I nod. "Since I brought you out here, my treat."

She scoffs. "Not hardly. Besides, my mother would lose her shit if she knew I allowed a stranger to buy me something. That's just begging for quid pro quo."

I shrug a shoulder. "She's not wrong."

Her mouth quirks into a half smile that strikes me as . . . wrong. Not exactly dry but full of a twisted humor that packs not just a story but a whole novel behind it.

"She never is," Zora murmurs.

Then, after turning, she heads back down the steps, preventing me from asking any more questions. As if it's going to be that easy.

For the next twenty minutes, I follow her as she peruses the book-shelves and selects and pays for her title. She at least lets me pay for her coffee in the café—as long as she pays for mine. I huff out a laugh as we carry our drinks and purchases over to a small section of crimson upholstered theater-style chairs. The polite thing would be to allow a chair between us, but I'm not known for being polite. And I'm not beginning with her. As soon as she settles into the seat on the end, I sink into the middle one right next to her.

She doesn't say anything as I set my bag on the floor between my ankles. Or when my knee presses against the outside of her jean-covered thigh. But I don't miss the tension that draws her body straight, pulls her shoulders tight. The hand wrapped around my coffee cup itches to ease around those taut shoulders, slide under her hair, and cup the nape of her neck. My fingers flex around the brew-warmed cardboard, aching to knead the stiffness from her muscles, feel her loosen and relax under my touch.

That's the problem, though, isn't it?

I can't tell if Zora wants that touch. She's offered no signs that she does. Hell, she could be here out of guilt, out of pity.

Yeah, fuck, I don't need her pity. Just the thought cools the flames licking at my skin. That's the last thing I crave from her.

The only thing I need is her cooperation.

"You saw what I bought." She nods toward the plastic bag with the store's logo on the floor. "What did you get?"

"Harlan Coben's newest release. I saw you bought Kimberly Belle. You read Coben too?"

"Of course. And binge all the Netflix series based on his books." She sips her coffee, eying me. "I hate to sound like a cliché, but do you come here often?"

I snort. "Is this where you tell me I've been running through your head all day?" A flicker of emotion in her eyes, and I'm slowly straightening from my casual sprawl. Leaning slightly forward before I can caution myself about violating her personal space. Those flames sputter back to hot, dancing life under my skin. "What was that?"

"What was what?"

"You haven't played games with me up until this point, Zora. Don't start now."

She glances away, and if possible, her shoulders draw tighter until they damn near bunch near her ears. Doesn't matter. I know what I saw. If she needs a martyr, I'll be a willing sacrifice.

"Me too." I don't touch her; the rigidity transforming her into a living statue doesn't invite me cupping that delicately rounded chin. But I inch forward on my seat and cock my head. Voice lowered, I say, "All damn day, Zora."

"What are you doing?" She whips her head to the side so our faces are only inches apart, and a light honey-and-almond scent envelops me, teases me. I inhale it, trap it on my tongue, in my lungs. "Why are we here?"

"I haven't quite figured that out yet," I admit.

It's not a lie. My hastily thought-of plan drove me here. But part of me hasn't decided if it also wasn't simply the desire to see her again. Or an exercise in self-control. Dangling what I shouldn't take in front of me to see if I possess enough discipline to keep my hands to myself, to walk away. Or tempt myself with this sensual form of edging by embracing what I shouldn't. The sweet disturbance.

The ambiguous answer seems to be the correct one, though. The tension slowly ebbs out of her body, and she props an elbow on the chair's arm.

"That makes the two of us, then, because I haven't figured out yet why I came here." She huffs out a soft breath and briefly dips her head to stare at her cup before lifting it again to look at me. "I'm certain of one thing, though. This isn't right or smart."

"Why? Because you're Val's friend?" I slice a hand between us. "She's already seeing someone new. Probably was before she sent you to do her hatchet job. So I don't care about that."

"Is that what this is, then?" she murmurs. "Revenge? Payback? You plan to throw"—she twirls a hand in the air—"whatever we're doing here back in her face one day for breaking up with you and moving on too quickly?"

I almost laugh long and loud at that bullshit.

"That's not going to happen."

"You were in a relationship for months. Possibly in love with her. You don't know what you'll do."

"There aren't many things that are a one hundred percent certainty. Weather, election outcomes, the price of gas, Hollywood marriages. But this I can state without a shadow of a doubt. Not happening."

She studies me, and I can practically read all the questions in those brown eyes. *How can you? Why? What happened?*

But she lifts her cup and drinks, and instead of asking what she so clearly wants to know, she says, "Not my business."

"Isn't it?" She frowns, and I absently rub the pad of my thumb over my denim-covered thigh, imagining it is that small wrinkled patch of skin above her nose. "When you chose to put yourself in the middle of our relationship, it became your business." The moment comprehension dawns, her eyes widen, then narrow. But I lean forward, a smile curving my mouth. And that smile? It's possible it isn't nice. Because *nice* doesn't accurately describe this uncomfortable and unwanted gnawing inside of me. I'm feeling hungry. "You owe me."

I both hear and see the hitch in her breath, but she doesn't let on. The almost nonchalant note in her voice belies the worry in her eyes. Too bad for her; I make a living at reading people. Too bad she's shit at hiding her emotions. God, I could fucking *feast*, become a damn *glutton* on her honesty.

"What?" she whispered.

"You heard me."

"Yes, I heard you." My own breath really shouldn't quicken or my blood pump hotter at the sound of those words coming through clenched teeth. Or the sight of her hand wrapped tighter around her cup. As if only her grip on the cardboard container is preventing her from transferring it to my neck. Hell, I almost remove the cup from her grasp myself. "But obviously I don't understand your meaning. I owe you for what?"

For witnessing my weakest moments since leaving my aunt's house. For reminding me that my life, my world, is not in my control. For throwing me back to that twelve-, fourteen-, sixteen-year-old uncertain boy again.

For refusing to be evicted from my head like a sexy, stubborn squatter.

For being my answer, my salvation, in this moment, when for years I've vowed to depend only on myself.

And her most heinous sin? For deviating from my carefully laid-out plans. For stepping outside those lines and hungering for something, someone, I have no business desiring.

But I say none of that because those reasons are mine and mine alone.

She gets, "For not stepping back and letting Val have the guts to do her own dirty work. Instead, you got involved where you shouldn't. You allowed yourself to be her patsy, and I'm pissed with you and her about that. I'm also mad as hell that you both stole the chance for me to have my say."

Stole my control in the situation. Left me rudderless, powerless.

Resentment stirs in my chest, mixing with the desire, creating a murky, swirling mess so I can't extricate one emotion from the other.

A starkness enters her eyes, and she briefly closes them before glancing away, her hair concealing most of her profile. Fisting those curls and moving them out of the way so I can see her expression, her thoughts, is such a fierce urge I shift away from her. As far back as the chair permits.

"I didn't think about that. About stealing your voice. I'm truly sorry for that."

I believe her. But I'm not letting it go that easily. It isn't in my interest to.

"Look at me," I say softly. I order softly. And a coil in my gut draws almost painfully, sweetly tight when she obeys. "You owe me. And I'm offering a form of . . . penance."

She loses that pained, haunted expression, and anger tautens the skin across her cheekbones, emphasizing their boldness, their strength. Her jaw flexes the tiniest bit, but I catch it, and as perverse as it might make me, my cock pounds at the signs of her ire. Yeah, I'm turned on, and part of me is hoping she takes it out on me with teeth and nails.

Well shit. When did I become a man who enjoyed an edge of pain with his pleasure?

The answer?

Zora.

When the possibility arose that I might be the receptacle of that pain/pleasure if she was the one doling it out.

"Penance?" She bites *penance* off in a way that should have my cock flinching in horror, but nope. Apparently, it's made of much sterner stuff.

"Or think of it as an arrangement. An arrangement between acquaintances." I shrug.

"Is that supposed to sound better?" she grinds out. "Why don't you explain what you mean by both before I pick up my coffee, book, and go home?"

I've never believed that bullshit cliché of women being beautiful when they're angry. Until now. She's absolutely transcendent. And possibly dangerous.

I slip her cup from her fingers while she's distracted and set it down on the floor on the other side of me.

"Let me start at the beginning." And I do, telling her the abridged version of originally being hired by Ryson, Dare, and Gregerson LLC, the culture there, being up for a partnership, and, finally, about the corporate retreat.

"You don't find that a little misogynistic at all?" she asks, nose wrinkled.

"How so?"

"They want partners who are solid, grounded, family oriented? What about the women who decide they don't want children—or a husband, for that matter?" She squints at him. "Here's another question. What's the percentage of women in your firm? Partners?"

I see where she's going with this, and she's not wrong. Out of thirty associates, five are women, and only one is being considered for partnership.

"Your silence speaks volumes." She snorts and curls her fingers at me. "Gimme my coffee. Your family jewels are safe from me . . . for the time being."

Controlling the smile that's fighting to slip across my mouth, I hand her the warm to-go cup.

"Good ol'-fashioned misogyny aside," she continues, dark eyes fixed on me over the coffee-cup lid. "What does this have to do with me or any . . . arrangement?" Her lips twist on the last word, as if sucking on a shit-flavored lollipop.

I inhale a long deliberate breath, hold it for several seconds, and then release it. Meeting that unwavering stare, I lean forward, voice lowered.

"This retreat is pretty much a casual vetting process for the associates being considered for partnership. Every person on that list will be bringing their wife, fiancé, or partner. Since mine just recently broke up with me, I find myself in need of a substitute. You."

She blinks, eyes going blank with shock for a moment. But as comprehension dawns in the chocolate depths, anger joins it. And another, foggier, murkier emotion that I can't . . .

"That's crazy," she snaps. "And if this is your idea of a joke or *penance*," she practically snarls, "then let me tell you what you can do with it. And be warned. It starts with *shove* and ends with *up your ass*."

Her glare and the blast of heat from her fury could peel the skin from my bones. And it requires every ounce of control I've earned and learned over the years not to lean closer into that fire, not to beg her to singe me with it. Lust battles with curiosity, the need to know where that anger originates. So I can extinguish it.

"It's not a joke," I say. "I wouldn't joke about something as important as my job and the future of my career."

Her lips snap shut, and she glances away from me.

What was that about?

The question leaps and dances on my tongue like a living flame.

"No one, and I mean absolutely no one in your firm, will buy that we're a couple."

Genuine curiosity ripples through me. "Why do you say that?"

"Are you serious?" she scoffs. "You previously dated Valerie Summers. Tall, blonde, rich, size two Valerie Summers. Among *other* things."

"And by other things, I'm guessing you mean white," I calmly add, though the irritation stirring in me is anything but *calm.*

"Since you put it out there. You've already said there are only five women in your firm. I'm almost afraid to ask the percentage of Black or nonwhite associates. So needless to say, I'm not encouraged to believe your coworkers will accept the *differences* that exist between me and Val. Significant differences. Enough that your colleagues would either think I was a plant, the rebound chick, or, worse, a random fuck you're trying to pass off as the new girlfriend. You're better off finding another Val look-alike for the retreat."

"I don't want a Val look-alike. I want you."

I want you.

The three words vibrate and shimmer between us like vapors of steam rising off a damp sidewalk after the blazing sun rises to its zenith in the sky. Hot and damn near visible. I should qualify it, explain what I mean by it, but I don't. I just leave the provocative statement hanging out there like dirty laundry between us, daring her to take it however she desires.

"Why should I?" she whispers. "Why would I ever enter into this . . . arrangement?"

I, again, prop an elbow on the armrest that separates us, leaning forward until her honey-and-almond scent teases me.

"You think I don't see the guilt in those pretty eyes, Zora?" I murmur, cocking my head, drinking in every feature of that beautiful face before coming back to her gaze. "I'm not going to need to force you, to coerce you. All that guilt swimming inside you is going to do the job for me. I could remind you again of how you owe me. But you want to make it up to me, don't you?" I lean closer, drop my voice even lower. "I bet part of you wants me to force your hand too. Do what? Threaten to tell Val how her little messenger failed on the job if you don't come through? Ruin that so-called friendship you two have going?" I narrow my gaze on her, catch the slight tightening of her mouth, the flash of emotion in her eyes. Straightening, I shake my head. "Yes, I think a small part of you would like that, Zora. So it would absolve you of having to make the decision. It might even absolve you of that guilt swimming in your belly. But I won't. I'm not taking the same choice away from you that you and Val took from me. Your decision. Are you going with me to the retreat? Do we have an agreement or not?"

Her inner conflict wars across her face. Indecision, anger, hurt, and, yes, shame.

"What are your terms?" she quietly asks.

Satisfaction and triumph pour through my veins like liquid gold, trumping the biggest case I've won in court and the wealthiest and challenging contract I've negotiated.

"No more Val. You're mine now."

Her full lips part, and she slowly straightens in her chair. Another myriad of emotions march across her face—shock, confusion, suspicion, back to confusion.

"Excuse me? You want me to be your . . . what? Pretend fiancée? Friend?"

Yeah, I don't blame her for requiring clarification. She's not the only one who's surprised at my decidedly possessive declaration. I had no idea that was coming out of my mouth, either, until it echoed between us. But it's out there. And the longer it sits there, the more certain I am this is what I want.

Mine.

That's it. Pretend fiancée. Friend. Whatever I need to make it through this fucked-up charade I'm asking both of us to play.

This isn't about lust. Oh, I still want her. The thick length pressing against my zipper attests to that. But I can easily find a woman to fuck. Not being an asshole; it's just the truth. But I've never had a woman simply as a friend, much less a fake fiancée. But as I stare at her, Jordan's words from earlier haunt me, and I want more. I want someone to give me advice on her beautiful but complicated sex. Someone to help me not to be such a rigid, well . . . asshole. Because I'm in panic mode. Val was my plan A, and I didn't have a B. If I'm going to go into the next long-term relationship and make it last—if I'm going to get my own laid-out plans for my life back on track—I'll need to do it differently this time.

My partnership at the firm depends on it.

My immediate goals depend on it.

My promises to my parents depend on it.

Bottom line, I need her friendship and her acting skills more than her pussy.

"Yes." I answer her question, setting my coffee on the floor next to hers. Like second nature, I smoothly slide into negotiation mode. "Here are the terms. First, you end any and all contact with Val. I can't have a double agent in my camp."

"Seriously?"

She thrusts a hand through her curls, and though I just convinced myself I need her cooperation more than sex, that doesn't stop me from wanting to bat that hand away and assume its place. It doesn't require too much imagination to feel the phantom caress of those thick strands over my palm, between my fingers, and over the backs of my hands. A little coarse but silken. Soft yet textured.

Your rules, I remind myself, curling my fingers into my thigh. *And you just made them five fucking seconds ago.*

"Seriously. And I don't care what you tell her to make it happen. Just make it happen."

After a long moment, she gives an abrupt nod. "What else?"

"If we're going to pull this . . ." Hell, words fail me at the moment on what to call it. "Off and convince people we are a real couple, then we need to spend time together. A lot of time since we only have a month. So I can't have you reneging on me later out of some misguided loyalty to Val."

"Hold on." She throws up a hand, palm out. "What exactly does that mean? 'Spend time together.' So if you call and want a playdate and I can't make it, what happens? Do you follow through on that threat to tell Val that I screwed up? That's not fair. I have a life. Family. Real friends. Suddenly rearranging my life so you're the center of it isn't easy or reasonable."

Real friends. Family.

I hate that those three words punch me hard in the sternum. Hate that she can claim those in the plural, and I can count only Jordan. I shove it off. Same as I don't address her assertion that I would go to Val. Not a chance in hell that would happen, but if Zora assumes that? I mentally shrug. This is a business arrangement. A negotiation. And in negotiations, it's about advantage and getting the most for your client, not always about what's easy, fair, or reasonable. In this instance, I'm my own client.

"Those are the terms," I say.

"Shit," she mutters, pinching her forehead. Then she blows out a low breath. "Fine. But can we add a clause? I'll be your beck-and-call girl like a good little *Pretty Woman*, minus the illicit paid-for sex, but I also get five get-out-of-jail-free times when I can say no without being penalized . . . or threatened."

"One."

"Three," she shoots back.

"Fine." I pause. Smile. "I would've given you five."

"You must be one hell of an attorney."

"Thank you."

"That wasn't a compliment."

Suppressing a rusty chuckle that scrapes at my throat, I rap my knuckles on the arm of the chair. "Back to the terms. This agreement remains between us."

She snorts. "Will you be sending me another NDA?"

"I don't think I need to. I trust you to keep quiet."

"Trust me." She shakes her head. "This is weird as hell. But fine. How do I explain this"—she waves a hand back and forth between us—"to someone anyway?"

"Good point." I shrug. "One more item." Dropping all pretenses of casualness and humor, I stare directly into her eyes. "No lies, Zora. Don't lie to me."

That something—that almost bleak, fearful *something* that I glimpsed earlier—passes through her eyes, darkening them.

This time I do reach for her. Lightly but firmly grasping her chin, I tip her head back. It's my first time touching her, and that skin is as smooth, as soft, as I imagined. But savoring it, indulging in the pleasure of it against my own flesh, takes second place to that flash of sadness, of fear. They cinch my ribs like the strongest of vises, and the primal need to confront, to tear down, whatever or whoever causes that emotion in her gaze surges within me.

"What's wrong?"

In her favor, she doesn't pretend to not know what I'm referring to. But not in her favor—and to my frustration—she shakes her head and circles her fingers around my wrist. My gaze dips, for some reason utterly fascinated that the tips can't meet. Heat flickers, then waves inside of me like a banner in a hot summer wind. Why I find that sexual, I can't explain and don't try to. But I lower my hand from her face, gritting my teeth against the instinctive need to rub at the place where her fingers wrapped around me, feeling their brand.

"Answer me, Zora. What's wrong?" I ask again, injecting a note of steel in my tone.

And like last time, she looks at me, obeys.

And like last time, lust licks at me, ravenous and insatiable.

"I have my own term to add," she murmurs. "You want my cooperation and . . . friendship. You want my honesty. Then we don't get personal. I'll go on this retreat, and I'll give you my assistance so you have a chance at winning this partnership, but you can't compel what I give you of myself. I choose that. Now, that's my stipulation." Her chin hikes up. "Take it or leave it."

Just because of my nature, I want to argue. But admiration rolls through me. So does curiosity. And greed.

What does she want to keep from me? And even without knowing, I crave it. Simply because she's hoarding it.

Did I forget to mention I'm a greedy asshole?

"I'll take it." Does that mean I won't try and dig or convince her to give me more and more of her? Hell no. There's that greedy-asshole part. "Do we have a deal, Zora Nelson?"

I extend my hand to her. And for several moments, she stares down at my palm. And I don't move, don't lower it. Just wait. Because this is another thing I've learned in my career.

When the other side is out of options and I've won.

Finally, she slides her palm over mine, enfolding her fingers around mine. And fuck. It's erotic. It's everything but *friendly*.

"Deal."

Triumph and relief sing through me.

But underneath?

Underneath is a thin but very distinct vein of foreboding that this arrangement is going to change everything. My careful plans. My life. Me.

Then again, I don't believe in superstitions.

Everything's going to be just fine.

CHAPTER EIGHT

ZORA

"Hey, I'm here! Where is everyone?"

I close the door to my childhood home behind me, shrugging out of my jacket and hanging it up in the hall closet. It's still September, and in the midafternoon, the temperature is in the midsixties. It's perfect sweater weather, and by all rights, I should be good rocking one outside and inside. But my father keeps it at a firm eighty degrees in the house all year round; he has since we were kids. Just another topic he and my mother have argued about for the past thirty-plus years. According to her, heat is nothing but a waste of money.

Personally, I think it's his way of reminding his kids what awaits us in the afterlife if we don't get our shit together. And by "get our shit together," I mean obey God's commandments *and* his. And Reginald "Reggie" Nelson has a hell of a lot more commandments than God's ten.

"In the kitchen," Mom calls out.

Sighing, I shut the door but don't immediately head down the hall in the direction of the kitchen. I pause and conduct a mental survey.

Hair up in a neat bun as if I didn't have a chance to take it down after coming from church today. Didn't go to church, but it's all about the appearance.

Burnt-orange, wide-legged romper that's stylish enough to satisfy my mother's pride in knowing she raised a daughter who isn't ashamed of the curves God blessed her with. And modest enough to appease the father who believes God wants only your future husband to appreciate and see aforementioned curves. It's a careful and sometimes treacherous tightrope I have to balance. Thanks to experience and painful—and very loud—mishaps, I mostly nail it. Hopefully, I did today too.

Loosing a sigh, I step forward, and the brush of metal against my neck draws me up short.

"Dammit."

Hurriedly, I remove the long dangling gold earrings from my lobes and tuck them into the pockets of my romper. How could I have been so careless? Just the sight of those could've caused an immediate argument between my parents. An old-as-Methuselah argument but one that hasn't lost its lasting power or venom.

And the blame for it can be placed squarely at my feet. Just because I wanted to get my ears pierced when I was twelve since it'd seemed like I was the only person in my seventh-grade class who still possessed virgin lobes. Mom had been all for it, but Dad? Hell no. And he had scripture to back his decision up; he always did. But Mom didn't let that stop her.

One day after school, she hustled me over to the mall, led me into the jewelry store, and convinced me it would be okay to get my ears pierced. I was twelve, dying not to be different from the other girls in my class, and since my mother said it was okay, well, I went with it. And I loved the little silver balls in my ears. *Loved* them . . . until I arrived home and Dad hit the proverbial roof.

That argument had been so bad I'd gone to bed and hadn't been able to leave it for a couple of days. I'd been sick to my stomach, throwing up, shaking. Not just because of my father's rage and the ferocity of their battle. But because of the knowledge that my mother had used me as a pawn in their ongoing war. I'd been a weapon to get at him, to one-up him. That had been devastating for me. And it'd taught me a valuable lesson.

Never give my parents ammo.

Never give them the opportunity for me to *be* their ammo.

So now, even eighteen years later, I wear discreet small earrings to family dinners so my mother doesn't feel like I'm surrendering to my father's demands, and my father can pretend they don't exist.

See? Careful balance.

Not trusting my memory, I turn, peering into the hall mirror and giving myself another quick scan. Patting my top bun, I nod. I'm good.

Seconds later, I enter the kitchen and find the rest of my family there. Surprise whispers through me. As soon as Levi, Miriam, and I hit eighteen, we all went to college and never returned home. It's become somewhat of a game for us to see who can arrive the latest to these dinners where, thankfully, Mom and Dad require our presence only once every two or three months.

Looks like I win this time.

My prize? Less time in the splash zone.

"Hey," I greet them, passing the table, where Miriam perches on a chair. She wrinkles her nose, and my stomach clenches. God, that could mean anything, but one thing for certain. Mom and Dad have already been into it. Turning up the wattage of my smile, I cross over to the stove, where Mom stirs a pot, and kiss her cheek. Even the heavenly smell emanating from it isn't enough to uncoil the knot tightening further in my belly. "Hey, Mom. Whatever you're cooking smells amazing."

"It's beef stew," she says with a sharp twist of her wrist. The spoon raps against the pot, declaring to everyone her agitation. "And it would've been finished thirty minutes ago if your father had bought the beef I asked him to instead of what *he* wanted. As if he does any of the cooking around here and knows better than I do what should go into this meal."

Whew, boy.

"If you'd been clearer about what you needed, then I wouldn't have had to make a guess. That's always been your problem, Monica. Expecting me to read your mind."

"No, since you're a full-grown adult, I'd expect you to use that cell phone in your pocket and place a call if you're unsure about something. It's not just a camera or paperweight."

"Maybe I didn't feel like hearing *this* in my ear while I was in the store."

Oh damn.

"Mom, I'm sure Dad did his best, and you're a genius at what you do. No doubt the food is going to be wonderful."

I take a glimpse at my brother and sister, who have suddenly transformed into selective mutes. Levi, who honestly just doesn't give a shit, leans against the kitchen wall, his thumbs rapidly flying over his phone. And Miriam returns my glance with a "You got this" look and thumbs-up.

So basically, I'm on my own.

Sometimes being the peacemaker fucking sucks.

Mom slides me a side-eye that's worthy of its own GIF.

"Always taking your father's side. I should've known."

"Oh, come off it, Monica," my father interjects, throwing his hands in the air. "She literally just called you a great cook. Which, while nice, she should be ashamed of lying on a Sunday." He stalks toward the kitchen entrance, ignoring the glare Mom buries in his back like a Roman dagger. "I'm done with this conversation. The game is on. Call me when dinner's ready. Come on, Levi."

Levi lifts his head, a frown marring his brow as he stares at Dad's retreating back. His lips part, and I don't need a twin bond to predict the "No fucking thank you" that's about to fall from his lips with full Levi disdain. He abhors sports. With the passion of a thousand suns. A fact our sports-apparel-store-owner and die-hard Denver Broncos–fan father can't understand or accept.

But I give him a small hard shake of my head. Oh hell no. Not today, Satan. He's got to take one for the team if we're going to get through this quickly and with as little damage as possible.

A sneer rides his mouth, but he pushes off the wall and strides from the room.

"Mom, how's the school year going so far?" I ask, turning back to my mother.

And thankfully, the question diverts her attention and bad mood. An hour later, when we're all gathered around the dining room table, bowls of beef stew and white rice with steaming-hot homemade biscuits and butter in front of us, I start to cautiously relax. Mom and Dad have sniped at each other as usual but just over small things. Nothing that has the capability of setting off a shitstorm. Miriam is her usual funny and charming self, even eliciting laughter from Dad. Minor miracle there. And Levi is taciturn, but nothing inflammatory has escaped him, so I'm counting it as a win.

We might actually make it through this dinner unscathed . . .

"Darlene said she saw one of your ads on the Facebook. She asked me if it was my kids' company. I had to lie at Bible study; can you imagine? I was so embarrassed," Dad says.

Oh *fuck*.

So close. We'd been so *close*.

I glance up from my dinner to meet my father's narrowed stare from the end of the table. He's silent, waiting on me. Probably to apologize. That's another thing. Technically, I'm not even the oldest child—Levi is by two minutes—but they treat me as if I am. Which includes when either my brother or sister gets in trouble, they look to me. I should've been watching out for them. Why didn't I know Levi had been writing essays for the other students and charging cash for them? How could I have let Miriam participate in that student protest about college tuition funding prisons? Well, that had been Dad. Mom had been positively giddy her daughter had ended up arrested for the cause.

Still, they both blamed me for dragging my siblings into this ridiculous business venture. As if Levi and Miriam didn't have fully functioning brain cells and hadn't contributed their unique skills to the company. We were equal partners, having invested the same amount of money, sweat equity, passion, and time. But no. In my parents' eyes, I'd failed in my responsibilities toward Levi and Miriam and them.

"So lying in the church parking lot would've been preferable to lying at Bible study? I'm not a theological student, but I don't think God cares where you lie. It's still shitty," Levi drawls.

Oh double fuck.

Dad slaps his hand to the table, jerking his glare from me to Levi. While the rest of us jump at the sharp sound, Levi doesn't even flinch, just calmly continues to spoon more stew into his mouth, completely unfazed by our father's show of temper.

"The. Hell," I mouth at him.

He arches an eyebrow back at me.

"Don't you speak that way at my dinner table, in my house. I won't put up with that kind of disrespect."

"But it's okay to disrespect our business? Do unto others as you would have them do unto you." More spooning of stew.

I love my mother's cooking, I do, but it's just not that fucking good.

"Honor your father and your mother so that you may live long in the land the Lord your God is giving you," my father growls.

"Fathers, do not provoke your children to anger, but bring them up in the discipline and instruction of the Lord."

"Levi, please," I murmur, praying—and I do mean *praying*—my brother hears the message in those two words.

If he doesn't stop, I'm afraid Dad is going to go apoplectic . . . well, more than he already is, and that won't be good for any of us. I just want to get through this dinner with as little conflict as possible. The arguments, the sniping, the digs—they don't affect Levi the same as me. Sometimes, he seems to thrive on it. Like just now. Especially with our dad. Miriam has always done what a glance beside me reveals she's up to now. Staring across the room, a tiny wrinkle above her nose. She loses herself in her head in a world where none of us can reach her. I've always envied her of that ability—that gift.

But the peacemaker? She can't escape. She has to remain on the battlefield, at her post. And suffer the physical consequences later.

"Dad." After a tension-taut moment where he continues to glower at Levi, who once again is dining on his stew like it's ambrosia, Dad drags his focus to me. "I'm sorry you felt you had to lie to your church member." I ignore my brother's snort. "That must've been uncomfortable for you."

I'm sorry you can't be proud of your children's hard work, initiative, and success.

But the words remain trapped in my head because, hey. Peacemaker.

"I just don't get why of all the businesses you three could've chosen to open, you decide on a breakup service, for God's sake. It's unheard of. And ridiculous. When people ask me what my children do for a living, I can't even begin to explain it."

"Not exactly unheard of. There are several companies like ours, but they don't offer the level of services, packages, and amenities that we do. And it's not ridiculous at all. If it were, we wouldn't be in the black this year. There's a need and a demand, and we supply," Miriam says, sounding as if she's reading from a financial journal.

Hell, I'm surprised she's back from . . . wherever to join the conversation.

"Oh, honey, I doubt if that's true." Mom goes so far as to pat her hand.

I've always wondered if she realizes how condescending she is toward Miriam. As if just because she's a genius, she's also void of common sense. It's maddening. If Mom had her way, she would've prohibited Miriam from leaving the house, Bubble Wrapping her room and keeping her locked behind the door.

"She has an IQ of one hundred fifty-one and is a member of Mensa. I think I'm believing the genius," Levi drawls.

"We get it." I hold my hands up, the meal a heavy, congealed weight in my belly. Cold fingers scuttle down my spine, and a faint throb pulses above my right eye, portending a tension headache. "You don't approve of our company." How can we forget when it's literally the only thing they agree on? "And if you choose not to tell your friends, congregation, or coworkers what we do, then fine. We wish you supported us, but we can't force you. But can we table your disapproval and moral outrage for now? At least until our next dinner? If we don't, we might not have anything to talk about."

My father's mouth thins, and Mom's chin jerks back toward her neck. I glance across the table, and though his expression remains impassive, Levi is my twin, and I can read that look.

And you talk about my sarcasm?

Oh, shut up.

He sniffs and spoons up more stew.

I'm asking Mom to box up my leftovers and give them to him.

"There was no need for that much tone, young lady," Mom says. After pushing back her chair, she picks up her bowl and rounds the table to grab Dad's and then walks toward the kitchen. That's how I know we've pissed her off. She's being polite to Dad. "I don't know what's gotten into you three tonight."

You. The word ricochets off my skull like a pinball. *You and Dad pretending like you don't recognize why we opened BURNED in the first place. You two acting like you don't have any ownership in who we are and our decisions.*

But . . . peacemaker.

And the peacemaker never misses a good opportunity to shut up. Especially when the crisis appears to be averted. Even if it's left her emotionally bruised and exhausted.

Just as I reach for my glass of wine, my cell phone vibrates against my hip. I startle, my elbow hitting the table. Frowning, I slip my hand under the table and into my pocket. It's Sunday. Who would be texting me? Unless Deanna thought of something important and decided to message me so it would be the first thing on our minds Monday morning. She's done that before.

"No phones at the dinner table, Zora. You know the rules," Dad reminds me.

Too late. I've already slid the cell free and peeked down at the screen.

MNBM.

My heartbeat stutters, slows, and then kicks into hyperdrive. The raucous pounding drowns out whatever else my father says as I shove back my chair and stand. Pasting a smile on my face, I swallow past the sudden thickness of my tongue and grasp for normal. As Miriam squints up at me, I'm going to take a wild guess that I'm failing.

"I need to take this. I'll be right back."

Before Dad can say anything else, I stride from the dining room and pivot sharply in the opposite direction toward the front of the house. I don't stop at the foyer, though. I open the front door and walk out onto the porch. Facing the cooler September air in a sleeveless romper is better than having one of my nosy family members sneaking in on me. Because no, they're not above it.

I move to the porch railing and lean my back against it, facing the front door. Only then do I open the text.

MNBM.

My Next Big Mistake.

I never did change how I listed Cyrus in my phone. Why should I? It's still true.

Shock still wavers through me that he messaged me. It's been five days since that night at the bookstore. Since he wielded his attorney-like magic like Thor's hammer and beat me down with my own guilt until

I yielded into being his fake girlfriend. God, even thinking those words sounds ludicrous. Five days later, and he hasn't been in contact to enlighten me on what this assignment entails. Just complete radio silence. I'd begun to believe he'd changed his mind. And I refuse to admit to, much less dwell on, the disappointment that slides through me. Relief. Relief has been my companion for the last few days.

Until now.

MNBM: First fake relationship duties. At 8.

I stare at the screen, blinking. Not believing what I'm seeing. But no, the message remains the same. And the pulse slamming against the base of my throat and hammering in my head like a mallet against iron assures me it's not changing.

Me: It's Sunday.

MNBM: That's usually what they call the day after Saturday and before Monday.

Smart-ass. Right. Best not to think about his ass right now.

Me: It's a rest day. Time to spend with family.

MNBM: Are you with yours?

Me: Yes.

Dots appear, then vanish. Appear, then vanish. Then . . .

MNBM: Are you using one of your free passes?

Dammit. I lift my head and stare at the front door. Seeing the dysfunctional family beyond. Weariness presses down on my shoulders at what awaits me when I return to that table. Thirty years with my parents. Thirty. They might let the topic of BURNED go, but there will be another one for them to snap at each other over. To argue and throw verbal punches over.

I rub the spot over my eye where the faint thrumming steadily increases. By the time I leave here in another hour or so, that drumming will evolve into a full-blown migraine.

Am I willing to use a free pass to stay here and suffer this broken merry-go-round?

Me: No. Where am I going?

MNBM: My house. I believe you know the address.

Blowing out a breath, I tuck the phone back in my pocket, noting the time. 6:38. Enough time to return inside, give my excuses, go home, and change and head over to my new fake boyfriend's house.

Pushing off the railing, I brace myself for the explosion of questions and attitude about to come my way. But strangely, it's not anxiety that bubbles inside me.

Anticipation carries me back into my parents' home and down the hall.

And maybe a little bit of excitement.

But damn if I admit to that.

This time when I knock on Cyrus's front door, nerves jangle just under my skin, and sweat dots my palms, but for a different reason. Because I'm here not to break up Cyrus's relationship but to learn more about him in order to make our charade more believable in front of his colleagues. I shake my head, crossing my sweater-covered arms over my chest. This is the kind of stuff that happens in cutesy rom-coms . . . or with stalkers.

Sighing, I study the gorgeous home sitting on the corner lot. When I initially drove up to the address Val gave me, surprise winged through me as I pulled up to the house. From Cyrus's picture and the little bit of information Val had provided about him, I'd assumed he'd live in a luxurious condominium or townhome. Definitely not this beautiful single-family home in an immaculate residential neighborhood that screamed carpools, PTA, and door-to-door trick-or-treating. Okay, so carpools in Lexuses and PTA meetings at exclusive private schools with tuition more expensive than some colleges, but hey, still family oriented.

Like I did weeks ago, I can't help but admire the white limestone exterior made up of slopes, angles, and arches. To the right, glass nearly encompasses an entire wall, providing a glimpse of a gorgeous winding staircase. A private walled space curves around one side of the house, and a garage occupies the other. So much house for one man. But maybe he bought it soon after meeting Val, planning on filling it with a family . . .

No, that doesn't sit right. I've known Cyrus for only a very short amount of time, but he doesn't really come across as the Taj Mahal type. Prenup, yes. And Val . . . well, while this house is stunning, I can't see it being quite palatial enough.

While I'm still scrutinizing the home and motives of the owner, the front door swings open, and said owner stands in the opening.

It's just not fair, dammit. He's as beautiful in his don't-look-directly-at-the-sun-or-risk-your-vision way as he's ever been. Possibly even more so in a thin but obviously expensive gray sweater, a white T-shirt, and faded blue jeans with frayed hems.

I swear there's going to come a day when my belly doesn't make a fast break for my feet when I catch sight of him. Or my heart doesn't throw itself against my sternum like a groupie at a rock concert with just a glimpse of that wicked, lush mouth and its slightly cruel edge. Or my sex won't quiver like a virgin with the vapors at the glimpse of her first bare male chest.

Apparently, lust transforms me into the queen of metaphors.

He continues to silently stand in the doorway, a hand palming each side of the frame, and his gaze trails over me. It requires the strength of Hercules not to fidget. Not to pat my hair as that inspection glances over my bun or tug my long cardigan sweater closed over my black tank top. When he returns to my face, every part of me tingles from the visual caress of his narrow-eyed study. Hell, even my knees, bared by the rips in my black jeans, prickle with sensitivity.

Whew, boy. Whatever this evening entails, it's going to be long.

"So do I require a password to gain entrance to the house?"

He doesn't reply to my snarky question, but if I'm not mistaken, the corner of his mouth twitches. I can't confirm as he steps back inside the house, silently granting me permission to enter. Inhaling a deep breath, I move forward.

"Shit," I breathe, pausing in the foyer next to a floating staircase and in front of a spacious living room that flows into a dining room with a masterpiece of a chandelier and continues on to what appears to be a minilibrary or reading nook, complete with a comfy chair and upholstered window seat.

At least ten-foot ceilings soar high above me, and church organs and pipes wouldn't be out of place. Another stunning chandelier hangs above my head, and to my right on the far wall loom a stone fireplace and mantel.

It's a combination of modern and classic styles. Elegance and comfort. Luxury and coziness.

It's gorgeous.

Cyrus glances over his shoulder, an eyebrow arched. "Excuse me?"

"Sorry." I cough. "Nothing."

He scans my face for a long moment, then finally turns back around. And I release my pent-up breath.

"I wouldn't say my house is shit. *The* shit, maybe."

I scowl at his wide shoulders. Damn the man and his bat ears.

Seconds later, he leads me to what can only be described as a man cave. But with roid rage. Of course, the requisite theater-size mounted television, entertainment center, and huge sectional that stretches half the length of the room. But a fully stocked wet bar and a refrigerator claim one wall, actual eighties' arcade games another. Gaming chairs, consoles, and another huge screen take up a corner in the back of the room.

Even Levi couldn't find fault with this room. Shoot, he might hole up in here for life and bar anyone from entering.

"Your home is amazing," I say, spinning in a half circle.

Curiosity still dogs me about why he needs all this house. The question leaps on my tongue like a kid in a bouncy castle. But I quell it. Asking him personal questions means opening the door for him to pose those same inquiries to me. And I can't allow that to happen.

A sour swill curdles in my stomach, inching toward the back of my throat.

His terms had included complete honesty, no lies. I'd violated that stipulation even before I'd agreed to his deal. Not in words, no. But in my silence. In my complicit agreement to his assumptions. I can mitigate my dishonesty only by not lying *more*. It's the only out he's left me.

Because not agreeing to this arrangement wasn't—and isn't—an option. Not only because Cyrus nailed it—my own guilt wouldn't allow me to walk away. And it's silly, really; this is my job. But being behind the desk allows me distance. And there's no point in denying to myself what I can't—absolutely refuse—to admit to anyone else. None of my other clients stirred this . . . connection, this draw that I have toward Cyrus.

Then there's the other side of him . . .

I don't doubt for a moment that Cyrus, with his eyes that can go from summer sky to winter storm in seconds, could be ruthless if the situation called for it. I could easily attribute it to the nature of his career, but . . . I don't know. It seems deeper than that. As if the profession grants him the freedom to use what's already inside him and excel in it. And though he didn't confirm that he would tell Val that I had fucked up in breaking up with him, he hadn't denied it either. I have to do whatever it takes to keep my name out of his mouth when it comes to Valerie Summers. Because if he discovers I've been lying to him about my job, about my very identity, I have zero doubts I will see that other side of him.

The thought of that ruthlessness sends a shimmer of anxiety rippling down my spine. But quick on its heels is a current of that excitement from earlier. I need my head examined. And apparently my vagina too. Is a pussy psychologist a thing? If not, it needs to be.

"Thank you." He walks over to the couch, jerking his chin toward the bar. "Can I get you something to drink?"

Thinking of the censorious looks and admonishments I left behind, I let "Anything with a hundred proof" slip out before I can trap it. And when his dark eyebrow shoots toward his hairline, I smother a groan.

"Water will be fine." Because imbibing alcohol around him is not a winning idea.

He doesn't say anything, but his lingering look is speaking a damn dissertation. Ignoring it, I head over to the couch and sink down on the far end of it. A football game plays out on the TV screen, and my father would probably sacrifice one of us to watch his beloved Broncos on this monster. Forget that ram-in-the-bush thing.

"Here you go."

A cold bottle of water with condensation running down the sides and a napkin appear in front of my face, and I accept both.

"Thanks." After twisting the cap off, I down a grateful sip, then glance at Cyrus as he sprawls out on the middle of the couch. I *don't* stare at his powerfully muscled thighs and how they press against the light denim. And I definitely don't imagine how they could so easily control a woman underneath him. Or over him, for that matter . . . shit. "So why am I here?"

He lifts a beer to his mouth, then peers at me while he takes a long drink. Another thing I don't do: stare at those beautifully cruel lips wrapped around the mouth of the bottle.

"Doing what couples do. Hanging out."

I stare at him. Blink. Stare some more. Because my ears have heard what he said, but my brain is having a difficult time computing the meaning.

"You mean to tell me you called me all the way over here from a family dinner just to sit on this couch and *entertain* you?" I narrow my eyes on him. "Is this a rich-people thing?"

"I wouldn't know."

I twist on the cushion, exaggerating as I scan the room and the obvious display of wealth surrounding me. "Excuse me; my bad. But I could've sworn I was sitting in your Washington Park house, where a high-end vehicle sits in your two-car garage, a chandelier that costs more than a year's rent of my Park Hill bungalow hangs from your ceiling, and a home bar that is better stocked than top shelves in some bars occupies your den. But like I said, my bad. Didn't mean to assume you were rich."

"Sarcasm duly noted." He folds his hands across his flat stomach, his measured gaze resting fully on me. I almost order him to look at the game. That blue-fire stare borders on too much. Too intense. Too invasive. Too. Damn. Much. "And thank you for enumerating the possessions in my home. I nearly forgot for a moment there."

"Now whose sarcasm is duly noted?" I grumble.

"But what I meant is," he continues, as if I hadn't interrupted, "I wasn't born wealthy. Didn't grow up in it either. So I don't understand entitlement since I've worked, bargained, and possibly schemed for everything I have. Although, that last one you'll have to prove because there's no evidence." A faint flicker of amusement barely curves his mouth before it disappears. "So like I said, I wouldn't know if that's a rich-people thing. I asked you over here to get to know you since we're friends now. I didn't intend to interrupt your family dinner, but I also offered you the opportunity to use one of your free passes. It was your choice not to use it."

Call me genuinely chastised. Because, dammit, I feel like a grade-A bitch. He's right. I did decide not to take the out; I could've stayed at my parents' house and finished the evening with them, Levi, and Miriam. But I didn't. Truthfully, I saw his text as an escape, a reprieve.

But I can't tell him that. Can't explain. Because that would be getting personal.

Speaking of that . . .

"I thought we agreed not to get personal," I remind him.

I *need* him to agree. Not just so I don't become more of a liar and leave him feeling more stained and dirty, but because knowing more about him forges connections. It transforms Pinocchio into a real boy. Just the bit of information about his past stirs my curiosity, feeds my insatiable hunger for *more*. I can't have more of him. More has the potential of threatening my business, my brother's and sister's futures.

Threatening me.

Because if I give myself that "more" and he finds out the truth about BURNED, about my connection to Val . . . unease curdles in my belly. He would leave scorched earth behind, completely razing me to the ground. I can't allow that.

"I did," he says, tilting his head. "You said, and I quote, 'You can't compel what I give you of myself.' But you failed to add a stipulation regarding what *I* give *you* of *me*."

My lips part. Then snap shut.

Sneaky bastard.

"How long is this arrangement supposed to last?" I blurt out. "We never discussed that."

And I need an end date for my sanity.

"You already want to get rid of me, Zora?" Another one of those faint not-quite-there smiles.

Yes. But not for the reason he probably thinks.

"Any smart business partner likes to know her contract end date."

"Fine. New Year's Eve. Start the new year a free woman."

I gape at him. Honest-to-God gape. *Yes, it's a little over three months. But it's three months.* With *him.* Pretending to be *his.*

"Why?" I ask. "The retreat is a little over three weeks away. Why aren't we calling it quits after that?"

"And how would that look to my coworkers, to the partners of the firm? Exactly like what we are—a fake couple who came together solely for the purpose of the retreat. No, Zora. I'm playing the long game. They'll announce the new partners about a month after the retreat, and I'll need you for at least a month after that to make this look authentic. Then we can quietly break up, claiming 'We just wanted different things.'"

I swallow a sigh. Okay, I could do that. I mean, three months of being in his space, inhaling his scent, calling him mine when he isn't, afraid this house of cards will tumble under the slightest breeze seems like a long anxiety-ridden time, but it's doable.

Hell, he could've said a year.

I nod and stretch my arm toward him. "Deal."

Cyrus hesitates for the briefest moment before wrapping his hand around mine, squeezing lightly, and abruptly releasing me. I start to frown but at the last second catch myself. No curiosity when it comes to this man. That's my new rule.

"I was going to order dinner, but since you ate, would you like dessert?" he asks.

My stomach chooses that moment to gurgle, reminding me and anyone within a five-mile radius that I left before Mom could serve up peach cobbler and butter-pecan ice cream.

"I take that as a yes?"

"A gentleman would've ignored that," I mutter.

He shoves up from the couch. "I'm no gentleman. We're both aware of that fact."

As he strides from the room, I briefly close my eyes, but that's a bad, bad idea, as my mind provides in vivid, exquisite detail how *it* believes just how *un*gentlemanly he is. Beginning with how he would tangle one of those big but incongruently elegant, long-fingered hands in a woman's hair and shove her to her knees . . .

A searing blast of heat surges through my veins, converging between my thighs. Leaving me hot and wet. Because that woman in my head has dark natural curls, and as she tips her head back to look up at him and await his next instruction, she wears my face . . .

Shooting up from the couch as if my ass is on fire, I follow behind him.

Friend. He wants a friend. Not a friend with benefits. Not that I'm offering that. Because I'm not.

Good God, girl. Who are you trying to convince?

Shut up, heffa.

I'm losing it. I'm calling myself out, and I'm losing it.

Cyrus leads me into a kitchen straight out of *Architectural Digest*. I instantly fall in love, and cooking isn't even my ministry.

"This is lovely," I murmur, brushing my fingertips along the marble countertops. "This room must be one of your favorites."

He pauses next to the island, studies me. Then slowly dips his chin. "Yes, it is." Another pause. "It's actually the room that sold me on the house."

"I can see why." I scan the unique wine closet, beautiful countertops, top-of-the-line appliances, airy spaces, eating nook, fabulous island . . . "Is that pie?"

"Dutch apple." He moves to the cabinets and pulls down two small plates, then retrieves forks from another drawer. "Do you want a slice?"

"Don't play with me. Do these hips look like I turn down pie?" I slap them for good measure.

He draws short, dishes and utensils in hand, his gaze dropping to my waist. And it stays there. The air catches in my lungs, and I'm afraid to move. To shatter this moment where that blue gaze strokes me as if the denim covering me has disappeared and nothing separates him from my skin but space.

A second later, he drags his gaze upward, meeting mine, and the breath that lodged in my throat expels on a low, harsh puff. Before, I'd compared his eyes to the blue heart of flames. But I hadn't seen them alit, burning. I hadn't been seared by them.

Until now.

"I'll take that as a yes too," he says, covering the remaining space to the island.

There's gravel in that midnight voice, and a shiver trips over my skin.

What was *that*? He hadn't been staring at my hips, at *me*, like he wanted to strip me out of my jeans and eat *me* instead of the dutch apple pie. That must've been a figment of my overactive, sex-starved imagination. Yes, that had to be it. After all, it's been . . . well, a while since I've had an orgasm that wasn't like frozen yogurt—self-served.

Cyrus lifts the crystal dome from the cake plate and cuts a healthy-size slice of pie, sets it on a plate, and slides it across the island to me. I tense, waiting for the comment; I can't help it. Call it a side effect from too many boyfriends who considered it their God-given duty and right to advise me on my health, dietary habits, and weight just because they stuck their dick in me. Other than platonic, professional handshakes, Cyrus has touched only my chin—and yes, I can still feel the brand of that grip without even trying—but it doesn't stop me from bracing myself for the verbal onslaught.

But it doesn't come.

Instead, he cuts himself a slice as big as mine, replaces the top, and tucks into his food. Surprised, I stand frozen, watching him. I'm not ashamed of my size 16 frame and the curves that pack it. Contrary to what some people have to say about my lifestyle, I regularly work out and eat a well-balanced diet, but I refuse to starve myself. And I enjoy food, especially treats like pie. And I don't see a reason to go without things I enjoy just because society frowns on it. Society can suck a fat bag of dicks. Skinny ones, at that. Still . . . I wouldn't be human if the comments didn't dig into my tender skin, if they didn't leave bruises. Particularly when they come from people I share my heart and body with. I would be a liar—more so than I've already been lately—to claim I haven't erected a sensitive wall when it comes to this issue.

"You're not hungry?"

"What?" I rasp. Giving my head a small shake, I cut off a piece. "No, this is great. Thank you." I slide a forkful of the dessert into my mouth, and *holy shit*. Did my eyes roll to the back of my head? Did I moan aloud? I think I did, and I'm not even sorry. "Oh my God. This is sex illegal. Where did you buy this, and can I purchase it in bulk?"

I open eyes I hadn't realized I'd closed and once more meet pure heat. The pie melts on my tongue, and unbidden, I slick the tip of my tongue over my lower lip. I tell myself it's to catch any wayward crumbs, but deep in that place where it's safe to be honest with just myself, I admit it's to see those flames jump in his eyes again. That can get addictive.

I *want* to become addictive, even though I know it's about as good for me as crack.

"I baked it."

My head jerks back, the fork nearly tumbling from my fingers. "Say what now?"

The corner of his mouth twitches. "I baked it."

"As in you made it? From scratch? With your own hands?"

"Sometimes I think we speak different languages. We'll need to work on our communication, as I understand it's one of the foundation stones of a good relationship," he drawls. "Yes, from scratch, with my own two hands." He holds them up, palms out, for emphasis. "It's my mother's recipe."

"Wow," I whisper. "Plot twist. Didn't see that coming." Then I pause. This was my stipulation, after all. But it can't go unsaid. "I'm sorry about your mother. From what you've said, I'm assuming she's gone. And I'm truly sorry for that."

"My mother and father. And thank you. It's been a long time, though."

"That doesn't matter. I can't imagine it mattering."

As dysfunctional as my parents are, if I'd lost one of them, much less both, I don't know how I would've managed. Who I would be today. How I would've recovered. Cyrus suffered the hell of losing his father and mother and still stands here today. The strength of that . . . the pain of that . . .

"At least I have this part of her." He tapped the edge of his dish with his fork. *More than that. She lives on inside you.* But I lock those words down. That's not us. "I'm glad you like it. Gives me brownie points toward making up for interrupting your family dinner. Speaking of family, your sister texted Jordan. He's utterly fascinated with her, by the way. Especially since she refuses to have anything to do with his community peen. Her words, not mine."

I snort, slapping a hand over my mouth to trap my loud bark of laughter.

Cyrus waves a hand. "No, go ahead and laugh. I did. Hard. Your sister is hilarious. Is it just you and her?"

"No, I have an older brother by two minutes."

"Two minutes? Twins?"

I nod. "Yes. His name is Levi."

"Levi." He frowns. "I assumed you were named after Zora Neale Hurston. Was he named after Primo Levi?"

I shake my head. "You're right about Zora Neale Hurston, but no. Since we were twins, my mother named me, and my father chose Levi's. It's short for Leviticus, the third book in the Bible."

"Got you." He forks up another piece of pie. "That explains Miriam, then."

I laugh, and it abrades my throat. Hearing it, Cyrus lowers his fork, his gaze watchful, careful. And I want to duck it, avoid it. But it's as if a switch flipped on my mouth, and it won't stop running.

"You'd think, but no. When my sister came along, my parents couldn't agree on who would name her. It was easy with me and my brother; they had a kid apiece. But this time they only had one, and they fought over who had the right to choose the entire pregnancy. I was only three or four, but I remember the loud arguments, the yelling. From what I understand, after my mom had my sister, she waited until Dad left the hospital room and filled out the birth certificate without his knowledge. She named my sister after Miriam Makeba, the South African singer and activist. My father has never forgiven her for that." That and a long list of other things. "When asked, he tells people my sister's named after Miriam, Moses's sister. But that's just to save face."

My words echo in the silent kitchen. Heat streams up my neck and pours into my cheeks, and I'm pretty sure I'm debunking the Black-people-don't-blush myth. Dammit. I hadn't meant to say all that. What happened to nothing personal?

"What's in this pie?" I huff out a soft, trembling laugh. "Truth serum? Because I honestly meant to wait until our second hangout to spill the sad story about my family's pettiness. Now you probably won't invite me over for pie anymore."

My joke falls flat. Mainly because even I can hear the strain and embarrassment in my voice, and he doesn't look the least bit amused.

If anything, the tight fold of his lips, the flex of a muscle along his jaw, and the frigid ice in his eyes scream anger. But at what? At . . . whom?

"Cyrus?"

"I'm suddenly not sorry for interrupting your dinner."

"Um . . ." Okay. "Why not?"

He splays his hands out on the top of the island, leaning forward. "Because if I was having dinner with my parents, I would've taken the damn pass. You can deny it to yourself if it makes you feel better, but you wanted to leave. You weren't just leaving them; you were running to me." He straightens, picking his fork back up, as if he hasn't left me broken. "Next time don't leave your brother and sister behind. Bring them with you."

Did I say he left me broken? No, he's left me *shattered.*

So I eat more pie, afraid of what might spill out of me next. Afraid I might tell him I feel safer here in this kitchen with him than I did at my parents' table. Afraid I might confide more about my chaotic childhood, about the war of wearing earrings, of how conflict twists me into so many knots I become physically ill.

Of how I opened a business inspired by my parents' craziness. And how that business brought me to him.

But I can't admit that. The time for admissions should've been earlier, when he wouldn't have felt lied to, played for a fool. When I wouldn't have placed not just me but my company and my brother's and sister's futures at risk.

So I eat more pie.

"I bake to feel closer to my mother."

I pause, the fork halfway to my mouth.

"When I was younger, she baked as an outlet for her emotions. When she was happy, she baked. When my father pissed her off, she baked. When she was sad, she baked. It was her happy place, and she always included me in her space. Never pushed me away because I was too young or small. She *wanted* me in her space. We bonded in the kitchen. It's where she'd ask me about my day, and I could tell her anything, and she listened. And I learned. After they died and I had to leave the house, I snuck into the kitchen that last night and stole her tin box of recipes. And no matter where they sent me, it went with me."

A fist squeezes my throat as I picture a small thin boy with Cyrus's eyes going from home to home, a suitcase in one hand and a small tin box in the other. More questions crowd into my mind, onto my tongue. What was your childhood like after they died? Did you have a good home? Were you okay?

Then I look at him. Really look at him and glimpse that shade of ruthlessness around his mouth. Recall the ice of his eyes. Remember the flatness his voice can take. And I answer my own questions.

Not good. No. And no.

But why is he sharing this with me? I didn't ask him to . . .

"You gave me a little of yourself, so I'm giving you a bit of me in return," he says, as if he heard my silent question.

This man is dangerous. If I didn't know it before, I do now.

Today taught me a valuable lesson. I can't let my guard down around Cyrus. He'll sneak under my shields before I've even mounted a defense.

Three months.

I just have to hold out for three months.

I can do it.

So why do I sound like I don't believe in myself?

Shit.

CHAPTER NINE

CYRUS

I watch the door of the Five Points restaurant that Zora suggested we meet at for lunch. Suggested, hell. She informed me the barbecue place was where she'd planned to eat today, and I could meet her there or have my lunch date over the phone. My choice. Seeing as how I'd called her about a half hour earlier and asked to see her, I guess she might be a little miffed.

I shake my head, a smirk tugging at my mouth. A sense of déjà vu descends over me. Not too long ago there was another time I obsessively studied a door, waiting on Zora to walk through it.

Only instead of a bookstore, I'm sitting in a restaurant, stomach growling at the delicious scents of sauce, pork, and coleslaw.

She's lucky I'm in the mood for macaroni and cheese and ribs.

"Can I get you a refill?" the waitress asks, a pitcher of water in hand. "And I can take your order if you're ready."

"No, thank you. I'm still waiting on someone—here she is now. We'll need a few minutes," I say, rising from the table, my gaze fixed on the woman striding through the entrance.

Does she feel the eyes that swing to her? Some admiring, some envious, most lustful?

She takes a simple emerald-green A-line dress and transforms it into a sexy number out of a lingerie catalogue with the thrust of those gorgeous breasts, a sway of those ample rounded hips, and her confident, sensual glide on navy stiletto pumps.

As she reaches me, a cloud of honey and almond teases me. Invites me to seek out its source. Her neck? Her wrists? The back of her ears? Between those beautiful thighs?

Fuck being an attorney. I'm ready to turn my law license in for a map and a new career in exploration.

"Cyrus." She nods at me, then gives our waitress a polite smile. "Hi. I'm sorry if I held you up." Not held me up. The waitress. I don't know if I'm insulted or impressed. "Could I have a glass of water?"

"Of course. I'll be right back with a glass." The young woman sets the pitcher on the table and returns moments later with a new glass, filling it. "I'll give you a few minutes to look over the menu."

"Thank you."

"Thank you for seeing me on short notice," I say, lowering back to my seat.

She flicks a glance at me over the top of the menu. A menu I'd bet my prized KitchenAid Artisan series stand mixer she knows by heart.

"I wasn't willing to use a free pass on lunch since I had to eat. Even if it was very short notice."

Propping my forearms on the table, I lean forward. "Nice spot. You work nearby in the Five Points area?"

She lifts her head from perusing the menu—or pretending to—and slowly lowers it.

"Now, where I work would fall under the 'my private life' part of our arrangement." She arches an eyebrow. "I made a slip last night, but that was an aberration, not the norm. And it doesn't mean the terms of our deal have changed. No personal questions or demands for information."

I cock my head, studying her shuttered expression, the stiff set of her shoulders.

"Is that what this"—I tip my head toward her—"is about?"

"What is *this*?"

"The ice-queen routine? Is this your attempt to place distance between us because you're regretting what happened last night?" I shake my head, lightly tsking. "Easy, Zora. You told me a little about your brother and sister, not your social security number and bank account information. I promised you I wouldn't violate your privacy, and I won't."

Not that I hadn't considered it. Well, not last night. But after I'd proposed our arrangement, I'd almost used the firm's PI to have her investigated. I've never trusted easily, and I'd wanted to know who I was involved with. But, in the end, I'd decided against it. One, because it would have betrayed our agreement. She'd asked not to get personal. Digging into someone's background was the definition of *getting personal*. And second . . . I wanted—want—to trust her. It's a novel feeling. Only Jordan has earned it. Not even the woman I'd planned to eventually propose to had. But Zora has been honest with me, and she deserves my loyalty in return. And that begins with honoring my word.

"It's not an ice-queen routine." She shoots me side-eye, wrapping those full lips around her straw and sipping her water. For a moment, I lose my train of thought, focusing on nothing but that mouth and imagining it pursed around something bigger, thicker, hotter . . . *Goddamn.* I tear my gaze away, scanning the full restaurant for our server. "I'm annoyed. And I have the right to be annoyed, because I'm wondering if this 'When I call, you jump' thing is going to become a habit. I have a life, and I hate to break it to you like this, Cyrus, but it doesn't revolve around you."

Now *I'm* annoyed.

"I didn't ask you to change your plans or your life to suit mine, Zora," I say, reclining in my chair, voice calm, soft. "Aren't we at the restaurant you chose? That you'd already intended to eat at today? At least those were your words. So let's cut the shit. What's the real issue? Get it out there so we can get past this."

Her eyebrows arrow down over her nose, and shadows darken her brown eyes. Before she can reply, our waitress reappears, and her expression clears, that polite smile replacing the frown.

Frustration and an electrified surge of anticipation race through me, and I have to restrain the part of me that almost demands the server to leave. I want that anger, that irritation. It's real. It's authentic. And fuck, in a world where everyone wears a mask of phony affability, it could become addictive. I need her to mark me with it.

I wait only seconds after the waitress leaves with our orders before I turn back to Zora.

"Tell me. And don't lie," I command, deliberately reminding her of my stipulation.

Again, those brows slam down to meet, and she glances away from me, her slender, ringless fingers toying with her paper napkin.

"Zora."

An almost strangled sound rumbles in her throat, but she turns her head toward me, and I embrace the lick of ire in those eyes. And hate the wisps of panic.

"I feel . . . almost powerless in this. And I don't like it."

Her words pummel me like tiny fists. But the blows drive the breath from my body. Bile burns the lining of my gut, and for a moment, I fear I'm going to be sick right here in the middle of the restaurant.

With a trembling hand, I pick up my glass of water and slowly sip, hoping to push down the acid and disgust.

"Cyrus?"

That frown still creases her forehead, but concern tinges it. Concern for me, and isn't that laughable?

"What do you need from me?" I ask, and there's shit I can do about the slight rasp in my voice.

She shakes her head, waving a hand. "What just happened?"

"What do you need from me?" I ask again. "To give you back your power. I don't ever want you to feel that way. It wasn't my intent, though I can see how it happened. What do you need from me?" I repeat.

And if there's a note of desperation in the question, I can't hide it. Can't take it back. Because that's what I am in this moment. A desperate kid who's been stripped of his own voice, his own strength and control. The thought of inflicting that on anyone else . . . it sickens me.

"Cyrus." She reaches across the table and covers the hand I hadn't even realized I'd fisted around my napkin. "Tell me. And don't lie," she softly says, handing my own words back to me.

But I can't.

The story of baking with my mother—that I can share with her. But this? I can't.

"What do you need from me, Zora?"

She stares at me, and tension beats like a heavy heartbeat in the silence between us.

"Boundaries," she finally says. "You believe I owe you because I stole your voice in the breakup with Val. And I understand that. But your price shouldn't be robbing me of mine. This arrangement needs defined boundaries. What do you expect from me and when? If it intrudes on my life, do I get to tell you that—and you trust that I'm not just trying to get out of our deal or using a pass? There needs to be some element of trust here because I can't be at your beck and call. I'm not that woman."

Our food arrives, and though it smells delicious and looks even better, neither of us touches it. All of our attention is focused on each other.

"Okay."

She blinks. Frowns.

"Okay?"

"Yes." I nod. "With my work schedule, I can't give you a firm *when*. But if I call and you tell me you're unable to make it, I can give you my trust. No more passes. Just trust."

Her lashes lower, hiding from me. I clench my jaw, trapping the demand to lift them so I can look into her eyes, read the beautiful, addictive truth there.

"I accept that," she murmurs, returning her gaze to me.

The power of the relief that pours through me leaves me shaken, unnerved. Deciding not to dwell on the why of that, I turn my attention to the food in front of me. We eat in silence for the next twenty minutes, until she sets her fork aside and, after pushing her plate forward, folds her arms on the tabletop.

"So . . . you said something important had come up. You said you needed me."

Yes, I'd said that when I'd called her. And hearing the words aloud in her voice . . . well, it's an erotic kind of torture I've brought on myself. I know how I meant it, but my body is throwing in its own two cents and interpretation.

"Yes." I set my fork down next to my plate, mimicking her and giving a small wince. "They moved the date of the retreat up. It's now in two weeks."

She squeezes her eyes closed, then tilts her head, her tight curls brushing her shoulder. "Two weeks? We have fourteen days to get to know each other to the point that we're able to convince people you've known for years that we're in love?"

"Worked with them for years, yes. But known them—I can't say that's true. They're my colleagues, not friends. So they won't be that hard to convince."

Admitting that, hearing the words out there, sitting on the table between us right next to the salt and pepper shakers, carries a certain . . . shame. I'm embarrassed by them. As if there's a deficit in me because after four years of working with people, I can't call them friends. What I know about them, other than caseloads and clients, wouldn't be enough to fill the plates in front of us. What does that say about me?

What is she seeing at this moment when she looks at me?

I'm afraid to consider it.

"Can I ask you a question?" she quietly asks in the silence that has fallen between us.

Risking a glance in her direction, I push my advantage and lob a question at her. "Can I ask you a question in return? Quid pro quo."

She inhales a breath, and I hold mine. Damn. When did it become so important to me to unearth layers of Zora, as if she's my personal archeological dig?

"Comparable to the one I'm posing to you, yes."

Satisfaction slides through me in a warm, golden glide.

"What's your question?"

"Despite us being in a serious relationship"—her lips curl in a sardonic twist—"we really don't know each other that well. Still, you strike me as smart, tenacious, and strong willed. And at times, you can even be a little . . . nice."

"Did that hurt? It looked like it hurt."

"It did." She fiddled with the edge of her napkin before shifting her hands to her lap, out of my sight. "Anyway, out of all the fields of law you could go into, why entertainment? No shade, I promise. But why not family or criminal? Where you can help people in need?"

Does she expect me to take offense? It'll take more than that to offend me.

I shrug. "Money. With the right clients, entertainment law is very lucrative." I catch the wince that flashes across her face and give her a half smile. "Did you grow up poor?"

"We weren't poor, but we weren't rich, either, by any means."

"But you've never known what it is to wonder whether or not your guardian will remember to feed you that night. Or if they will buy you new shoes since yours has a hole in the bottom or if they will spend that government-issued check on a pair for themselves since they're going to the club that weekend. You've never known what it is to have to hide what few clothes you have or risk having others steal them while you sleep or go to school. If you experienced any of this, then you wouldn't disparage pursuing a career because of the earning potential."

"There's more to life than money, Cyrus."

I arch an eyebrow, trapping a scoff. "Like what? Integrity? Respect? Love?" I can't help but sneer at the last one. "You're being naive if you believe money doesn't influence and, in some cases, buy those."

"That's so cynical," she murmurs, her gaze dark with . . . I don't want to know. Because if it's pity, I won't be able to handle that. "And you're right. I haven't experienced that kind of need or lack. And I'm sorry you have."

"I don't want or need your pity," I say bluntly. Brutally.

"You don't have it," she replies, voice softer but just as brusque as mine. "You're a successful, wealthy, beautiful white man. You had a rough start, and I sympathize with it, but this system was created for you to win. The fact that you're in the running for partner at a prestigious law firm at thirty-three proves that. So yeah, sorry. No tears from this Black woman for you and your privilege."

She's lying.

And it's the first time since we've met that I know it with a certainty. Oh, the words are true—very true. But those eyes . . . they say differently. She has tears for me. Not for who I am now but for the boy I described. For him, she would cry a river.

My chest swells, my ribs expanding under the pressure.

I intended to leave my answer at *money*. To let her think what she wanted about me. Truthfully, I hoped she would assume the worst. It's easier when people do; then you don't have far to go to live up to their expectations. You can't disappoint them, and they damn sure won't be able to disappoint you.

Yet I find myself seeking to mitigate her impression of me. Later, when I'm alone, I'll analyze why.

Or maybe not.

"Most of my clients are like Jordan—athletes, actors, musicians, or artists who aren't born into wealth but because of their talents find themselves millionaires and even billionaires. There are companies out there that would use them, capitalize off their names, their brands, and images without fully compensating them. Or tying them up in unfair contracts that resemble something given to an indentured servant. These businesses that are bigger, with more resources, money, and attorneys, would take advantage of them simply because they can." I've been on the receiving end of being taken advantage of because I was smaller, powerless, and voiceless. "There's a sense of fairness in ensuring my clients are given their due, are compensated for what they bring to the table. Someone needs to protect their interests." Protect theirs like I wish someone had been there to protect mine.

A weighty silence descends over our table, so thick it seems to block out the chatter and clamor from the counter and kitchen. Regret creeps under my skin, an itch I can't scratch. What magic does she wield? It's a fucking superpower that should earn her a spot in the Justice League . . . or the Legion of Doom.

"You might want to keep that under wraps if you want that partnership," she says, picking up her fork and scooping up macaroni and cheese.

"Keep what under wraps?"

She slips the food between her lips, chewing and staring at me, and no one—not my aunts, not old social workers, not opposing council, not senior partners—has ever stirred the urge to fidget in me. But this woman . . .

Suddenly, I'm rethinking the reason I asked her to meet me here. She threatens me in a way Valerie never did.

"That heart," she continues, circling her fork in the direction of my chest. "The powers that be might be okay with it growing three sizes bigger during Christmas, but the rest of the year?" She shakes her head. "Do better."

I stare at her. Then snort. Christmas was—and still is—another day for me, but even I catch that Grinch reference.

"My turn to ask a question."

It's a phenomenon watching the warmth ebb from her eyes and witnessing a brittle cold seep into her features. If I hadn't been studying her so closely, I might've missed it; she covers that ice with a small polite smile so fast it must be practiced. And it serves to deepen my curiosity about her profession. Service industry of some sort. Because a distant but conciliatory expression like that comes only from working with the public.

Here's where I should let her off the hook since she so obviously doesn't want to answer any of my questions.

But I don't.

I'm too insatiable for more information about her.

I prop my folded arms on the tabletop, my gaze tracing the delicate arch of her eyebrows, the proud slope of her nose, the flagrantly erotic curves of her mouth.

"What's your idea of a romantic date, Zora?"

She blinks, then in the next second narrows her eyes on me.

"What are you playing at?"

I shrug a shoulder, anticipation beating inside of me like falcon's wings. Hard. Loud. Determined. "Just what I asked you." I lean closer, peering into those chocolate, perceptive eyes. "Do you want to know one of the reasons I asked you to be my friend as well as my fake girlfriend? I need you to teach me to be different. One of the lessons I learned early in high school and college was behave your way to success. And though I'm not an idiot—Val was obviously fucking another man behind my back before she sent you to my house—I own some of the fault in why our relationship failed. So I need to do differently the next time around. And that's where you come in. Show me where I can be a better partner, what a woman wants from her man."

Somewhere during my explanation, she went as still as that brick wheel sculpture I passed on the way here. Her normally expressive eyes are shuttered, and even the polite smile has disappeared.

"You need me to tell you what a woman wants," she says slowly. Flatly. And rife with disbelief.

I give an abrupt jerk of my head. "I know how to fuck a woman, Zora. But Val was my first attempt at a long-term relationship. And apparently, I'm not that good at it. So yes, I do need you to show me what a woman needs."

She glances away from me, her curls a barrier between me and even a glimpse of her profile. And like in the bookstore, I fight the urge to fist those dense strands and pull them up and away so I can read what she's trying to conceal from me. Because that's what she's doing. Hiding. A silent but visceral growl rumbles inside me, and only years of control lock it down. *Look at me,* it howls. *Don't hide from me. Give me every thought,* it demands. As if I have the right to those. None of it makes sense. But I want it. I want to strip her mind as bare as her body.

I want her totally naked before me.

Just her, me, and that addictive honesty.

"Just so I'm completely clear. Our arrangement is not just about making you look like a committed family man to the law firm partners but to prepare you for the next Val," she says, finally turning back to me, and the satisfaction is tempered by frustration. Nothing. That same closed-off expression offers me nothing.

"Yes."

Why lie? I demanded truth, and she deserves it as well. So why do I suddenly feel like I disappointed her?

I mentally shake off that burden. Ridiculous.

"Good to know." She dips her chin. "As far as my idea of a romantic date," she says in a clipped, no-nonsense voice that scrapes over my skin, "I'm like any other woman. Dinner, wine, movie. Nothing special. I'm afraid if you were expecting something earth shattering from me, you bet on the wrong horse."

"Liar," I whisper.

Her breath catches, the sound soft, low, but I hear it, and for an insane moment, I consider stretching my arm across this table, curling my fingers in the front of her dress, and drawing her forward so I can taste that vulnerable puff of breath on my lips.

I ball my fingers around my fork instead.

"Excuse me?" she whispers back.

"You're lying." My focus drops to her mouth again, waiting to see if there will be a repeat of that sound. To my regret, there isn't. Lifting my gaze back to hers, I say, "You're not like any other woman. And you're holding back. Where's dinner? At a restaurant? At a park on a blanket? In bed?"

There's that hitch of air. Is she imagining dinner in bed now? With whom? Is the meal before or after she's been thoroughly fucked? Or is *she* the meal?

Lust crackles and pops inside me, an electrical current that sizzles along my sensitized skin, runs through my veins . . . pulses in my dick.

"Zora?" I press. Because no way in hell am I letting this go.

"At my house. On my couch." The admission is reluctant, tremulous. And sexy as fuck. "All day long I . . . people. So I don't want to go to a restaurant or a park. I love the privacy and sanctuary of my house where I can be me. I don't have to smile or make small talk if I don't feel like it. I can just . . . be. And the man I'm with would not just respect that but understand it. And my needs would be so important to him—I would be so important to him—that when I arrive home, he would be there, waiting with food from my favorite place. He would undress me, not because I can't do it for myself but simply because he believes I deserve to be pampered like a queen. And after we ate together, he'd hold me, ask me about my day, and then actually listen to the answer. Then, we may or may not watch a movie. Maybe we'd just talk or make love. But whatever we did, it would be because the other needed it. Because we needed it, wanted it from each other, and it would be our pleasure to give it to one another."

Air propels from my lungs like from Scottish bagpipes.

How is it possible for me to be this hard?

As she talked, painting an erotic portrait, I envisioned everything. Peeling away every article of clothing, skimming my lips over the delicate but strong curves of her shoulders before draping them in clothes that she finds comfortable. I wouldn't care. This woman's body could transform a gunnysack into a merry widow. I'd feed her, hold her between my legs, in my arms, wrap my body around her. Give her my ear, my words, my cock—whatever she needed from me.

"Is that your favorite place to have sex? On the couch?" I rasp.

"That's two questions."

"Mine is against a wall. There's something about having a woman in my complete control—whether it's pressing her against it or holding her in my arms—that's hot as fuck."

She goes still again.

Except for the rapid rise and fall of her chest.

"Why do I need to know that?" she whispers.

Because I want to know if you'd let me have you against that wall. If you'd let me slide deep into you, until you took every inch of me without complaint. If you'd give me your pleasure, take mine . . .

"Because as my woman, that's something you should know," I lie, falling back on the charade as my safety net. I lower my arms, leaning back against my chair, inserting much-needed space between us. Space that doesn't include her sweet honey-and-almond scent. "We have two weeks to pile as much knowledge of each other into our brains as possible. If you're going to pretend to be my girlfriend, then you'll need to know all my likes. And convince everyone you love them."

Bullshit. She grips the edge of the table, and her lovely yet tight face with its narrowed eyes fairly screams it.

Yet underneath it . . .

Heat hums within me, purrs. Yeah, I recognize that emotion she's trying to conceal. What she's probably denying.

Excitement. Pleasure.

Common sense cautions me the next words on the tip of my tongue might not be wise.

Fuck you, common sense. Mind your business.

"Are you going to be able to handle making people believe you know what it is to give me that control? And to crave it? To crave it from me?"

My growled words vibrate between us.

They're dangerous, heavy. Alive.

I glimpse the unease in her eyes. But I also see what she would rather I not—the flash of heat like dry lightning.

"I think you're asking the wrong question," she throws back at me. But I don't miss the rasp in that voice. I know that rasp. Know what's behind it. Intimately. "It isn't whether I'm a good enough actress; it's whether *you* are. Do you really believe your esteemed colleagues are going to buy you craving *me*? Losing control for *me*?"

I still, her words from now and the past running so fast through my head they crash into each other like a pileup on I-70.

"You said something similar when I originally proposed this arrangement. Tell me why you think we wouldn't be believable as a couple. And don't avoid the question this time."

Her lips flatten, her throat working as if she's physically swallowing her answer. But finally she says, "Because men like you go for women like Val. As you've proven."

"Men like me." I pause. And here I thought I wasn't hard to offend. I'm fucking offended. "Explain."

"God, Cyrus, are you being deliberately obtuse?" she huffs. "Beautiful men who drop three thousand dollars on a suit, drive luxury cars, and think nothing of paying thousands of dollars for a plate of dry chicken at charity events. *That* kind of man."

Beautiful men.

My dick jerks, focusing on those two words, but my mind zeroes in on the rest of her explanation.

"Better question, then. What makes you think a man like me wouldn't want a woman like you?"

"Even better question," she lobs back. "When was the last time you were with a woman like me?"

Shit.

Shit.

At my silence, Zora nods, her mouth twisting into a caricature of a smile. One that cuts me to the quick.

"Right," she drawls.

After gathering her purse from the back of her chair, she removes several bills from it and places them next to her plate. She rises from her chair, slipping her purse strap over her shoulder.

"Thank you for lunch."

With a tight smile that doesn't reach her eyes, she pivots on her heel and exits the restaurant.

Dammit.

That did *not* go as planned.

CHAPTER TEN

ZORA

"You lied to me, wench."

I look up from my computer monitor as Miriam closes my office door behind her with a snap and stalks across the room. Her brown eyes narrow on me, and even her dyed-blonde curls seem to bounce in outrage. She draws to a halt in front of my desk and crosses her arms, glaring at me. When she doesn't speak, I sigh and fall back in my chair.

"Care to specify?"

I mean, these days, I have quite the tab going.

"You told me you were cutting off all communication with Cyrus Hart. But according to Jordan, you two are quite the BFFs." She bends forward from the hips. "But how can that be when you promised me you wouldn't see him again? Dad would be so disappointed in you breaking the eighth commandment."

"And Dad would be equally disappointed in you having premarital sex with Jordan Ransom."

She gasps, splaying her fingers over her chest like a Victorian virgin. "What? How'd you know?"

I gasp right back at her. "I didn't. But I do now, you hussy!" I jack-knife from my desk chair, slapping my palms to the desktop. "You had sex with Jordan Ransom?" I hissed. "What were you thinking? I thought you'd friend zoned him?"

"I don't *know*! And I *did*!" she wails, sinking down into the chair in front of my desk, her hands covering her face. "I swear I'm still confused about what happened. One moment we were on his private range hitting baseballs, and in the next I was playing with *his* bat and balls." She groans while I throw up in my mouth a little. "I'd always rolled my eyes at women who'd slipped and fell on men's dicks, but now I get it. But it wouldn't be so bad if it only happened that once. But I did it again. And again. Three times in a night. I'm fucking accident prone, Zora." She drops her hands and looks at me with such a miserable expression that I'm caught between going and hugging her and laughing in her face. "Are you judging me right now? You're so judging me, aren't you?"

"No, of course not." I round my desk and take the chair next to her. Cupping her knee, I shake it. "Hey, you know I was just kidding when I called you a hussy, right? What you and your vagina do is your business. You're a fully grown woman, and you don't have to ask anyone's permission about who you do or owe anyone an explanation. I was just shocked because I thought you were adamant about not partaking of community peen; that's all."

"I was." She groans again, shaking her head and staring down at her palms. As if she's still shell shocked. "But apparently there's a reason why it's community peen. He knows how to service it *real* well." She sighs, and her eyes glaze over.

I snap my fingers in front of her face, and she starts, blinking several times. I don't know where the hell she just went. And I'm afraid to ask.

"Sorry," she mumbles. "Anyway, I can't go there again, and I've made that abundantly clear to Jordan. Contrary to recent events, I don't do athletes." Her mouth flattens, and her brown eyes harden into shards of flint. Yes, I remember very well why she doesn't do athletes, which is why I was so shocked when she agreed to give Jordan her phone number in the first place. "But he's a nice guy, and I'd like to be friends. If he can't accept that, then . . ."

She shrugs, but I catch the flash of pain in her gaze.

"He'll accept it." I squeeze her knee. "Something tells me he'd rather have you as a friend than nothing at all."

She shrugs a shoulder, but I've been my sister's protector since she was born, and I know her inside and out. This relationship matters.

"Anyway, turf burn with Jordan is not why I'm in here." Okay. *Ew.* "You lied, Liar McLiarson." She jabs a finger toward my chest. "Imagine my surprise when Jordan casually drops that you and Cyrus are hanging out at his house, all cozied up. Good thing I'm a fabulous liar myself or I wouldn't have been able to cover my shock."

I snort. "Well, thank God for small favors."

"Damn straight. What happened? I thought we agreed you continuing to see him wasn't a good idea."

"We did." I rub a hand over the nape of my neck. "But it got a little more complicated, where I couldn't just walk away."

I tell her about my arrangement with Cyrus. Everything, leaving nothing out. Not even the conversation from the restaurant today. That's the thing about Miriam. There isn't anything too out there, too off the wall, for her to accept. She listens with a thoughtful frown, and when I finish, she thrusts her hands through her hair, drawing the curls back from her face.

"Wow. That's some shit."

Why, yes. Yes, it is.

"So basically, you're going along with this whole fake relationship thing and going on this corporate retreat because of your pesky conscience and the chance that his ex, our client, might discover you've been making time with her ex. Which makes you—and our company, by extension—look shady as hell. And this Valerie Summers doesn't sound like the reasonable or forgiving type if she believes she's been played. Do I have all the facts?"

I nod. "Basically."

She holds up a finger. "Okay, first things first. After your months of relationship-itude are up, what is your endgame? Are you going to just walk out of his life, and he's going to disappear from yours? You never plan to reveal the truth about BURNED to him? You do realize the longer you keep this from him, the angrier and more betrayed he's going to feel when the truth comes out, right?"

Mimicking her earlier gesture, I burrow my hands through my hair, gripping the strands.

"Don't you think I've thought of that? A lot? I don't have those answers. But he and I . . . we don't belong in the same worlds. If not for Valerie Summers, our paths would've never had any reason to cross. And I don't see why, after our bargain is up, we can't return to normal. We won't have any reason to talk, to be in each other's lives anymore."

Miriam snorts. "Keep telling yourself that if it helps you get through these next few months." She peers at me, and it's unnervingly . . . kind. "Zora, this isn't going to end well. Regardless of how much you protest, you're more invested in Cyrus Hart than you want to admit. Somewhere along the line he became more than a client's ex and a pseudo boyfriend. And when the shit hits the fan—because, babe, it has no choice but to hit the fan—you're going to end up hurt. And I hate that for you."

My chest tightens with each foreboding word that falls from her lips. Dread twists inside me, and I briefly close my eyes. She isn't saying anything that hasn't whispered through my head in the deepest, darkest part of night when work, clients, or people aren't there to distract me from my thoughts.

During those hours, when I close my eyes, I can't help but see Cyrus's face when he discovers the truth. And it's cold. So cold with anger, with . . . hatred.

No lies, Zora. Don't lie to me.

And that's what I fear as much as the threat to BURNED, to Miriam's and Levi's investments and livelihoods. I'm terrified of seeing that loathing in his eyes. Terrified of knowing that he despises me.

I can justify my reasons for not telling Cyrus the truth, but it doesn't change that I'm lying to him. And he'll never forgive me for it.

I'm a coward when it comes to him.

"You think that's why you dumped your shit on him at lunch about his people not possibly believing he could want you?" she softly asks. "Because you do know that going off on him was about you, not him, right?"

"I didn't go off on him."

She arches an eyebrow. "Just 'cause it was nice nasty doesn't make it any less of a read, ma'am."

Guilt buzzes in my belly like a swarm of angry bees. "Doesn't make it any less true, though. We don't make sense together. I know it. He knows it. His colleagues will know it. The more I think about it, this thing is ridiculous."

"You're projecting. And like I said, that's your shit, not his."

"Miriam, he couldn't even answer about being with a woman like me before. Why? Because he never has. So it being *my* shit doesn't negate the fact that I'm right."

"And what exactly do you mean by 'a woman like me'? Black? Thick? Natural hair? *Buffy* fan?" She shrugs. "So what if he hasn't? I've never dated a half-human, half-Atlantean with a predilection for beer and a chip on his shoulder, but that doesn't mean I wouldn't give him a try. Now, I'm not saying you don't love yourself or aren't proud of who you are, because I know you better than that. But I *am* saying there's something in here"—she twirls her fingers in a tight circle over my heart—"you need to clean up if you believe that man couldn't possibly be attracted to you because what? He's too pretty? Too rich? Too successful? Too . . . white? I gotta say, Zora. That day in the parking lot, from the way he couldn't take his eyes off your ass, it didn't seem like he gave a fuck about your tax bracket. So maybe, just maybe, it could be he doesn't have the issue, but *you* do."

I stare at her, that tightness in my chest slowly squeezing and squeezing until my ribs creak in protest.

She reaches over and clasps my fingers. "It's just . . . you've been through hell with a couple of the douches you've been with, and no one could've come out of that unscathed, unchanged. It could be not just Cyrus but any man who would come under suspicion—no matter if he was wealthy, poor, Black, white, gorgeous, facially challenged . . ."

A snicker slips free of me, and Miriam grins.

"You'll think on what I said?"

"Yes." How will I be able to think about anything else? "Thanks, Miriam."

"No problem." She squeezes my fingers, then stands. "You're still a Liar McLiarson, though. And you're making me one too. Because I have to keep the truth about our company from Jordan. And though I'm a fabulous liar—we're talking superspy level, here—it doesn't mean I want to do it in this case. You shouldn't start any relationship on lies." She claps me on the shoulder. "No worries, though. I'll be here with strawberry-cheesecake ice cream, bags of sour-cream-and-onion chips, and a Netflix binge ready to go when this blows to hell. 'Cause that's the kind of loving sister I am."

"'Preciate it, Miriam."

"You got it."

She strides across the office and out the door, leaving me alone with my murky thoughts and her crystal-clear words swirling in my head.

Damn.

I hate when my sister makes sense.

After Miriam left my office, the afternoon flew by in a blur of meetings, interviews, and invoices. By the time I park in the two-car garage of my Park Hill bungalow, I'm more than ready to shower, order dinner, park it in front of my television, and not move until it's time for me to go to bed. It's been a *day*.

I exit the garage and round the walkway that borders my private gardens and tiered deck. Pride beats within me as it always does every time I arrive home. Maybe it's utterly shallow, but I bought this house with money I'd started saving before I'd left my parents' home for college. I knew even then I wouldn't be returning there. But it's more than pride. There's a warm peace that settles in my bones. A sense of safety. Beyond those brick walls, there's no arguing, shouting, or threats. There's no walking on eggshells or waiting for the proverbial shoe to drop. This picturesque Craftsman bungalow with its swing on the front porch is my haven.

So focused on getting inside my haven and anticipating the hot drum of water on my tired muscles, I don't notice the man on my flower-upholstered swing until he rises.

I jerk to a stop, my heart lodging in my throat.

Holy *shit*.

"What the he—" Then it fully registers who is standing mere feet away from me. And my heart takes on a different rhythm. No less fast, no less heavy, but . . . different. "Cyrus. What're you doing here?"

Instead of answering, he holds up a large brown paper bag by the handles. The logo from one of my favorite restaurants is printed across the front of it.

I stare at it, swallowing hard. My explanation of a romantic date plays back in my head. He'd listened. But why wouldn't he have? He would've either been taking notes to woo Val's replacement or to make sure our charade at the weekend retreat was believable.

Yet even as the cynical questions roll through my mind, a need burrows so deep inside me I can't tell where it begins or ends. It's just *there.* And a seed of fear takes root that I won't be able to evict it. That one glance at this man, and it will always be there, a part of me like my arm or leg. Even if amputated, their phantom presence will continue to be felt.

I drag my gaze up from the paper bag to meet his eyes again.

"Come on in, then."

After turning to my front door, I open it and step inside my home. And battle the urge not to peek over my shoulder and glimpse how he's taking in my sanctuary. Why I care how he views my home, I choose not to dwell on because that'd probably require another conversation with Miriam that I'm not ready for, so I unload my purse, laptop bag, and keys on the dark walnut end table next to my couch.

Still, I scan my home, attempting to observe it through his eyes. Wondering if he'll see the coziness in the beamed ceilings, period fixtures, brick fireplace, gleaming hardwood floors, and huge picture windows. Unlike his home, mine doesn't have an open floor plan, but he can still glimpse the wide arches that lead to a dining room and large kitchen. And the sturdy carpeted staircase that leads up to the second level and master suites and bedrooms. When I bought this home, I wanted a safe space for not only myself but Levi and Miriam too.

"This is a great place, Zora."

"Thanks." I cross my arms and nod toward the bag. "Do I want to guess how you know Jax Fish House and Oyster Bar is my favorite restaurant?"

"I might've asked Jordan to do some research for me."

"Miriam."

"Miriam." A smile flickers across his mouth, there and gone in the next instant. "I might also owe her tickets to the next Lizzo concert."

That little . . . "That heffa sold me out for Lizzo?"

He nodded. "With anatomically impossible threats to my balls, but yes." Holding up the bag, he tilts his head. "Show me to your kitchen? By the time you shower and change, the food will be ready."

He would undress me, not because I can't do it for myself but simply because he believes I deserve to be pampered like a queen.

Are my words tripping through his head like they are through mine? Because they're taunting me, and I can't unhear them.

I lift my head, meet his blue gaze and the flash of fire in them.

Yes. I'm going with yes, he's recalling the same thing I am.

Clearing my throat, I thread my fingers through my hair. And when Cyrus's scrutiny drops to my curls and that fire leaps higher, an unrecognizable part of me whispers that I should walk over to him, ask him if he'd like to touch my hair. Burrow his big hands with his long elegant fingers in the strands, fist them . . .

I want it.

Sighing, I point toward the doorway to the right. "Kitchen's through there. I'll be back in twenty."

I don't run out of the room—but my pace could be described as a good power walk. Dammit, the man is lethal. Questions bombard me as I dash—no, briskly march—up the stairs, past my home office, and to the first master bedroom and en suite bathroom.

Why is he here? How long was he waiting on my porch? What does he want? Which isn't to be confused with "Why is he here?" because there are subtle differences. How much of my romantic-date scenario does he plan to reenact? Will or won't we watch movies? Will he . . . no, not going there! We're just friends. And not even that. We're fake friends with blackmail elements. Apparently, it's a thing.

By the time I'm showered, dressed in black lounge pants and a slouchy gray off-the-shoulder shirt with a bra—because seriously, that perky braless shit with women my size happens only in movies—none of those questions have been answered, and I'm just as much of a nervous wreck descending the stairs as I was climbing them half an hour earlier.

"Sorry," I call out, hitting the hardwood floor, hating the breathless quality to my voice. "That took longer than . . . I . . . intended . . ." My eyes widen. "What's all this?"

He's moved aside the centerpiece on my coffee table and laid out several plates filled with all of my favorite foods from Jax. Fried calamari, lobster rolls, shishito-dusted scallops, summer squash, and a slice of flourless chocolate cake. It's a feast, and my stomach chooses that moment to rumble, adding its vote.

"Sit." He enters the living room from the kitchen with a bottle of wine and two of my fluted glasses. As if his voice flips an instinctual switch in my body, I obey and shift to the couch. After lowering to a corner, I tuck my legs up under me and silently watch as he pours me a glass of wine and hands it to me. "This is the same sauvignon blanc you were drinking at the restaurant the second time we met. I figured I couldn't go wrong with it."

I sip, and its fruity flavor slides over my tongue. Closing my eyes, I hum my appreciation. "No, this is perfect. Thank you."

A moment later, I lift my lashes, and his sky-blue gaze traps mine.

"If I didn't know better—if I didn't feel like I knew *you* better—I'd think you did that on purpose."

"Did what?" I whisper.

"Tease."

I frown. "I'm not—"

"Yeah, I know." His tone is a blade, razor sharp, and as he pivots back to the table, it leaves me sliced wide open. "Here." He returns to me seconds later with a small dish piled with perfectly fried calamari in one hand and the remote to my TV in the other. "I was afraid to ask Miriam about your favorite shows on Netflix just in case she demanded a kidney, so you pick. I don't watch that much television, so I'm open to pretty much anything."

I woodenly take the remote and plate and set them both on the end table.

"Thank you, but we need to talk first."

To his credit, he doesn't wince or flinch at the announcement, but a shuttered mask slips over his face as he sinks to the middle of the couch, allowing distance between us.

"Cyrus, I need to apologize for earlier at lunch. My reaction was disproportionate to you asking me to accompany you on the retreat. As it was pointed out to me later, that had more to do with me than you, but I took it out on you, and I'm sorry for that."

Surprise flashes in his eyes like lightning across a summer sky, though his expression remains aloof.

"Want to share any more details about why that has more to do with you?" he calmly asks.

"No." I really, really don't.

He nods. "Fair enough. It's my turn to apologize, then. Given my profession, this might sound contradictory, but outside of the court-room or mediation, I'm not great with words. It's why I prefer contracts. Everything is written down, clear, concise, in black and white, with no room for misunderstanding." He pauses, and his jaw clenches, flexes. As if he's fighting the next words, battling to keep them in. "The past has taught me words can be twisted and turned against me, and silence is not only golden, but it can't be misquoted. But today, I realized it can be misinterpreted. And harmful. So I'm sorry that I hurt you, Zora."

No personal questions. No personal questions. I'm not curious in the least.

Screw that, I am. What in his past taught him that silence was better than having his words twisted and used against him? Who did that to him? Who'd hurt him? Better question . . .

Who I gotta fuck up?

Down, girl.

Shit, right. Not my business. And Cyrus is a big boy now. Way more than capable of fighting and winning his own battles.

Still doesn't mean I don't want to grease up, slick my hair back in a ponytail, and have somebody catch these hands . . .

My mental sigh could part the Red Sea.

"It's fine, Cyrus. We both didn't have our best moments today. There's something symmetrical in that." I shake my head, giving him a small smile.

He studies me, and the heat that had ebbed to a simmer flares higher. *Don't you dare squirm,* I order myself. *Don't you do it.* I manage to remain still under that intense scrutiny, but my panties have given up the ghost, surrendering a humiliatingly easy defeat.

"What?" I breathe.

"I told you I know how to fuck women, and I do. I've fucked white women, Black women, Latina women. Thin women, plus-size women. Poor, wealthy—honestly, I don't know or care, because when I'm inside them, I'm not questioning how many zeroes are in their bank accounts. It might make me sound like a dick, but sex comes easy to me . . . dating does not. Which is why Val is the first woman I was in a serious relationship with, period. I can only imagine how . . . weird that makes me look in your eyes. A thirty-three-year-old man involved in one relationship. But there it is. So when you asked me if I've ever been with a woman like you, what I should've said was no, I've never been with another woman like you, because there *is* no other woman like you, Zora. I've never had a woman who is sexy as all fuck but is my friend, not my lover. You are a beautiful novelty."

I know how to fuck a woman, Zora.

I've never had a woman who is sexy as all fuck but is my friend, not my lover. You are a beautiful novelty.

I can't breathe. My lungs and heart—hell, all my organs—have gone on strike while my vagina has happily taken the reins. And she is throwing herself at Cyrus with all the zeal of a pagan sacrifice.

I'm in so much trouble.

Because nothing in me right now is Team Friends. As I stare into those eyes, drink in the rest of his masculine perfection, and willingly drown in it, I'm all Team Fuck a Woman.

Because Cyrus Hart thinks I'm *sexy as all fuck.*

"Forgiven," I whisper.

For another long tension-filled moment, he doesn't move; then he stands, leans over me, grabs my plate, and hands it to me. Muscle memory has me reaching for it, and the delicious aroma compels me to eat the first bite. When my dish is clean, he's there to remove it from me and replace it with my entrée. We eat in companionable silence, one of my favorite Sherlock-influenced series on the television. The food is perfect, the show, though I've seen it several times, engrossing. And yet I can't help but peek at the man sitting next to me.

His very aura is a distraction. Power and animal magnetism emanate from him like a force, and it brushes against my face, the skin exposed by my shirt, the soles of my bare feet. I once thought of how all that intensity that seemed to hum below his skin must be an aphrodisiac. To have all of it focused on a woman must be almost overwhelming. And I was correct. Though his gaze is centered on the TV, any time the food on my plate runs low or my wineglass needs refilling, he's right there without missing a beat, fulfilling my need before I recognize it. It's . . . arousing. It's comforting. It's exactly what I described to him at lunch.

"You must be a serious Sherlock Holmes fan," he says, taking my empty plate and switching it out for a smaller one with a slice of chocolate cake on it.

Damn. It's enough to make me consider forgiving Miriam for selling me out for Lizzo. A moan works its way up my throat, but remembering Cyrus's reaction last time, I lock it down. Although an imp I didn't know existed inside me tries to cajole me into loosing it. I'm tempted, if only to see that hot flash in his eyes again . . .

Giving my head a mental shake, I fork another piece into my mouth. That's not me. I don't think . . .

"I am," I say, waving my fork toward the television. "What's not to love? A brilliant detective who solves crimes Scotland Yard can't by deducing the details that most of us miss along with his faithful partner, Dr. Watson? I know some people aren't fans of the recent versions and retellings of Sherlock, but I appreciate almost all of them. They reveal faceted personalities of the flawed man, just as we're all flawed. And you have to imagine that a man who is so brilliant would have demons.

There would be a price to pay for a mind that bright. So I love them all. Benedict Cumberbatch. Jonny Lee Miller. Robert Downey Jr."

He shakes his head, reclaiming his seat on the couch. "My father was a Sherlock purist. It was Basil Rathbone or no one. He'd watch all his old movies over and over, and I never could understand why. I mean, after the first time, the mystery was no longer a mystery. But he'd laugh and tell me one day I'd understand."

I smile at him. "And do you?"

His mouth curls at the corner. "Yeah, I do."

"I got my love of Sherlock from my brother. I think Levi felt an affinity toward him. Logic. Deduction. Dependence on science and reason, not people." I softly laugh, but it rubs my throat like old carpet. Scratchy, thin. "My father couldn't stand the movies. Well, actually, he couldn't pretty much stand anything Levi did. They were—are—like oil and water with a blowtorch set to it."

"Maybe your parents thought he was too young for the subject matter?"

I jerk my attention back to him, not realizing until that moment that I'd been blindly staring over his shoulder, my mind in the distant past. My laugh this time grates my throat, leaving abrasions.

"Oh no. My mother might not have been overly fond of Sherlock, but she wouldn't have agreed with my father. She purchased Levi every Sherlock movie and TV series DVD she could get her hands on. She even bought one of those deerstalker hats online just to irritate my dad. It was no longer about my brother but how they could use him to get back at each other. So then Levi and I pretended not to care about Sherlock. And we learned that whenever we had an interest in something to keep it from them, or it became fodder in their personal war."

Whoa.

Whoa.

Chocolate cake curdles in my stomach, and the thought of another bite is enough to send bile racing for my throat. Gingerly, I lean down and set the plate on the floor. Here is where I need to segue into something, anything, lighter. Distract him from the big toxic heap of truth I just dumped on him. Where did that come from? All he did was ask me about Sherlock Holmes, and like a door on creaking, broken hinges, it swung wide open, and I allowed all of that . . . *shit* to spill out.

Say something, dammit.

The weather.

The cake. Talk about the fucking cake.

But my tongue, suddenly made of the heaviest concrete, sticks to the roof of my mouth.

"Makes sense now," he murmurs.

What does? burns in my mind, but again, I can't voice it. And what's more? I'm afraid to hear his answer. Yet I sit there. I don't get up and leave to the kitchen, the stairs, or even the damn front door. Because more than my need to escape is my desire to be *seen*.

"Why you left your parents' home the other night," he continues, as if I did pose the question. "But more importantly, why you volunteered to break up with me on Val's behalf."

Oh God.

"Cyrus, I—"

He narrows his eyes, and my voice fades away. "I respect your no-personal-questions stipulation, and I won't pry any further into what you've just admitted. That's safe with me. But I'm not going to ignore it either." He shifts closer on the couch until my knee nudges his muscled thigh, and his cedar-and-leather scent reaches out and wraps around me in an ephemeral embrace. "All this time I couldn't understand why such a strong-willed, sharp woman would allow herself to be used by Val. But it wasn't that at all, was it?"

His gaze roams my face, and I curl my fingers into the cushion next to my thigh to keep from stroking my fingertips over all the places it lands on. My forehead. My nose. My mouth.

"It's because of them, your parents. You did it because you can't stand to see anyone end up like your parents. I bet you were the peace-maker in your house. And now you're doing the same for your so-called friends. Am I right, Zora?"

I'm speechless.

Had I said I wanted to be seen? Old sayings are old sayings for a reason: because they're true. Be careful what you wish for. I'm sitting here vulnerable, feeling more naked than I have when I've been stripped of clothes. And it's uncomfortable. It's frightening.

It's *exhilarating*.

I choke back a cry and dig my fists into the couch cushions. My nails bite into the flesh of my palms, and the sting should ground me, center me, but it doesn't. It only serves to heighten the vivid intensity of this moment. I'm seeing in sounds, breathing in colors, hearing in scents—everything is upside down because he's ripped me open.

Those eyes that never miss a thing drop to my stiff arms, to my tightly curled hands, and then slowly rise to my face. He studies me for several long moments, and I struggle to remain impassive, to conceal the emotional maelstrom whipping me to shreds.

"Do you want to touch me?"

"No." My answer is reflexive, born of years of learning to depend on myself.

But inside . . . inside, a wail shouts at me to take, take what's being offered. But I can't. Old habits die hard. And at this point, I don't even know how to take what I want. The one time I did, I ended up in my current situation: lying to him.

"Do you want me to make you touch me?"

Take the choice from me? Let me lean on all that strength for this moment? Let him hold me like in my description of my perfect date?

I can't . . .

"Yes," I whisper.

He moves closer. And closer still. Breathing is a precious memory. Thinking is an outdated ideal.

His big hands gently grasp my wrists, and his fingers wrap around them, branding my skin. He lifts my arms, and I watch them, as if they don't belong to me. I watch as he guides my hands to his wide dress-shirt-covered chest. One by one, he uncurls my fingers, running his fingertips along their lengths. That caress to each digit streaks down my palms and my arms to my breasts, my nipples, reminding me I'm very much attached. I'm very much present and *alive*.

He flattens my hands to his chest, and the beat of his heart echoes between my legs, my sex picking up the rhythm, and I squeeze my thighs against the ache that takes up residence there. It's useless, though. I'm becoming that tempo, everything in me transforming to surrender to it.

A moan slips up from the core of me—that hot, slippery, empty core of me—to my throat, and I sink my teeth into my bottom lip to trap it.

"More?"

More?

I lift lashes I hadn't realized had drifted down and meet ice-blue fire. There's more? I'm already on fire and so wet. And hurting. It would be the height of greed and foolishness to reach for *more* . . .

"Yes."

Without breaking our visual connection, he strokes his hands up my arms and curves, then over my shoulders. Slowly, as if granting me time to object, he draws me forward until he's sitting in the couch's far corner and I'm tucked between his sprawled legs, curled against his chest. His body heat envelops me, warming his wood-and-leather scent so it's rich and heavy on my tongue and nostrils. His arms and legs brace me, enfold me . . . protect me. I'm sheltered on all sides. And at my hip . . .

The rigid, thick length of his cock. *Oh God.*

.I close my eyes.

My sex spasms. Hard. And I clench my teeth against the sweet pain of it.

That big heavy dick against me should be enough to prevent me from relaxing, but it doesn't. It has just the opposite effect. I melt into his frame like butter left out in the sun.

How long we sit there, I don't know. One episode plays through. Then another. At the start of the second one, his fingers feather through my hair. Hesitant at first, but then, when I don't object, with more confidence and . . . enjoyment. His nails scrape my scalp, and I shiver. His big body stiffens behind me.

Then he does it again.

I shiver again.

Those fingers tangle in my curls, fisting them, and tiny pinpricks scatter along my scalp. A gasp slips free from my mouth, and I tip my head back, my lips grazing the underside of his jaw. Just that—just that slight, accidental brush—leaves his flavor on my skin. Slicking my tongue over my bottom lip, I sample him, and *damn*. He tastes so *good*. The musk of cedar, the earthiness of leather, and the indescribable but wholly unique tang of him.

It's my new favorite meal.

He remains so still, and I should heed that as a sign. But he has his hand in my hair, and hunger is a real thing now. Besides, he invited me to take. And I'm taking.

Shifting, I rub my lips firmer against his jaw, my tongue peeking out to lick. That fist tightens, and fire dances across my scalp. In retaliation, I bring my teeth into play. Grazing. Nipping.

His harsh breath punctuates the room, and only his fingers move, flexing and straightening in my hair.

"More?" he asks, voice no longer smooth but churned-up gravel.

"Yes," I say against his skin.

There's no hesitation now. Not here, with the sweet narcotic of his arms around me, of his catering to me, of his giving me control by shouldering it. For seeing me in a way no one has bothered to take the time to do.

So yes. I need so much more of him.

"You sure?" He tips his head down, at the same time using his grip to pull mine back so our mouths are inches apart. My heart pounds against my chest. So hard I can barely hear his question. So I read his lips. Those full, cruel, beautiful lips. "This what you need? If it is, I'll give it to you."

He'd been listening at lunch because he's returning my words to me. A man who listens.

I could fucking orgasm from that alone.

"More," I whisper.

He doesn't ask me again.

That mouth descends on mine and changes my world. Changes me.

This time I don't lock down my moan. I let it go. And I go with it. One of his arms wraps around my waist while the other rises, his hand cupping my chin, tilting it, holding me steady as he takes my mouth, fucks it, corrupts it.

That last *You sure?* was the last permission he requested. His tongue dives between my lips like my mouth belongs to him and he just returned to reclaim what was his. Over and over, tangling, twisting, and sucking. He sweeps in, leaving no part of me a stranger to him. And I open wide for him. Offer myself up for him. Because this pleasure he's giving me . . . *oh my God.* This kiss is better than all the sex I've ever had. Dirtier too. All due to the things this man can do with his tongue. He's gifted.

I circle his wrist, hold on, and let him drown me. He doesn't hesitate to take me under again. And again. With each lick, suck, bite, I'm lost, and I don't want to be found.

In one instant I'm drenched in passion, and in the next, I'm shivering in the abrupt abandonment of his mouth and whimper in disappointment.

"Dammit." His rumble vibrates against the corners of my lips, and his grip on my curls tightens before loosening. "This isn't why I came here, baby."

Baby.

I close my eyes, letting that roughly spoken, sexy-as-hell endearment caress me. Stroke over my nipples. Circle my clit. My body stiffens and melts at the same time. But then his words penetrate. This—holding me, kissing me, blowing my mind with unprecedented pleasure—isn't why he's here.

In other words, mistake. This is a mistake. *I'm* a mistake.

Goddammit. When am I ever going to learn? Especially when it comes to this man?

The hand that I just used to grab ahold of him I now use to push at his arm. After sitting up, I shift away, inserting space between us, until his powerful frame no longer aligns with mine. Until his scent no longer embraces me.

"Sorry." My mouth tingles, feels swollen, sore, and it requires every bit of my control and pride not to brush my fingers across my lips. "That shouldn't ha—"

"Don't say another fucking word, Zora," Cyrus snaps.

I jerk my head in his direction, not a fan of his choice of words or his tone.

"Excuse you?"

"I'm beginning to get an idea where the roots of that disproportionate reaction came from." Before I can reply with what he can do with his "idea," he moves from one breath to the next, closing the space I injected between us. And my chin is recaptured in one of his hands while the other grips the back of the couch, and his body borders my front. "Look at me, and listen to me. Don't get in your head, and for fuck's sake, don't listen to whatever demons you got stalking you. I meant what I said. I didn't come over here for that kiss, to finally get my mouth on you. But I damn sure don't regret it."

Finally get my mouth on you.

Finally?

Maybe he reads the question in my eyes because that brief half smile flickers over his lips. "Yeah, finally. I dare anyone with a dick—or without—to take one look at that mouth and not fantasize about getting theirs on it. But I wanted your friendship. Still want it. And you know what, Zora?" He leans closer, his breath coasting over my lips, and I can taste his kiss again. "The two don't have to be mutually exclusive."

Wait.

What?

He's not saying . . . "Cyrus, you don't mean—" I stop, draw in a breath, and gather my thoughts because I need every single one of them. "This isn't supposed to be real. That's not what you want from me."

"It's up to you what we are, Zora. I'll be what you need."

"What the hell is that supposed to mean?" I demand. And yes, I hear the desperation in my voice, but I can't help it.

Because Cyrus is flipping the script and not handing me a copy. I don't know the ending of this version, and it terrifies me. Part of me wants him to take the choice out of my hands like he did earlier. Make the decision for me so I can just enjoy the results without the weightiness of the responsibility.

My mouth tingles in warning . . . or temptation. I honestly don't know which one.

"It means we have several more episodes to watch. Now"—he bends down, picks up my forgotten plate of cake, and hands it to me—"let them eat cake. Or you. You eat the cake."

I stare at him. Blink.

And burst out laughing. And laugh. And laugh until my sides hurt. Until tears burn my eyes.

And it feels damn good.

CHAPTER ELEVEN

CYRUS

"I think I'm in love with you."

I jerk in the driver's seat of my Audi A6, my foot reflexively slamming down on the accelerator. Thank God the gear is already in park and the engine is shut off. If not, the front end of my vehicle would be tossing the salad of the Range Rover in front of me.

"Excuse me?"

Zora laughs, the sound light and thoroughly delighted.

"Calm down," she says, patting my thigh. "I'm not planning to get down on one knee and propose. At least not until we're at the retreat and in front of your coworkers on the last night. You're safe."

Ha ha. Funny.

And awesome. Now I can't scrub free the image of her down on her knees in front of me. Fucking great.

After shoving the driver's side door open, I climb out of my car, breaking free of the close confines that are permeated with her honeyed scent like an escaped convict. I round the hood of the vehicle and move to the passenger door, open it, and extend my hand toward Zora. She arches an eyebrow, just as she did when I held the door open when I picked her up earlier, but I don't blink. Ingrained manners I learned from watching my dad with my mom haven't disappeared in twenty years.

The question here isn't why I open doors for women but why she's so unused to men paying her the common courtesy of opening them for her?

Who the fuck did she date, and where can I find them to beat some basic etiquette into them?

The press of her smaller, softer palm to mine distracts me from my bloodthirsty musings, and I temper my strength as I guide her from the car, shutting the door behind her.

"This place is *gorgeous*. I've lived in Denver all my life, and can you believe I've never been here before?" she whispers, her tone almost reverent as she drops my hand and spins in a tight circle.

I don't blame her. Red Rocks is an awesome sight. The open-air amphitheater is actually built into a rock structure. Behind the stage, a disk-shaped rock sits, and to the right another huge rock angles up and outward like Noah's ark. It's like being surrounded by sky and earth, and it's breathtaking.

A beautiful smile lights up her whole face, and she closes her eyes, tipping her head back to the last rays of the setting sun. I jerk my gaze away, but lust punches through my chest with a ham-size fist, propelling the air from my lungs. A fist of pure heat grips my cock, squeezing, pumping, and that quick I'm transported back to the night in her living room where I waged an epic battle not to fuck her into her couch.

Then, I won. Barely.

But in the days since, I haven't been convinced the outcome would be the same if I were faced with the situation again. Even now, her sweet, toasty scent of honey and almonds lingers in my mouth, my nostrils. Hell, even my skin. She has become a fucking obsession that's far from "friendly."

That ship has sailed so fucking far and fast.

And my dick could be the mast.

She hunkers down, sliding a medium-size case off her shoulder. I'm not an idiot; I've seen camera cases before. But seeing Zora walk out of her house with it sent shock snapping through me. How did I not know she was a photographer? Or at least was into photography? There's so damn much I *don't* know about Zora. And that lack of knowledge drives me crazy.

This trust shit is not only new; it's frustrating as hell.

With quick, expert hands, she removes the camera from the case, attaches what looks to my amateur eyes to be the lens and the flash, and then stands, looping a strap around her neck.

Beautiful.

Confident.

Sexy as fuck.

I stare, damn near spellbound, as she holds the camera up, adjusts the lens, and starts shooting. The people gathered in the parking lot for the concert. The huge stunning rock formations beyond the stage. The darkening sky. The stage. The park.

Me.

And me.

"What're you doing?" I ask, resisting the urge to hold up a hand and block my face. Discomfort crawls through me. I might represent clients who are used to being in the spotlight or even crave it, for that matter, but that has never been my addiction. Unlike some of my colleagues.

Yeah, not thinking about work tonight.

Which is a first.

I frown.

And there goes another flash.

"Zora," I growl.

"Sorry," she says, lowering the camera and not sounding the least bit sorry. Her fingertips glide over the lens, and the touch strikes me as oddly sensual. Or that's how my body interprets it. A sheepish smile curls one corner of her mouth. "You're very photogenic. Since the first time I saw you, I've been itching to catch you on film."

"That right?"

Why do I find that hot?

"Yes, it's your face. All those sharp angles and slants. The symmetry is perfect. But then you have the tiniest nick through the end of your eyebrow, and in the sunlight, you have the faintest of freckles across your cheekbones. And your mouth, while beautiful, has a hint of hardness about it. It's those tiny flaws that take your face from boring perfection to wonderfully interesting."

"I don't know whether to be flattered or to feel like I've been pinned to a corkboard and eviscerated," I say dryly.

"Both are forms of admiration, so why choose?"

I snort; seeds of curiosity burrow deep, their roots spreading and digging for purchase. And finding it.

"When was the first time you saw me?"

She bows her head, fiddling with her camera before lifting it once more and firing off more shots. A heaviness settles on my shoulders, my chest. So she's not going to answer. Maybe that question is filed under *personal* . . .

"Val showed me a picture of you." She exhales, and though it's soft, I catch it. In the dying light of the day, and with splashes of orange, purple, and dark blue streaking across the sky, across her, I want to taste that exhale. She raises her eyes from the camera to meet mine. "I thought you were the most beautiful man I'd ever seen in my life."

I don't say anything; I can't. Because I'm certain *Forget this concert. Get in the car so I can take you back to my house, where I'm going to fuck you until even your soul walks funny* won't go over well.

But that's the ferocity of the lust roaring inside me right now.

All due to her thinking I'm beautiful. Not that I haven't heard that before from women and men, for that matter. But most of them possessed an agenda or wanted something from me, even if it was a fuck. None of them were Zora Nelson.

"I should put this back in the car. I don't think they allow cameras in during the concert," she murmurs, squatting down again and avoiding looking at me.

Quickly, she packs up her equipment, and by the time she stands again, I've located my voice.

"I didn't know you were a photographer."

She huffs a laugh. "That's a bit overstated. Could you unlock your car for me?" I press the key fob, and she stores the bag in the back seat. "I love photography; I have since high school. But I'm not a professional. It's just something I enjoy doing."

"Those photos of City Park hanging up in your living room. Those are yours, aren't they?" Her head sharply swings my way, eyes narrowed. I arch an eyebrow. "You didn't think I'd notice? News flash, Zora," I murmur, stepping closer, and she turns in the opening of the back door. "There wasn't one thing in that house that I didn't study seeking more clues into who you are. My hands are tied in asking you personal questions, so I've become somewhat of a student in everything Zora Nelson." I cock my head, spying the flicker of emotion in her eyes. "That scare you?"

"What have you learned so far?" she asks instead of answering my question.

As a diversion tactic, it's a good one. But it's not going to work. Nothing can erase that from my head. We'll be getting back to that.

"From your house?" She nods, and I shift closer still, erasing the remaining space between us. Lowering my head, I stare down into her eyes, silently demanding she not look away from me. Because I need to see everything—every feeling, every thought—that moves through them. "That place is your sanctuary. It's obvious from the care with each detail no matter how small. From a figurine to the cedar hutch to the perfect complementary fireplace poker set right to putting your own stamp on it with your photographs. You're about comfort, ease, and being secure in a place you call yours. How am I doing?"

Once more, she nods.

"You don't like to cook, but the meal-delivery service schedule on your refrigerator tells me you pay attention to what you eat. That fancy coffee maker is a dead giveaway about a full-blown caffeine addiction, as is the complicated espresso machine next to it. Looks like something out of the space station. You love to read, and your go-to are thrillers and suspense with some horror thrown in. That reading nook with the cramped and overflowing bookshelves off the dining room is a dead giveaway."

"You were pretty busy while I was taking a shower."

I shrug a shoulder. "Never pretended I wasn't going to snoop."

"Anything else?" she whispers.

"You didn't buy your house only for you." *There it is.* That glint of . . . something. "With most people who buy a home with more bedrooms than they could use or sleep in, I would say it's about show, status. But you're not most people, and you don't give a fuck about show. But there's at least two bedrooms on the second floor with an upper level that wide, and there's another on the main level. Which means you likely bought this home with your brother and sister in mind. Giving them a place to stay if they ever needed it."

"You have more bedrooms in your house than you could ever sleep in. Which is it? Status or something else?" she shoots back at me. Desperation tinges that accusation. As if I've poked at an emotional sore and she's batting my hands away from it.

Interesting.

We're coming back to that too.

"I bought my house for my parents." Her eyes widen, and her soft gasp brushes my chin.

"Cyrus," she breathes. "I'm sorry. I didn't . . ."

I shake my head, cutting her off. "No way you could've. They've been gone for twenty years, but . . ." *I'll never stop being their son. I'll never stop living for them.* "When my parents died, we lived in an apartment, but their dream was always to own a home with a backyard for me to play in, for Mom to have her garden and Dad to grill out. Even though he'd never grilled in his life." I smile at that dust-streaked memory, so old I'd forgotten about it. "They didn't have the chance, but buying the house was my way of giving them—giving us—what we should've had—what they deserved. It's too little, too late, and logically I recognize they couldn't possibly know, but . . ."

Then there's the fact that my parents' deaths stole the ideal of *home* from me. Forever. And for the last two decades, I've been trying to find it again, to replace it. That house is my latest attempt.

"It's never too late to honor our loved ones. And I can't tell you if they know or don't know, but I also don't think it matters. Buying the house was for you to feel closer to them, to show your respect and admiration for them as persons and for their lives and their sacrifices for you. That doesn't require an explanation. Although, just from how you've described them to me, I'd guess they'd say who you've become is honor enough."

I turn my head away from her. This time it's me not wanting her to glimpse what's in my eyes. Because how can the pressure of gratefulness, of grief, of need for this woman that's waiting against my chest like a hailstorm not be reflected in my eyes?

"We should head over. The concert's going to start shortly."

I don't see her dip her head, but I feel it. Stepping back, I give her room to move forward, and I close the door, then lock the car. As we thread through the crowd, I settle a hand on the small of her back, and yes, it's to help guide her through all the people headed to the venue. But it's also an excuse to touch her, even in this small way. And just the press of palm to shirt-covered skin brands my palm. Stirs images of the night she welcomed my hand on her chin and the other on her stomach.

The night she eagerly tipped her head back and sought my mouth, my tongue, my kiss. The night she'd gifted me with her control, leveled me by surrendering her choice.

Decimated me with her trust.

Once we're seated close to the stage in the amphitheater, her excitement and energy emanate, infecting me. She's not the only one who hasn't ever had a chance to visit this place. I haven't either. My life has been about survival and then studying and then work. Not a lot of room for play that wasn't directly related to work or the plans I set out for my future. But this . . .

This is one of the few inexplicable splurges I've indulged in that have nothing to do with clients or partnerships or ironing out contracts. This is . . . mine.

"I would've never guessed you for a Chicago fan," Zora says, a grin flirting with a corner of her mouth. "Lemme guess. It was *Karate Kid* that did it? 'Glory of Love' made you a lifelong fan?"

I slide her a look packed with all the disdain I can muster. "Technically, 'Glory of Love' was only Peter Cetera, not Chicago. And to answer your question, no. I grew up loving them. Maybe I didn't have a choice in the beginning since they were blasted in my house from the time I could walk, but I soon got with the program. They're the shit. Not to be confused with *Karate Kid Part II*, which was just shit."

Her grin grows, and laughter warms her eyes to a golden brown.

"Fact. Finally, something we agree on." She tilts her head, her gaze roaming my face. "Thank you for inviting me. I, uh . . . I . . . well, damn, this is awkward." She chuckles, giving her head a small shake.

"Say it."

"I figure when you bought the tickets, you thought it would be a completely different woman sitting beside you. I'm sorry if this brings you any kind of hurt."

And she means that. I barely manage to swallow my loud bark of laughter. Who *is* Zora Nelson? If it'd been Val, she would've been livid that I invited her to a concert intended for another woman. She would've ripped the ticket in half and stormed off in a dramatic exit worthy of an Oscar. Or a Golden Raspberry.

"It doesn't hurt."

A crease appears between her eyebrows, and doubt shadows her eyes. She doesn't believe me.

"True, I did purchase the tickets while Val and I were together, but I never invited her to go with me. She wouldn't have enjoyed this."

And we weren't *this*.

Hell, I doubt she even knows I like Chicago, much less why. We didn't share personal things with each other. Not like . . .

I yank my gaze from Zora to the stage. But that doesn't halt the confusion and, dammit, anger from mating and swirling inside me in a crazy, elemental dance.

What am I doing with Zora? And not here, in Red Rocks. I mean period. What am I doing? That day in the restaurant, Zora told me we didn't belong. She's not wrong. For years, I've forged this careful schedule and agenda about how my future should and will go. No deviation. No surprises. The first half of my life was filled with surprises and uncertainty; I can't stand them. Now, lately, that's all I've been thrown. One monkey wrench after another, and my carefully organized world has become fucking unrecognizable. I've become unrecognizable to myself.

And this woman is the epicenter of that chaos.

And I've kept her here with this admittedly out-there fake relationship. I don't do *out there*. Or I didn't, before her. Just like I didn't do sharing. I didn't do evenings of Netflix and chill. I didn't do Saturday nights at concerts.

She . . . scares me.

No, no. That's not fair because it places the blame for my fear on her.

My lack of control around her—the fact that I don't care and find reasons to justify not caring—terrifies me.

"Cyrus." A small hand settles on mine, but it might as well weigh a hundred pounds. It grounds me back in the present. "Are you okay? I'm sorry. I shouldn't have brought up a sensitive subject."

"Stop apologizing." I temper my sharp tone with a gentle squeeze before shifting her hand off my leg. Right now, when I'm on the edge, tense with a revelation that isn't exactly pleasant, I can't bear her touch. I barely tolerate my own skin. "You never have to apologize for being honest with me."

I feel her eyes on me even though mine are focused on the stage.

"Okay," she murmurs.

At that moment, the lights flicker on the stage, and the audience cheers and yells in anticipation of Chicago finally appearing.

Zora leans over and whispers in my ear, "Just in case I forget to tell you later, I had a really good time tonight."

I tip my chin down, humor bursting inside me. "Did you just quote *Pretty Woman* to me?"

"Did you just admit to knowing I quoted *Pretty Woman* to you?"

"Zora, I'm sitting at a Chicago concert. I have zero problems admitting I can quote *Pretty Woman* backward and forward."

She throws her head back, laughing. "You win."

Seeing her laugh like that, and knowing I'm the cause of it?

Yeah, damn right, I win.

"Oh my God, I had the best time!" Zora claps, practically bouncing in her seat. "That concert was amazing. *If you see me walking by* . . ."

"Yeah, no."

She glares at me, then starts laughing, her head falling back against the headrest.

"Fine, whatever. I know singing isn't my gifting. Still, you shouldn't judge."

I glance at her. "I'm not judging. Just stating facts. You sound like a dying cat staring down the barrel of his ninth life."

"Wow. That's hurtful." She snickers. "Seriously, though, I haven't had that much fun in a long time. When you drop me off, would you mind waiting while I do something?"

"It's not serenade me, right?"

"You're not going to let that go, are you?"

"Not in this lifetime."

She sighs. "No, no serenading." Pause. "Jerk," she mutters.

I smother a chuckle.

Thirty minutes later, I pull up to the curb outside her house. She reaches for the door handle, but when I growl a "Don't," she sighs and waits for me to exit the vehicle and come around to her side and open her door.

"Thank you," she murmurs, sliding her hand in mine and allowing me to help her out of the car.

As soon as she steps free, she turns back, pulls open the rear door, and removes her camera case. With the same quick, efficient skill she employed at the concert venue, she gathers her equipment, fixing the lens and flash. In moments, she sets the camera on the hood of my Audi and turns to me. Her small white teeth sink into her full bottom lip, and she raises her hand to her forehead, but before her fingers make contact, she drops her arm back to her side.

"I could see back at the amphitheater that you weren't entirely comfortable with having your picture taken, but if you don't mind, would you take one more with me? I'd like to have a picture as a souvenir of this night."

She waits, an air of nervousness about her, as if she half expects me to turn her down. And there's a part of me that's leery of being the focal point of that lens. But a bigger part, a needier part, craves for this moment to be captured. Craves for this moment to be immortalized . . . with her. Because in three months, we're walking away from one another, and that part selfishly needs for her to remember me. And not just as the pretend boyfriend.

"Yeah."

She smiles and fiddles with the camera once more. Satisfied, she moves toward me and steps into my body. Our sides brush, but I'm not happy with that. When she looks at this picture later tonight, a week from now, in another year, I want her to *feel* me.

I curl my arm around her shoulders, bringing her breasts into my side. Her hand flattens on my stomach, whether to brace herself or hold herself closer, I'm not sure. I'm not sure I care. I do care that her other hand slides under the shirt at my back. I care that her soft palm presses to my sensitized skin.

I care because now I'm hard, throbbing, and greedy for more.

The click and flash of the camera distract me for as long as it requires to take the pictures. And I can only imagine what it catches. I'm not that damn good to hide the lust that's no doubt hardening my features or my eyes.

We continue to stand there, her breasts cushioning my side, her thighs spread on either side of my leg. Her hand splayed over my rigid abdomen, her fingers caressing the patch of skin above my waistband.

My dick a goddamn flagpole shoving against my zipper, ready for her to run her hand up it.

"Get your camera, and I'll walk you to your door."

My voice is rough, almost angry, but that's lust, not rage. That's the heat pumping through me, agitating an appetite that has no hope of being satiated.

I fucking crave this woman.

Is there another word? Something else to describe how even just a simple touch of her fingers stroking my lower back can have a vise grip seizing it? Have the soles of my feet sizzling? Have my balls drawing tight and me tingling, staring an orgasm in the face?

She's dangerous.

No, no. She's fucking heinous.

And yet I'm walking her to her door, ready to plead, if necessary, for more of that touch. More of that mouth. That tongue.

I'm not even going to think about that pussy because I've never done anything that goddamn good to deserve it.

She stares at me, and I believe those dark-chocolate eyes peer into my thoughts. It's ridiculous, fanciful, and yet I wait for the shame to rush in. But it never appears. There's no guilt, not even a residue of shame when it comes to this clawing *thing* inside me. It's too consuming, too ravenous.

After several moments, she steps back, and I lower my arm. She packs up her camera, and then I'm walking beside her up the steps to her porch. I silently watch as she opens her front door, and tension creeps into my body. My gut clenches, and I feel like an utter animal, a predator, watching her, studying her body language, her cues.

Invite me in. Take me in.

I'm talking about her house. Her arms. Her mouth.

Nothing else.

Nothing else, dammit.

That flash of fear flickers inside me again, and for a second, I almost back off that porch. This is physical. Purely physical. That's *it*.

Zora glances over her shoulder at me, and that's when I realize I actually did backpedal a step. And just that one look centers me. And by *center*, I mean burns away the doubt, the uncertainty, and dials up the electricity snapping inside me.

"Do you want more?" she whispers.

This woman. Turning the tables on me. I knew she saw through me.

She runs a finger down the middle of my palm, then tangles my fingers with hers.

"Do you want me to make you take more?"

Grabbing my words and throwing them back at me. No, not throwing. Gifting them to me.

She pushes the door open and leads me in, and as soon as it closes, I'm on her.

I can't help it. With those words, that gift, she unleashed something inside me, and my hands, my mouth, my body—they're everywhere. Backed against the wall next to her front door, I fist my hand in her curls, because, *God*, I can't get enough of them. Of the rough silken strands between my fingers, over my palms. Because I can, I turn my face into them, inhale, rubbing my skin against them. Feeling their caress over my chest, abdomen, thighs . . . cock. Shit. My grip tightens, and she whimpers. I pull back, peering down into her face, gauging if I've hurt her, even unintentionally. What I glimpse . . .

"Fuck, baby."

Pleasure suffuses her features. Desire glazes her hooded eyes; color rides the high arcs of her cheekbones. Her lips, already swollen from my kiss, are wet, parted as if begging me for more.

That seems to be our theme.

More.

I can't resist the call, the lure of that mouth. Rubbing my thumb over the lush bottom lip, I press it inside, her teeth grazing the tip. Not satisfied, I push my thumb farther, claiming more of her mouth, sliding it along her tongue. Lashes fluttering down, she curls around me, sucking, drawing hard, and that suction pulls directly on my dick. I groan, and it's long and thick with lust. Abandoning her hair, I punch my fist to the wall above her head, grinding my erection against her hip, seeking some kind of temporary relief. But who the fuck am I kidding? There's no relief that doesn't include sliding deep inside the place my thumb is enjoying or the dark, tight, wet core her thighs are shielding.

"Tell me what's too much," I order, watching my hand with complete fascination as I pull it free of her lips.

Another moan slips free of me as I study my thumb, glistening from her mouth. Goddamn. Will my cock be as shiny from her pussy once I get it inside her? Because if I do nothing else before I leave this earth,

I'm going to push slow, firm, and without mercy into her. I'm going to know that hot, slick clasp of her sex strangling my dick. I'm going to find out the exquisite pleasure of her milking me dry and leaving me drained.

Taking her mouth again, I tangle my tongue with hers and lower my arm from above her. Slowly, I drag the backs of my fingers down her temple, her cheek, and her jaw until I reach her throat. There, I circle the elegant column, palming the front of her neck, fingers and thumb cupping the sides. I pause, staring down into her eyes, granting her time to tell me no, she's not comfortable with this hold or push at my hand and pull free. My grip isn't tight, but it is firm. I want her to feel me, to know what I want from her.

Which is her control.

But she doesn't speak. Doesn't push me away. Doesn't even reach up to circle my wrist like she did that night on her couch.

A primal, roaring satisfaction rises in me, and I bend my head, brushing a grateful kiss over her lips.

That soft kiss belies the firm rub I apply to her clit.

She cries out against my mouth, and I'm there to swallow it. And demand another one. Because it's sweet. It's addictive. It's mine.

I cup her, grinding the heel of my palm to that perfect little bundle of nerves, circling it. She arches hard, pressing her throat to my palm, crushing her breasts to my chest. Her nails claw at my back, and I count each tiny bite of pain as my reward, my due.

Her hips twist and buck, and I lean back to watch the show. Watch those thick, gorgeous thighs spread to accommodate my hand. To silently plead for me to finish what I'm giving her.

"Make me come, Cyrus. Please. I need to come."

Fuck. Not so silently.

Snatching my hand away, I devour her cry of disapproval, and shoving in between her thighs, I cup the backs of them and hike her high against the wall. That cry transforms into one of alarm, and she shoves at my chest.

"No," she rasps, breathless, shaking her head. "You can't—"

"I can and I am. Now put your arms around me. Hold on to me, baby. Kiss me like you mean it. Like you want what I have for you."

The panic doesn't completely ebb from her eyes, but the passion crowds in again. Especially when I drag my cock up her jean-covered folds, pausing to work it over her clit. Blazing-hot fire streaks down my spine, and I close my eyes, praying that this doesn't end with this one stroke.

"Kiss me, Zora." I need that connection with her.

Need her to hold me, just as I'm holding her.

She captures my mouth, thrusting her tongue between my lips and taking me in the same way I want to claim her body. It's a lit match to the powder keg inside me.

Pinning her tighter to the wall, I move, thrusting against her. If our jeans were to miraculously disappear—and shit, where's a miracle when you need one?—I would be buried inside her right now. This, though . . . I drive forward again. And again. And again. It's good. So fucking good. Having this beautiful, sexy woman tremble and moan in my arms? I'm transfigured into a god. A pagan god whose sole power is doling out pleasure to one Zora Nelson.

"Cyrus." She tears her mouth away from mine, buries her face in my neck. Her mouth opens on my neck, teeth grazing, tongue licking. "Please."

I can't deny her. Everything in me demands I give her the ecstasy she deserves.

"Keep me wrapped up tight in these gorgeous legs, baby," I whisper, reaching between us, releasing the button on her jeans. She stiffens, and I pause. "Your pace, on your word."

I might probably go to my car, huddle on the floorboard, and cry after I leave her house if I don't get to feel her come, but I'll survive.

Barely.

My hand continues to rest on her sweetly rounded lower belly, my thumb sweeping back and forth just inside the opening of her jeans, our fast, loud breaths the only sounds in the room. Finally, several moments later, she raises her head from my neck and meets my gaze. Even in the dimness of the living room, I glimpse the shadows in her eyes. But they take a back seat to the bright glimmer of lust.

And to the "Make me come" that falls from her lips.

On a growl, I wedge myself between her thighs, spreading her wider. A slight tremble afflicts my hand as I slide it between denim, cotton, and skin. Excitement and anticipation race neck and neck with desire, and when my fingers slide through slick, soft flesh . . . *fuck.*

Our twin groans melt on the air, and I press my forehead to hers, biting the inside of my cheek. Her head tips back, pressing to the wall, twisting from side to side. One day—one day soon if I have my way—I'm going to have a front-row seat to the beauty of her pussy parting for my fingers, my tongue. But tonight, I'm studying her face as if there will be a test on it later. Studying it for telltale signs at my every caress, circle, stroke. Studying it for that particular tautened expression just before . . .

I rub her clit. Hard.

Her cry trips free, and I slam my mouth down on hers, taking it, owning it as my due, and not letting up on her flesh. I pluck and caress, drawing out the release until she whimpers into my mouth and her hips flinch. Only then do I slowly withdraw my hand from her pants.

And lift it to my mouth.

Her hooded gaze flares as I slip my drenched fingers between my lips and suck her from my skin. Her taste—tangy, fresh, and so *her*—explodes on my tongue, and it only whets my appetite to gorge on it directly from the source.

I pull my fingers free and slowly lower her to the floor. Her arms, which were still wound tight around my neck, loosen, and she drops them to her sides. She flattens her palms to the walls on either side of her lush hips. The vulnerability of the move hits me in the chest. Is she afraid of me? Or of the pleasure we just shared? Because even though I'm still hard and hurting, giving her release—having her swollen, wet flesh under my fingers—was pure rapture.

"Zora." Her gaze lifts to mine, and the shadows are deeper now that the glaze of passion starts to fade. My gut clenches. "Talk to me."

Her glance drops down my body to the erection no doubt fucking with the seam of my jeans. I don't try to adjust or hide it. Hell, if anything, I want her to witness what effect she has on me. See how much I desire her.

"You," she whispers, jerking her gaze back up to mine. "You haven't—"

"I don't give a fuck about that." I slash a hand through the space between us. "And you're not ready for that." The brief slump of her shoulders confirms my guess. I'm not even sure she realizes her body revealed that small tell. "Only you are," I murmur, cocking my head.

She averts her gaze. "Cyrus, I'm—"

"Don't you dare apologize." I cut her off. "What just happened here was all my pleasure. It was my damn honor. If I don't get to do anything else but touch your sweet little pussy—because goddamn, baby, it's so fucking sweet—and have you come on my fingers, then I'm happy with that. If it's your choice not to go any further, then we'll end this right here. Not the friendship, Zora. Just this part of it. But you don't want to end it, do you? You want me, baby."

I lower my gaze to the obvious beads of her nipples under her white thermal shirt. And the evidence of her desire is still thick on my tongue. And her sex no doubt still pulses with the echoes of her release; her thighs are still damp with her cream.

"Your choice, Zora." I skate my fingertips over her temple and cheek and across her jaw. "You decide whether we continue as we've been, just friends. Or do we become lovers as well, enjoying each other's bodies, giving each other pleasure? Using each other to beat back the loneliness neither one of us wants to admit to but we both know we have. Either way"—I shake my head—"three months. No strings, no demands, no expectations." I drop my arm and step back. "Think on it, baby. Your choice," I repeat. "And whichever one you make, I'll honor."

Shifting forward, I brush a kiss over her forehead, her honey-and-almond scent filling my nose. I inhale, closing my eyes.

I step back.

"Night, Zora."

Then, without looking back, because my masochism has its limits, I walk the short distance to the front door and let myself out. On the other side, I pause, waiting until I hear the turn of the lock before descending the steps to my car.

Only then do I glance at the house.

And it's harder than it should be to get in my car and drive away.

CHAPTER TWELVE

ZORA

"Hey, Zora."

I glance up from the cup of coffee I'm brewing toward the door of the small break room. Deanna stands there, wearing a smile as bright as her voice. But as soon as she steps through the doorway and closes it behind her, her mouth flattens, and her brows crease into a frown.

"What's wrong?" I turn from the one-cup coffee machine and face my office manager and friend. "Your mom? Warren?" A couple of weeks ago, she'd met this guy, and I'm praying he's the one to get her over her crush on Levi.

"No, no, they're both fine." She waves a hand, and her smile makes another brief appearance. "More than fine, actually. Warren, I mean, not my mother. Although, I'm sure she's doing great, too, but I didn't wake up next to her this morning—"

"Okay, yep, I get it." I twirl my fingers. "Carry on."

Wow. Is everyone getting sex but me?

By choice.

Shut up, bitch.

I smother a sigh. I hate know-it-all, smug self-consciousness.

"Right." Deanna flicks her ponytail over her shoulder and, after casting a furtive glance at the closed break room door, inches closer to me. "Uh, did Valerie Summers have an appointment you forgot to add to the calendar or tell me about so I could add it to the calendar?"

I slowly straighten, ice crackling along my veins. Alarm bells clang in my head, and I can barely hear myself speak to Deanna. Guilt streams through me like a swollen spring flood.

"What? No, I didn't schedule an appointment."

Relief flashes across Deanna's face, followed by confusion.

"That's what I thought. And I would've remembered if you'd told me. I mean, Ms. I'd Never Dare Step Foot in Five Points is pretty unforgettable," she mutters. "But she's here in the lobby and is insisting on seeing you. Appointment or no appointment."

I turn on the pretense of tending to my coffee when I really don't want Deanna to see my trembling hands. Dread clenches my belly in its taloned grip and squeezes, digging its claws in until bile whips and burns a path for the back of my throat.

Valerie Summers. Here in my office. Without an appointment. After I've been spending time with her ex, and some of it not in private.

There can be only one reason for her sudden appearance.

To rip me a new asshole. And I deserve it.

Miriam had warned me, hadn't she? This couldn't end well. And the time had come to pay the piper. I couldn't hide from this. No matter how much I hated conflict, this situation I created. Hubris. This is the result of hubris. Not only have I continued to see the woman's ex behind her back, but not just in secret. Hell, only two evenings ago, I'd been at a rock concert with him. In public.

And you've had your tongue down his throat and his hand down your panties. Let's not forget that.

Shut. Up. Bitch.

Lobotomy. Do they still perform lobotomies?

Pivoting back around, I face Deanna again, pinning my polite, professional smile on my face. My only armor at this point.

"That's okay. I think my schedule is clear at the moment. Let me finish up in here, and I'll be right out."

Deanna frowns, and I read her mind without her speaking a word. She doesn't like making an exception for Val since she views the other woman as entitled. And under ordinary circumstances, I would agree with her. But these are far, far from ordinary circumstances.

"I'll let her know." Deanna turns but halts before she leaves, studying me over her shoulder. "Zora, are you okay?"

"Yes, I'm fine." To emphasize my fine-ness, I dial up the wattage on my smile.

But that's the thing with friends. They don't easily buy your brand of bullshit.

Her lips part, probably to argue with me, but I pop up a hand to ward her off.

"Seriously, Deanna. I'm good. Thank you for worrying, though."

One last long look, and then she nods. "You're welcome. I'll go let Queen Val know you'll be with her in a few minutes."

As soon as Deanna exits, leaving me alone, I heave a deep, low breath and clutch the edge of the counter, my head bent low.

I can do this. I can do this.

But I *can't* do this with coffee sloshing around in my stomach. It might end up on Val's shoes.

Grimacing, I take the freshly brewed cup and pour it down the sink. Such a waste.

Inhaling, I quickly rinse the cup out, place it on the draining mat, and trace Deanna's path out the door. No use stalling. Striding down the hall toward the lobby, I fix a smile on my face . . . and pray. Although, I doubt God is itching to cut out time for liars and wannabe fornicators.

My only saving grace is that I didn't take Saturday night any further—even though, *good God*, I so wanted to. Cyrus Hart is carnally gifted with his mouth and fingers. And that mouth. *Holy hell.* I came so close to slapping my hand over his lips to prevent him from talking me right into another orgasm with that whiskey-and-sin voice and sinful words. But it felt . . . dirty, as if I was once again stealing Cyrus's choice when I'm lying to him about who I am, how we met. I couldn't do it.

It's one thing if this happens to blow up in my face now when I've been deceiving him. But for him to discover my deception after I've had sex with him? That's theft on a whole different level, a betrayal that I can't come back from—that *we* can't come back from. Come the end of the year, my hope is that we can walk away from each other as friends. But if the depth of my lies is exposed, I would lose even that part of him. I would lose him to his hatred of me.

As soon as I reach the mouth of the corridor, I spot Val sitting on the same couch in the same spot she did when we first met. It's a case of déjà vu. Except then, she was just a new client. And now . . . well now, she's not.

"Hello, Ms. Summers." I extend my hand toward her, not sure what to expect as she stands and turns her unblinking, steady blue gaze on me. And yet when she slides her palm against mine and shakes it, it isn't relief that flows through me. It's more tension. "Though it's a surprise to see you today, it's a pleasure."

I haven't seen the other woman since that initial meeting in my office, and she's still as beautiful and perfectly poised. Today, she's exquisitely stylish in a winter-white, midlength sheath dress with a draped waist and front slit. Her long blonde hair falls in a shining sheet over her shoulders, and honestly, does she wake up like this?

"Yes, I'm sorry. It must've been my oversight if I neglected to schedule an appointment with your secretary. I thought I did."

A cough behind me portends Val's imminent demise if I don't move her into my office. And blood is hell getting out of the carpet . . . and explaining to future clients.

"Well, our *office manager* is very organized, so she was a little confused, but she also adapts quickly. So no harm done. If you'll follow me. Would you like coffee or tea?"

"No, thank you."

Smart woman. After that secretary crack, I can't protect her from Deanna's wrath. Not that there's anything wrong with secretaries—nothing at all. But Deanna runs this place like a drill sergeant and has earned her title.

Moments later, we enter my office, and I close the door behind her.

"Please, have a seat." I wave a hand toward the visitor chair in front of my desk and round the furniture to take my seat behind it. Somehow, I'm retaining my calm demeanor, but inside, I'm a shaking mass of nerves. "What can I do for you today, Ms. Summers? It must be important to bring you all the way over here."

I hold my breath, and the knocking of my heart against my ribs reverberates like a drum kit.

"Yes, it is." She pauses, and though only seconds pass as she sinks into the chair, slides the thin chain of her purse from her shoulder, and tucks the accessory beside her thigh, it stretches by like an eternity. And it's torture. Pure torture. "The first time I was here, do you remember I mentioned finding someone else who gave me the attention I needed that my ex wasn't providing?"

"Yes, I recall that."

Vividly.

"Well, as soon as my relationship with Cyrus ended, I pursued my own happiness. And it was wonderful. Just what I imagined and deserved. But lately . . ." She tilts her head, the sheet of hair falling behind her. "Lately, he hasn't been the same. Not answering his phone when I call. Preferring to party with his friends instead of spend time with me. Disappearing without an excuse. I don't need it spelled out for me. There's another woman, and I don't play second to anyone."

Relief, astonishment, and a healthy dose of WTF sweep through me like a summer tornado. Thank God I'm sitting because light-headedness is a real possibility.

Relief for obvious reasons. She isn't here to call me out on buddying up with her ex-boyfriend behind her back—and kissing him—and threaten my family's business in the process.

Astonishment because she's here in my office admitting to me that she hooked up with the sidepiece and now it's gone to hell. I usually don't receive updates after the breakups.

And the WTF . . . because this is *not* headed where I think this is headed. It can't be.

"I came here to hire you again to break up with my new boyfriend."

It's headed *exactly* there.

"Ms. Summers, while I appreciate repeat business like the next company, are you certain this is what you want to do? It's only been a few weeks. Of course I want to help you, but I also want to ensure you're not moving too hastily."

"If they'll do it with you, they'll do it to you."

Mom, please, I silently plead with my mother's voice in my head.

Now is so not the time for her know-it-all advice.

Especially when I'm attempting to convince an ex-client to not become a current client. Not only would it be messy as hell for me to work for Val while I'm . . . whatever the hell I am with Cyrus, but I also promised him I would cut off all ties with her.

When I initially agreed to this arrangement with him, I didn't expect things to become so damn . . . complicated. But every time I turn around, more and more strings appear, and they're snarled and dirtied with deception. And I'm choking on them.

"I appreciate your concern," she says, the cool note in her tone belying her words, "but I'm certain. Of course, if you'd rather not have my business . . ."

I smother a sigh. Yes, I'd rather not have her business. For personal reasons. But personal reasons have no sway here. They can't have reign when it's not only myself I have to consider. And not when it would take only one negative, well-placed comment in the right ear from Val Summers to hurt our reputation and all that we've built.

"No, it would be our pleasure to help you again. I'm sorry for the circumstances, though."

She shrugs. "These things happen. Actually . . ." She sighs, threading her fingers through her hair. Glancing away, she briefly closes her eyes and rubs her fingertips against her breastbone. A moment later, she drops her hand and faces me again, that pensive expression vanished, as if it'd never happened. "Actually, I've been thinking about Cyrus lately. About how if I was too hasty, it was with him. The grass definitely wasn't greener on the other side. Being with this other person made me appreciate Cyrus's stability and dependability more. And I can say what I want about him being a workaholic; Cyrus would never see another woman behind my back."

Then you shouldn't have cheated on him and dumped him for some pretty superficial reasons.

Shit.

I didn't think this could get worse. But I was so wrong. I've lost all objectivity. Our cardinal rule is not to get personally involved with clients. And while I haven't broken the letter of the law, the spirit of the law? I've shattered that and then stomped the pieces to dust.

I can't, in good conscience, continue to work for Val. Not while I know what her ex—the man she now seems to be pining for—feels like, tastes like, kisses like. Not when I know what it is to receive pleasure at his hands, his mouth.

Oh God. Getting hot at the memory of Cyrus has to violate some clause in my contract with her.

There's one silver lining. With the flu no longer running rampant through our staff, I'm no longer required to pinch-hit on the actual breakups. Still, the wisest play here is to pass off Val's file to Miriam. It lessens the messiness of the already messy conflict of interest, and Val won't have to know. Besides, nothing in her contract specifies who will be over her file, nor does it prohibit me from assigning her to another owner of the company.

And why, yes. Yes, I am justifying my actions.

"I think it's perfectly natural to think about what-ifs," I say, and how I utter that so calmly with guilt swaying in my belly like a drunken sailor is a minor miracle. "Especially when you're about to come out of another relationship."

"Maybe." She pauses, as if considering my explanation. "And maybe it's a reminder to go back and reclaim what you've lost before it's too late."

Dread crashes over me in icy waves, and if I wasn't going to be ill when Deanna announced Val's presence in my lobby, I just might be now.

Images of this woman and Cyrus together rush to the forefront of my mind. Of their perfection as a couple. Of how they seem to fit. To belong.

Stop it.

Just because Val wants to revisit the past doesn't mean he is up for a trip down Memory Lane. Besides, hadn't he said—

Oh my God, what am I doing? What am I thinking? Another wave of terror crashes over me, dragging me into its frigid undertow. I can't get invested in Val or Cyrus. Not like this. Like, like . . . *shit.*

And what happens if he eventually does decide to go back to her? What does it matter to me? Because if it's not her, it will be another woman like her. He admitted as much to me. So the worst, most idiotic thing I can do is become attached to a man who slapped a three-month expiration date on our fake relationship/friendship, much less . . .

There is no *much less.*

I'm not even a rebound girl.

I'm penance. An arrangement. A teaching tool.

As long as I keep that forefront in my mind, I'll be fine.

I'll be just. Fine.

"When the shit hits the fan—because, babe, it has no choice but to hit the fan—you're going to end up hurt."

Damn. There are way too many people in my head today.

Forcing a smile, I tap the space bar on my keyboard to bring my monitor alive.

"Okay, Ms. Summers. Let's discuss which package you'd like to book with us."

In the end, it all comes down to business as usual.

CHAPTER THIRTEEN

CYRUS

"Why am I here again?" I ask Jordan just as my cell phone vibrates. I remove it from the front pocket of my black dress pants, glance at the screen, and decline the call.

This shit again. What the fuck?

"Because you ain't doing sh—jack else," he says, quickly correcting himself for the benefit of the preteen holding the basketball jersey out to Jordan. "What's up, lil man?"

Jordan greets the boy, scrawling his name across the number. For the next couple of minutes, he talks with the kid, and by the time the youth leaves, he's grinning and grasping the top to his chest like it's a treasure map.

And so on and so on with all the middle and high school children who approach him to have jerseys, basketballs, posters, photos, and even limbs signed. The charity event, held at one of the local middle schools, invited several athletes from various Denver professional sports teams to come and speak to handpicked inner city youth from several different schools, hand out sports paraphernalia, and sign autographs. It's a great event, and the smiles on the kids' faces, even those who appear determined to remain unaffected by all of this, are inspiring.

Still . . . I'm not sure why Jordan called me at the ungodly hour of 4:00 a.m. and demanded I accompany him here. Not when he has an agent and a manager.

My cell vibrates again, and though I'm 50 percent certain whose name will occupy the screen, I can't risk ignoring it. Not when I'm hoping to see *another* name.

It's been a week since I left Zora's house. A week since I've heard from her.

I could've called, sent a text, tugged on the fake-girlfriend arrangement. But I meant what I said to her. This is her decision, her choice. And I won't influence her in any way. No matter how much it goes against the grain not to do just that.

I remove my phone from my pocket and peer at the screen again. And hit decline *again*.

This is getting ridiculous and annoying as hell.

Several hours later, the crowds start to thin, and Jordan walks up to me where I've found a shadowed corner, a wall, and relative privacy. As much privacy as one can find in a gym full of excited middle and high schoolers.

"Hey, ready to go?" Jordan appears in front of me, interrupting an email reply to my legal assistant.

I don't bother looking up at him as I continue to type out my message.

"In a minute. Let me finish this. In the meantime, mind answering my question from earlier? Why am I here?" I hit send on the email and tuck the cell in my pocket. "Not that this hasn't been a great event."

He slaps me on the shoulder. "Shit, I did you a favor and saved you from yourself. If I hadn't called, you either would've been holed up in your office working or holed up in your house working. On a Saturday. You're welcome."

"So you've appointed yourself my personal savior now? No thanks. And you don't want that job. It's a thankless post. Ask my last guardian angel. You can probably find him at the local bar or on his therapist's couch."

"Savior?" Jordan snorts. "Martyrdom is so last year. Honestly, I just didn't want to come alone, and since my agent would annoy the fuck out of me, I chose you. So here we are. Now"—he claps his hands and rubs them together—"let's go eat. I'm starving. And on the way, you can tell me who's been blowing up your phone."

Shit. He would notice that.

I sigh, and he smirks.

"Val."

Jordan skids to a stop in the middle of the gym floor and scowls down at me from his six-foot, nine-inch height.

"You're shittin' me."

Several adults within earshot throw disapproving glances his way, but he either doesn't see them or just doesn't give a damn.

"No, I'm not shittin' you."

If possible, his scowl deepens.

"I thought you weren't talking to her anymore."

"I'm not. We haven't spoken since—" Since she sent Zora to my house to dump me. "Since we ended things. That's been weeks. I have no idea why she's suddenly calling me now. And don't care."

"It's obvious." He crosses his heavily inked arms over his chest, arching a dark eyebrow. "She wants you back."

It's my turn to snort. "Bullshit."

"Why bullshit? As Mom always says, 'The grass not only isn't greener on the other side, but the neighbor's dog takes regular dumps on it.'"

"I don't . . . I don't even know what to say to that." Mrs. Grace Ransom is a lovely woman, but I swear to God she comes up with her own sayings, and they don't always make sense.

"Okay, I'll clear it up. This new motherfucker either didn't kiss her ass enough, or she realized he didn't have enough money to keep her how she's accustomed to living. I'm just saying, she's not suddenly hitting you up 'cause she misses your conversation." Jordan cocks his head. "Could be she miss the dick, though."

"For fuck's sake." I whip around on my heel and stride toward the gym doors.

"What?" He laughs, and it's diabolical. His long legs bring him by my side. "It's an option." His laughter ebbs, and he slides me a look. "The question is are you going to fall for it?"

Seriously? He knows me better than that.

"Hell no. Once I'm done, I'm done." I press the bar handle on one of the large gymnasium doors, pushing it open. "No offense, Jordan. But why do you give a damn?"

"Are you kidding me?" He frowns, his strides stiff, abrupt. Yeah, he's offended. "Yeah, bruh, you're my attorney, but you're also my friend. And I know you and Valerie had some kind of quid quo pro arrangement going on that, personally? Was fifty shades of fucked up, but I hate to see you used. And ol' girl was using you."

"I wouldn't paint her as the bitch in our relationship," I say. "I was using her too."

"Like I said, fifty shades of fucked up. But it was your shit, your arrangement. And in the end, she betrayed it. Betrayed you. She shouldn't get another chance to do it again. Nobody should get another shot at shoving a knife in your back."

I look at Jordan's dark expression and wonder if that last part is as much about him as it is about me. Curious, I study him closer. I thought I knew my friend well, but maybe that's not exactly true.

"Yeah, well, that's over. I don't go back once it's over."

Jordan absently nods, but then he draws to a halt in the middle of the emptying hall. His attention no longer on me, he stares down the long length of corridor. A smile curves a corner of his mouth.

"Huh. It's a good thing you mean that, or else that one right there might make things a little more complicated."

I follow his gaze, and . . . *damn.*

My cock recognizes her the moment my eyes do.

Zora.

After a week, it's as if I've been on a hunger strike. My stomach tightens damn near to the point of pain, like cramps, and only a taste of her can satiate it. Her thick hair is pulled up in a curly crown, and big golden hoops decorate her ears. A white turtleneck embraces every curve, flaunting her gorgeous breasts, and dark-green wide-legged pants hug rounded hips and long toned legs. She's beautiful. She's a goddess. She's breathing and walking sex.

Part of me wants to go stand by her side, see if she'll claim me.

The other part wants to march over there and snarl and snap at the men sniffing at the six-foot table she's standing behind. Let them know she called *my* name as she came all over *my* hand. Let all those motherfuckers staring at her like she's a goddamn steak dinner know that she's fucking *mine.*

But that's not true.

Her silence in the last week speaks volumes.

Doesn't stop me from craving it to be true.

At least to the end of the year.

As if sensing my gaze on her, Zora's head turns in our direction. I can't see her eyes with the distance of the hall between us, but judging from the stiffening of her frame, she notices us.

"Friends." Jordan hums, humor lacing the sound. "Are we still rocking with that story? I just need to know how I'm playing this before we go over there."

"Fuck you," I mutter, walking down the hall. Toward Zora.

He chuckles, following behind me.

I don't stop until I reach the table with a last few baseball caps, shirts, and socks on it. Zora doesn't take her gaze from me, and I briefly remove mine from her to take in the older woman next to her. Tall, with natural curls like Zora, although with gray sprinkled throughout, identical-color eyes, and the same full mouth. Even the curvaceous figure reminds me of Zora. It clicks that this woman must be her mother or at the very least an aunt.

Jordan's presence draws the attention of the people lingering around the table, and in seconds a small crowd forms around him. Never more thankful than I am now for my friend's fame, I skirt around them and approach Zora.

"Cyrus." She greets me first, her gaze shifting to the woman next to her before returning to me. If I'm not mistaken, an edginess threads through her voice, and her normally elegant, graceful frame is rigid, tense. "What a surprise seeing you here."

"Zora." I nod. "It is. A good one, though." Turning to the older woman, I extend my hand. "I'm sorry, it's not my intention to be rude. Cyrus Hart. It's nice to meet you."

"Monica Nelson. Social studies teacher here and mom to this one." She takes my hand and shakes it, giving me a curious once-over. "Likewise. I gather you and my daughter know one another."

"Yes."

I cast a glance at Zora, who's remained silent. Uncertainty crawls up my spine. I'm in a position that's unusual and uncomfortable for me. I'm not sure what or how much to say. And I sense . . . I sense Zora is afraid of what I'll say. I'm treading on dangerous ground here, and Zora will be the casualty.

When she sees I'm leaving my answer at yes, her mother grimaces, tossing an eye roll at Zora. "Just for future reference, I'm your mother. Which means I have a God-given right to be nosy."

"I don't think that's how that works, Mom," Zora drawls. "And Cyrus and I are friends. We've only known each other a few weeks, so sorry. No plans to elope. No secret babies on the way. Sad to disappoint."

Her mother's mouth twitches. "Smart-ass. You totally get that from me," she boasts, sliding an arm around Zora's shoulders and pressing a kiss to her temple. "So tell me, Cyrus Hart, since my daughter won't. How do you know my brilliant daughter? Where did you meet?"

Until now, I haven't had the best impression about her parents. But it's plain to see that Monica loves her, is beaming with pride over her. It's how I imagine my own mother would've been with me had she lived. Dad too. Despite the obvious dysfunction that exists in Zora's parents' relationship, I'm glad she has this, at least.

"We met through work," I answer.

From one instant to another, Monica's expression transforms from one of glowing delight to weary distaste. It's so surprising I step back from the table, glancing between mother and daughter.

"Oh, please, God, don't tell me you're talking about that little business of hers." Her mouth twists as she slides her arm from around Zora's shoulders.

That little business of hers?

What the hell does that mean? And what exactly is the "little business"?

I flip through the mental files of all our conversations, and the only thing I know is she works somewhere within driving distance of the Five Points area. That could cover a considerable part of Denver.

Other than that? Nothing.

But that was our agreement, wasn't it? No personal details or questions.

Yet . . . she's a businesswoman, an entrepreneur? I study her, picturing her lush curves clothed in those suits, those prim blouses and figure-hugging skirts. I'm not surprised. She's brilliant, assertive, driven. And she wears command and authority as easily as one of her pantsuits.

"Mom, please." Zora shifts away from her mother, that edginess that had crept into her voice invading her expression. Small lines bracket the corners of her mouth, and her silken skin pulls taut over her cheekbones.

"What?" Monica holds up her hands, palms out. "All I'm saying is I was hoping when you finally did meet someone, it didn't have anything to do with that sor—"

"That's enough."

Zora doesn't yell at her mother, but the arctic tone has my shoulders snapping back. As does the hurt glinting in her eyes. Does her mother not see it? Does she not give a fuck?

"Really, Zora—"

"I was referring to my job, actually," I interject, careful not to look at Zora. If I do and glimpse that pain in her gaze again, I'll lose my shit. "We met through my work. But even if we hadn't, it wouldn't matter. Your daughter is a smart, self-assured woman. And she brings those same qualities to her business. And no one should make her feel less than brilliant for that."

Silence descends over the table, and it's so thick, so taut with tension, that cracks would probably spiderweb through it at the slightest breath. Monica's eyes narrow on me, and I don't need a second career as a mentalist to interpret the message there: *She's my daughter, and you don't know what you're talking about.*

Yeah, a daughter you have no problem tearing down and embarrassing in front of a person who's a stranger to you.

She's a puzzle. That pride had been authentic. But so had her disdain.

I don't know what Zora's business is—and I would be lying if I claimed curiosity didn't beat at me—but derision? What could Zora, one of the most sensitive, most honest people I know, do that could possibly merit that?

"Hey, what's good?" Jordan appears at my side again, wearing his trademark wide bad-boy grin. "Nice to see you again, Zora."

"You too, Jordan."

"My, my, you're keeping quite the interesting company today," her mother murmurs.

Jordan switches his smile and attention to Monica. "If by *interesting* you mean gorgeous, rich, and gifted, then yes, you're right. She's been leveling up."

Despite the outrageous arrogance of that reply, Monica smiles up at him.

"I didn't have the opportunity to meet you earlier," she says. "But I want to personally thank you for investing in our students. Especially when so many aspire to be you. Having this chance to listen and talk to you—it means the world to them. I appreciate you sacrificing your time for them."

"Of course," Jordan says, dipping his chin. "I'm just paying it forward. If someone hadn't done the same for me when I was younger, I might not be where I am today." His grin returns. "We were just headed out to grab some food. Did you two want to join us? My treat."

Finally, I glance at Zora.

And the vestiges of panic in her eyes before she lowers her lashes have me curling my fingers into my palms. Somehow, I doubt she wants me reaching out and hauling her into my arms in front of her mother and Jordan. But especially her mother. So I tuck my hand in my pocket to further prevent me from making that mistake.

"I'm sorry, Jordan," Zora murmurs. "I already have plans that I should be leaving for in the next few minutes. But thank you for the invitation."

"Really? You didn't mention these plans before." Monica arches an eyebrow. "They're pretty convenient all of a sudden."

"It's not convenient at all. But I'm glad I could help out today, Mom." She ignores her mother's direct barb, leans in, and kisses her cheek. Straightening, she gives me and Jordan a polite, small smile. "Cyrus, Jordan."

Then she turns and walks the few feet to the exit and pushes through the doors, disappearing to the other side.

"She didn't deserve that."

Her mother glares at me, and if it wasn't for a flash of guilt in her eyes, I might've written her off.

"You don't know us," she snaps.

Right. Doubling down.

"You're right. I just met you, and I've only known your daughter for a short while. But in that short amount of time I've become acquainted with a woman of strength, integrity, and loyalty. So I'll repeat—she didn't deserve that." Turning to Jordan, I hike my chin. "I'll meet you outside."

And with one last look at Monica, I follow in her daughter's wake. There's no sign of Zora in the parking lot, and there's the primal animal in me that snarls to go after her, make that hurt, that edge of panic in her eyes, disappear by whatever means are at my disposal. My words, my arms, my body. My cock.

But it's her decision to come to me, and I'll respect that.

Even if it kills me.

CHAPTER FOURTEEN

ZORA

There's a word for me.

Idiot.

Moron.

Dumb as a box of rocks.

Though that last one's a phrase, it still fits.

Because it takes a total lack of sense for me to be sitting outside of Cyrus's house at ten o'clock at night. I press my forehead against the steering wheel. Serves me right if someone called the neighborhood watch. How would I explain my presence?

Hi, Officer. I promise I'm only contemplating a little ill-advised hot sex, not a B&E.

That should go over swell.

A knock echoes on my window, and I jerk my head up, fully expecting to see a uniform.

But it's not.

It's Cyrus.

He crosses his arms over his powerful chest, cocking his head. The gestures snap my paralysis, and I shove the driver's door open and climb out of the car. Shutting the door behind me, I can't look away from his hooded gaze. He's a master at concealing his thoughts. And his shuttered expression doesn't aid me in deciphering what's going on in his head either. What is he thinking of finding me parked outside his house like a groupie? Especially after I haven't talked to him in a week? Especially after the shit show of earlier today?

"So you've made your mind up about coming inside?"

"Seems so." When he arches his eyebrow, I sigh. "Yes."

He doesn't say anything else but pivots and walks toward his house. I lock my car, glancing down and noticing his bare feet under the frayed hem of his jeans. I've seen him in jeans and a T-shirt before. But not bare feet. It's oddly . . . intimate. And that's saying something since I've had his fingers on my clit. Yet desire stirs low in my belly, and I'm glancing down to check if my sweater sufficiently hides my already beading nipples.

I silently heave a sigh of relief. Looking good down there.

Moments later, that relief deep dives into a jittery anxiety as I step over the threshold of Cyrus's home and he leads me past his living and dining rooms into his kitchen. The heartbeat of his home, I'm quickly learning.

He makes a beeline for the refrigerator and pulls free a bottle of wine, then detours for a cabinet, removing a wineglass. Just one. After pouring a healthy amount of the golden alcohol in it, he gently sets it in front of me.

"Take it," he softly orders. "You look like you need it."

Liquid courage. Seems like such a cop-out. But these are extraordinary circumstances. It isn't every day I pop up at a man's house to . . . to fuck, I don't know. But hell, that's it, isn't it? To fuck.

If I can just admit it to myself.

If I'm brave enough to ask him and take it for myself.

If I'm brave enough to be truthful with him.

And it's the last one that has me terrified.

Because being truthful doesn't just mean placing my career at risk. It also means walking out of here and never seeing him again.

So yes, I pick up the glass and take that wine to the head. And feel his scrutiny on me the whole time. Only when the last drop is gone do I lower the glass and meet his curious but somehow understanding gaze.

"Better?" he asks.

"No."

A faint smile ghosts over his mouth. "Should I refill it?"

I shake my head. "No." And I push the glass away from me, just in case. "First, let me apologize for showing up at your house unannounced in the middle of the night."

"Tell me why you're here. That'll determine whether or not I'll accept your apology."

I stare at him, then huff out a dry chuckle.

"Thank you," I softly say. "For today. You didn't have to . . ." *Blindly defend me. Go toe to toe with my mother. Be you.* "Well, you didn't sign up for Monica Nelson today. Thank you for being kind and respectful when she wasn't."

"Is this your role? Has it always been?"

His voice doesn't alter, but an intensity enters his ice-blue gaze, and suddenly I'm feeling like a black-and-white x-ray image. It borders on too much.

"What are you talking about?"

He gives me a look that can be described only as chiding. And it's deserved. I'm not dense; I get his meaning. But do I want to? No.

"Peacemaker. The diplomat. In families, most of us assume roles, and I'm just wondering if that's the one you chose or the one forced on you?"

Okay, so we're going there. Bending my head, I close my eyes, pinching my nose. Maybe I should've had more of that wine. But no amount of alcohol can drown out the anxiety, the guilt, and the embarrassment that crawl beneath my skin like a rash. A rash I can't scratch or cure.

A large hand cups the nape of my neck, squeezes it. And a quiet enters me like a soothing balm. It settles my mind long enough for the words that whirl in my head to pass my constricted throat. There's resistance, as if I'm disloyal by sharing anything about my past, my family. But I'm tired of bearing this load on my shoulders by myself. Of being silenced by my own anger, fear, and shame.

"I had my first ulcer at fifteen. Stress. Because kids find the damnedest ways to hoard the blame for their parents' issues and behavior—if I'd asked for lunch money the night before instead of in the morning, maybe Mom wouldn't have screamed at Dad over cornflakes and sent Levi, Miriam, and me to the bus stop with their argument ringing in our ears. If I'd just gotten an A on that earth science test instead of a B plus, then maybe when Miriam's friends showed up for her sleepover, they wouldn't have had a ringside seat to our parents' knock-down, drag-out fight. Miriam's first and last sleepover."

It doesn't require a stretch of my imagination to feel the trembling of Miriam's body or the dampness of her tears on my shirt as my sister cried in my arms after our parents humiliated her in front of her friends. And as a genius, Miriam had already felt different from other girls her age, so the sleepover had been a huge deal. And they'd ruined it for her.

"It became my responsibility to try and keep the peace as much as possible in my house. To try and alleviate the tension or avoid a blowup. That was my job. And even at thirty, I haven't resigned from it. I'm beginning to believe it's a lifelong assignment." I laugh, and it's harsh, the bitterness and self-deprecation scratching my throat. "God, I sound so pathetic and weak."

"Weak? There's nothing pathetic or weak about you, Zora." He squeezes my neck again, and it isn't to offer comfort but to gain my attention. I tip my head back, staring into his face. "I don't want to hear those words come out of your mouth again. Not pertaining to you. It takes strength to be the one not to break. The one who stands in the gap for others so they can breathe or gather their own strength before fending for themselves. It takes strength to be quiet when you want to rage. So no, Zora, you are not weak. Not pathetic. You might very well be one of the strongest people I know."

I blink. Blink again. Battling the sting of tears. I duck my head, but he doesn't allow it. Clasping my chin, he tilts it up, granting me no choice but to meet those brilliant eyes. Offering me no shield against what's in mine.

"Cyrus," I whisper. Pause. Nerves beat at me like I'm a punching bag, and I clutch the edge of the island behind me for support. This is going to hurt. Seeing his disappointment, his anger, his . . . rejection is going to rip a hole in my chest. But it must be done before we go any further. "About today. What my mother said—"

He shakes his head once. Hard. Cutting me off.

"Is this about your job? Your business?"

"Y-yes," I stammer. "I need to—"

"No," he interrupts again, voice smooth steel. "You don't need to tell me anything. And I don't want to hear it or know it."

I lift my hand to his that still pinches my chin and, twisting my head, remove it.

"Cyrus, stop. Please, listen . . ."

"I said no." He steps back from me, his mouth flattening into a grim line, eyes gleaming chips of ice. "And you listen to me. I don't want to know because this information isn't freely given. You're only telling me because of what your mother insinuated today."

"She's not the only reason," I murmur.

"I don't believe you. And since I'll never be sure you weren't pressured or shamed into it, I don't want to know. Because it comes down to this, Zora. I don't give a fuck. You could be a preschool teacher by day and a kindly madam by night, and I would still want to be buried balls deep inside you tonight and have lunch with you tomorrow." He lunges forward, reclaiming the space he placed between us. His mouth hovers a mere inch above mine, his breath a hot blast of a caress. "I. Don't. Give a. Fuck. I just want to fuck you." He cants his hips, and there's no possible way I can contain the whimper that climbs my throat like a ladder and escapes me as his cock drags over my clit. "Now tell me that's why you came here, and put us both out of our misery."

He does it again, pumps his hips, gives me a preview of what I can have tonight if I'm greedy enough.

If I'm willing to acquiesce to his demand to let my confession go and see this—this temporary fake-relationship friends-with-benefits arrangement—through to its natural conclusion.

I can make him listen. If I say stop, he will. But do I want him to stop? No. The dirty, sinful truth is I *am* greedy enough. I want him so bad—have from the first time I stared down at his picture on a phone—that I'll grasp on to the flimsiest of excuses to have him. I'll let him convince me to let it go. To take this slice of time, these three months, and hoard it for myself. And at the end, walk away as he promised. As we agreed. No strings, no harm.

I exhale, breathe out that weight, that guilt. I have no doubt it'll be waiting for me when the sun rises—I'm not in the habit of deluding myself. But for this moment? I'm diving. I'm drowning. And I'm not coming up for air.

"Yes," I admit, and lust flares in his eyes.

"Yes what?" He fists the bottom of my sweater, tugging me the small inch closer, and he utters the words against my lips. "Tell me exactly what you came here for."

"For you to fuck me."

Bending, he sweeps me up in his arms, and like that night of the concert, panic bolts through me in a footrace with excitement. I'm not a small woman, and no man has ever carried me around as if I'm this doll. But him . . . he does it so effortlessly, and dammit, I bury my face into the crook of his neck, breathing in his wood-and-earth scent.

He doesn't carry me far. Before I can become too used to being in his arms, my back and ass hit the couch, and his big body is straddling me.

And *holy fuck.*

The breath propels from my lungs on a hot blast of air.

I'm surrounded, covered, and, oh my God, mounted.

Big clever fingers thrust through my hair, pinning me to the back of the couch. Then his mouth is on mine, devouring me in a feast of senses that leaves me drunk, full, and yet ravenous for more, more, more.

His tongue duels with mine, encouraging me to engage, to take, to give as good as I'm getting. And I follow every last instruction. I pursue him, sucking, licking, demanding he surrender even as I submit.

Abandoning my mouth, he trails his cruelly beautiful lips down my cheek to my neck, nipping and sipping at my collarbone. I arch into the sensual caresses, loving his mouth, teeth, and tongue on me. Loving the pleasure that contains the barest hint of pain. And when he slides to the floor, his fists balling into the hem of my sweater and tearing it over my head, I eagerly raise my arms.

For the first time, I'm half-naked in front of this man. This man who is as close to physical male perfection as I've ever seen. And for the glimmer of an instant, it occurs to me that I should be modest or a little concerned about my lack of perfection by society's standards.

But then Cyrus sits back on his heels and stares at me. And that isn't disgust glittering in his eyes. It's not disappointment slashing red across his killer cheekbones. It isn't resignation making his lips appear even fuller. It isn't repulsion lifting his chest up and down on harsh inhales of breath.

No, all of that is due to lust. Pure lust.

And it's for me.

Me with my size 16 frame, big breasts, three-pack stomach, and round hips.

A glow that momentarily capsizes desire builds and builds inside me, radiating so bright I'm surprised the room isn't illuminated with it.

I accepted and learned to love myself a long time ago. But finally being intimate with someone who not only accepts my body but desires it heals something inside me that until this moment, I hadn't realized had remained so broken. Was it sore to the touch? Yes. But no longer broken.

Leaning forward, I clasp his face in my hands and bring his lips to mine. This kiss is slow, not as ferocious and wild as the previous ones. It's a thank-you, and though there's no way he can understand the meaning behind it, he accepts it. Sinks his hand into the curls at the back of my head and lets me give to him.

But the gentleness can't last against the gnawing passion that's never quiet for long between us. Not when the air in the room brushes across the tops of my breasts and teases my nipples. Urgency to touch him, to be touched by him, rides me, and I lower my hands to his T-shirt and mimic his actions, grabbing it and yanking it up and off.

He doesn't offer me a chance to admire—because, God, that could take *hours*—instead, he gently pushes me back against the couch cushions, and with a reverence that parts my lips on a soft, surprised gasp, he cups my breasts, lifting one to his mouth. Even through the silk of my bra, he sucks on my nipple, flicking it, teasing, worshipping. But apparently, that must not be enough, because he reaches behind me and, with expert hands, releases the clasp. My bra loosens, and he drags it off, baring me to his gaze and hands.

"Beautiful. So fucking beautiful." He rubs his lip back and forth over the neglected tip while his thumbs circle the damp one. "How are you this goddamn gorgeous?"

I'm guessing he doesn't expect me to answer since he draws on my flesh again, rendering me incapable of speech. My cry bounces off the walls of the room, and I clutch him to me, holding him close. Back arching, hips gyrating, trying to ride that perfect ladder of muscles he calls an abdomen, I'm a wild thing under him. There's a direct sizzling current of electricity that travels from my breasts to my sex, and it's crackling with lust and energy, lighting me up with dizzying speed. I've always figured orgasming from breast stimulation was a myth. But Cyrus is about to become a myth buster.

He releases my breasts with a soft pop and trails his lips down my belly, lingering to tease the shallow dip of my navel with his tongue. But soon, he's unbuckling my jeans, his movements hurried and, *damn*, his hands slightly trembling. Biting my lip, I smooth my palms over his short hair, silently letting him know I'm all in. I want this. With him. Even if this has never been my favorite sexual activity. Before this has always seemed like a chore with the other men I've been with, so I could never relax enough to enjoy it or just opted to skip altogether.

But with Cyrus . . . with Cyrus, I trust him.

The cool air hits my bared hips and thighs. Cyrus shifts back between my legs and, palming my knees, spreads my legs, and that same air grazes my hot, dripping sex. Because, good Lord, it is dripping. Moisture gleams on my inner thighs; that's how aroused he's made me. The modesty that was missing earlier after my shirt came off decides to make an appearance, and I tense my thighs, but Cyrus shakes his head, leaning over me. His tongue peeks out, and he takes a long luxurious lick up one thigh, gathering the wet there. When he lifts his head, my breath catches. His lashes flutter, and his lips curve on a smile of such complete satiation that hunger clenches my belly in sympathetic pangs.

"Don't hide from me," he rumbles, and it vibrates over my swollen flesh, sending quivers through me. "That's what I want. What I need from you."

Splaying his fingers wide on my legs, he holds me open to his gaze and then to his mouth. A cry rips from my throat, and yeah, tomorrow I'll be feeling that one. But tonight, with his mouth sucking and circling my clit, I don't give a damn. It's decadent. It's indulgent. It's messy. It's raw.

It's perfection.

One hand gripping the edge of the couch cushion, and the other clutching his head for dear life, I whimper as he opens me further using his thumbs, exposing all of me. Feasting on every part of me. He nibbles and sucks on my folds, flattens his tongue, and licks a wide path between them to torture my clit, only to start all over again.

A fire builds inside of me, stoked by his dedication to my pleasure, to my demise. I can't remain still under his erotic ministrations, and the wilder I become, the more gleeful he seems. The more determined he seems to send me careening over the edge, as if my total lack of inhibitions is his endgame.

"Cyrus, please," I whine. Because that's what I've been rendered to. Whining. Begging. Pleading. "I need . . ."

Everything.

Nuzzling my mound, he licks the tight bundle of nerves cresting my sex, then presses two of those elegant artist fingers to my entrance, sliding deep, so deep, filling me. And with only a crook and rub of his fingertips, I'm flying.

No wings. Who needs wings when Cyrus can make me free-fall like this?

When I finally fall back to earth, he's there, like I knew he would be. Still, I trail my hands down his hard, wide chest, luxuriating in the tight, golden skin. The light dusting of dark hair across his pecs and the silky line that bisects his abdomen and disappears into the waistband of his jeans.

Jeans that need to come off.

Maybe he hears me. Or the more reasonable option is he wants to get inside me as much as I want him there. Still, he strips off his jeans, removes his wallet and a condom, quickly sheathes himself. Moving back between my legs, he cups my hips, sliding his hands under my ass and lifting me to him.

"Zora," he murmurs. "Look at me."

I drag my eyes from where his cock is notched at the entrance to my sex. My chest rises and falls, rises and falls. When I meet Cyrus's gaze, he nods.

"Eyes on me, baby. Be with me. Breathe with me."

I inhale, exhale. Following his lead. Leaning forward, I press my lips to his.

"Come inside me," I invite him.

He doesn't wait. Doesn't hesitate. He thrusts forward, burying his cock, stretching me, filling me, branding me. I whimper against his mouth, and it's part plea, part demand. And they're the same word: more.

His arms wrap around me, holding me tight, even as his hips buck and grind, driving into me. Winding my legs around his waist, I open up to him, allow him to claim all of me, pound deeper, giving me all of his long thick length. As if in thanks, he strokes a hand up my back, tangles it in my hair, and tugs my head back, capturing my mouth. His tongue strokes inside, mimicking his cock, taking, claiming, leaving me thoroughly fucked.

Lifting his other hand to the back of the couch, he steadies himself and rides me hard, offering me no mercy. Pleasure sizzles and snaps through my body. My sex quivers as every one of Cyrus's thrusts rubs the base of his cock against my clit, setting off minifireworks. I'm shaking—my thighs, my belly, my arms.

"Let me have it, baby," he growls, reaching between us and strumming his fingers over my clit. "Give it to me."

One more caress. Then another. And I'm exploding. Scattering in pieces. Even as my cries bounce around my head and ricochet off the walls of the room, his cock jerks within me, setting off another, smaller but just as intimate orgasm. I clutch him close, trusting him to be my safe place to fall.

Even if only for a little while.

CHAPTER FIFTEEN

CYRUS

I watch from the predawn shadows of the kitchen, coffee in hand, as Zora creeps down the staircase and soundlessly makes a beeline for the clothes scattered on the living room floor. She shimmies into her jeans, and despite coming three times with her, my dick stirs at the unselfconscious sensual dance. I sip my coffee, leaning my hip against the counter, and continue to take in the show.

She rummages among the couch cushions and finally locates her bra and then her sweater. As she's about to pull on her boots, I move from the kitchen to the living room entrance.

"Were you going to say goodbye?"

"Holy *shit*." A boot flies from her hands and hits the chair leg across from her. Spinning around, she glares at me, splaying a hand across her chest. "Could you maybe *not* scare the living daylights out of me?"

"Sure." I sip my coffee. "The next time you're not sneaking out of my house at the crack of dawn, I promise not to."

"I'm not *sneaking*," she hisses, appearing offended.

I arch an eyebrow.

"I was being considerate and trying to clear out before you started your day."

"Did I ask for that . . . consideration?"

We stare at each other, her with narrowed eyes and me over the rim of my cup.

"Fine." She throws up her hands, then plops them on her hips. "You got me. I was trying to avoid the awkward morning after."

"Well, you definitely accomplished that," I drawl.

"You're enjoying this, aren't you?"

I shrug a shoulder. "A little."

Sighing, she digs in her jeans pocket and, a moment later, ties her hair in a messy bun on top of her head.

"Can you at least offer me coffee?"

"I can do that," I rumble, battling the lust rapidly firing inside me at that simple, easy gesture.

Maybe because I want my hands in those thick strands, tugging, tangling. You'd think I would've had my fill last night. But apparently not. When it comes to this woman, I'm insatiable. That, I should've known. Pivoting on my heel, I pad on bare feet back to the kitchen. In moments, I hand her a coffee mug and remove the creamer and sugar for her to doctor her brew how she needs it.

"Do you regret last night? Is that what"—I hike my chin in the direction of the living room—"your escape attempt was about?"

Head lowered, she stirs her coffee, the clang of the spoon against her cup the only sound in the room. I wait for her response, outwardly calm, but inside I'm tense, anxious. The last thing anyone desires to hear is they're a mistake.

"No," she murmurs, setting the spoon aside on the saucer the cup sits on. "I don't regret that or you. I just . . ." She lifts her head, shadows shifting in her brown gaze. "Where do we go from here? Sex complicates . . . everything. It always does."

"Not if we agree that it won't."

She smiles, and it strikes me as wistful. "Just because you will it not to be doesn't mean it won't be." A sigh escapes her. "I'm not going to lie, Cyrus. I'm worried. I'm terrified I'm going to be your biggest regret when all of this is over."

"Come here."

Her gaze sharpens, and just like that, I'm hard. Shit. It's her effect on me. I should be alarmed by it. And if she wasn't circling the island, those rounded hips gently swaying, maybe I would be. Later. Right now, though, I can concentrate only on getting my hands on her. Again.

Once she nears me, I grasp her hips and bring her into the cradle of my body so we're perfectly aligned. Cupping her cheek, I rub my thumb over her cheekbone and watch myself caress her. Because I can, when just days ago, I wasn't permitted to do this.

"Will boundaries make you feel better?" I murmur.

"Yes," she whispers. "It will."

"Okay. If you want me, I'm yours. Feel free to use me for your pleasure; I'm here for it, for you. And the same for me. Because I intend to be inside you as often as possible, Zora. I've fantasized about you for so long that I don't know if three months will be enough, but it's going to have to be. Because at the end of our arrangement, we walk away. No strings, like we agreed. No entanglements, no expectations. And if at any time you want to end this, we do. And we go back to how we were."

"Same for you too. If you want to end it."

I smile at the thought. "Baby, that's not going to happen."

A shiver courses over her, and it reverberates through me.

"This is crazy." She balls her fingers into the loops of my jeans, pressing her forehead to my bare chest. Rolling her forehead back and forth, she repeats, "This is so crazy. *I'm* crazy."

"Sex with me? I'm not sure if I should be offended or not."

Her huff of warm breath to my skin isn't a laugh or a sigh; it's somewhere in between.

"Cyrus, I'm not . . . this isn't . . ." She tips her head back, and the faint smile that curves her mouth isn't humorous. "You just got out of a relationship. And yes, this is just physical, but I don't know if I'm cut out to be the rebound girl. I don't—"

"Say it, Zora."

Her throat works for several seconds, as if she's battling the words, but eventually she blurts them out. "At the restaurant, I asked you about the Dear John letter, and you said it didn't tear your heart out. But I remember the devastation on your face when I read it. Your face revealed how you felt—"

I step back from her, inserting space but cradling her neck, my thumbs on either side of her jaw.

"Look at me." I need her to get this, and I harden my voice. Zora obeys, and I pause a moment, ensuring she's meeting my gaze and really seeing me. *Hearing* me. "What you saw on my face wasn't about Val. Not specifically. Since my parents died and I left my aunts' homes for college, I've planned out my future. High school. College. Law school. The law firm I would join. And eventually when I would date and marry. I've stuck to those plans; they've guided me through rough and lean years, gave goals to work toward. That's what you saw on my face, Zora. The devastation of deviating from my plans. The fear of failing, of insecurity and the unknown. The fear of failing and disappointing my parents. Not about losing Val."

Her gaze roams my face, searching, and I hold still, letting her see the truth. After several long moments, that gaze softens into warm, melted chocolate.

"That's why the partnership and the retreat is so important to you, isn't it?" she murmurs. "It's in your plan."

"Yes."

She nods.

Then her arms wrap around me, holding me close, and I shut my eyes, inhaling her scent, feeling her body. Savoring every curve, every dip. The lust is there—it's never far. Yet here, in this moment, there's something softer tempering it. For how long before the desire overtakes it? I don't know.

But I stand here, holding her.

Wondering when that started to feel so natural.

And a little terrified that it is.

CHAPTER SIXTEEN

ZORA

So this is how the other half lives.

Private jet. Travel by high-end SUVs fully stocked with alcohol and food. Full-service, luxury resort in western Colorado, four hours outside of Denver.

Stepping into the main lobby with its cathedral ceilings, gleaming stone floors, floor-to-ceiling windows that invite the gorgeous Red Rock Canyon beyond inside, and elegant yet rustic decor, I try to prevent my jaw from dropping and embarrassing Cyrus. It's tough, though. Because this place's beauty is like nature on steroids.

What have I gotten myself into?

You don't belong here. You don't belong here.

That insidious voice whispers through my mind, and I mentally shake my head, attempting to rid myself of the self-destructive thought. But it refuses to release its talons from my psyche. Maybe if I weren't standing with a group of people who all could've stepped straight from a *Real Housewives of PickaCity*, it wouldn't be as difficult. But everything from their clothes to their jewelry to the self-entitled demeanor screams wealth and privilege. I don't belong among these people.

And I don't know if I want to.

But Cyrus does.

He's a chameleon.

No, no, because that makes him sound like a hypocrite or a poser, when he's absolutely not. The man who can sit on my couch eating takeout and watching Netflix or singing to "Baby, What a Big Surprise" at a Chicago concert is also the same man fully capable of adapting to this group. He's in his element with them. He shines with them.

Unease squirms in my stomach.

"You okay?" Cyrus murmurs in my ear, squeezing my hand.

That quick, with just the whisper of his warm breath against my skin and his touch, my disquiet dissolves, and I tip my head back, smile at him.

And I'm reminded why I said yes to accompanying him here to this retreat. Not just out of my guilt. But because from the beginning of our unique . . . relationship, he's not only cared about my feelings; he's sought to protect them. He's been a defender of them. Somewhere along the line, we really did establish a friendship.

No real relationship can be built on a lie.

I fidget under that soft reminder that ghosts through my head like a dark harbinger. Shoving it aside, I mouth to Cyrus, "I'm fine."

He studies me for a long moment but then dips his head and returns his attention to our resort host. Or at least most of his attention. He lifts my hand to his mouth and brushes a kiss across the back of it. Now, I'm sure the PDA is for the benefit of his colleagues, but the shiver passing through me is all too real. So is the catch in my lungs and heart.

"The Red Plateau Resort wants to thank you again for choosing us for your retreat. We offer several amenities to ensure your experience with us is the most enjoyable possible. Just to name a few, we have four restaurants and cafés, stables, a spa, two outdoor pools and hot tubs, HD theater with stadium seating, as well as state-of-the-art conference meeting rooms. There will be booklets in your rooms containing complete details regarding all of our services and opportunities."

The young brunette dressed in a sandstone-colored linen shirt and pants turns and beckons several staff members forward.

"I'm sure everyone would like to freshen up after traveling. We'll show you to your rooms."

By *rooms*, I discover ten minutes later, she means our own little house that could've been carved directly from the surrounding red rock. With cathedral ceilings, huge windows, a living room, a fireplace, a private deck that includes a firepit, a fully stocked kitchen with top-of-the-line appliances, and a bedroom with breath-stealing views, how do the owners get anyone to leave?

Strolling through yet another living area with an inlaid gas fireplace, I surreptitiously pinch myself. How has this become my life? Even for a weekend? I wonder if Cyrus would be cool with me opting to stay right here for the rest of the retreat.

"It's a lot, isn't it?"

His arms wrap around me from behind, his lips grazing my ear.

I nod. Pause. "Is this the life you want? The one you planned for?"

He's quiet; then he palms my shoulders and turns me around. His blue eyes search my face.

"What's your real question?"

I swallow a sigh. We've known each other only a handful of weeks. How does he know me better than people I've known for thirty years?

"Zora?" He pinches my chin, tilting my head up.

"There's nothing wrong with this world. The private jet. This place. People waiting on you hand and foot. It's the mindset that can come along with it. The one that convinces you the world revolves around you and your needs and others are only here to serve those needs. That you are entitled to this. I'm afraid that if your plan includes pursuing only this"—I wave a hand, encompassing the gorgeous room—"then you'll lose who you are. Who your parents meant for you to be."

Tension invades his body, but he doesn't release my chin. Which is good, considering I knew even as I spoke the words that I might be treading too far. He'd shared some of his past with me, but it could be a little presumptuous of me to assume I'd know what his parents would want for him. But because I know him and I've heard the love with which he speaks about them and the life he's built for them, I can say it.

"What do you think you know about who my parents meant for me to be?"

The words are harsher than his tone, and I focus on that.

"I know they wanted you to be who they were. Your parents were your example of how you should walk in this world. The values and memories they instilled in you? That speaks volumes about the boy they were raising and the kind of man they wanted him to grow up to be. Kind. Generous. Empathetic. Hardworking yet fun loving. Protective of those who are weaker. Loyal. Good. Lover of Chicago, baked goods, and great wine."

The corners of his mouth quirk. "Two out of those last three aren't bad. But Dad appreciated a good beer, too, so I think he'd forgive me."

I smile and brush the back of my fingers down his cheek. "You're *all* of those things. And I just don't want you to lose them. Lose you."

He threads his fingers through my hair, drawing my head back. If I didn't know any better, I'd think he had some kind of obsession with it. Images of what he did with the curls just last night flash through my mind. Heat rushes up my chest and pours into my face. If not an obsession, maybe a fetish.

"What are you thinking about?" A smirk rides his mouth, and he raises an eyebrow. "Care to share with the class?"

"This isn't show-and-tell, so the class can mind their business," I mutter.

He chuckles, and the low sound strokes over my skin underneath my jacket.

Tipping my head back even farther, he presses a soft peck to my cheek. "So you think I'm kind." Kiss to the other cheek. "Generous." Kiss to my nose. "Empathetic." Chin. "Hardworking and fun loving."

Forehead. "Protective of the weak." Temple. "Loyal and good." Back to my mouth. "Sounds like you like me, Zora Nelson."

"Who knew you had an eidetic memory?" I grumble. "And you aight."

I bring my hands up between us and lightly push him away, needing space that isn't filled with his cedar-and-leather scent. Needing space that isn't filled with *him*. His body, his power, his intensity . . . he can be overwhelming. Especially when my defenses are particularly dented, pockmarked, and weakened.

Another one of those delectable, wicked laughs caresses my ears and other senses, and I'm seconds away from clapping a hand over his mouth and issuing a restraining order on that sound. It's dangerous to my nipples, vagina, and . . . well, it's dangerous.

"So what's on the agenda?" I move to the refrigerator and pull it open. Wow. So many options. Wine. Beer. Juice. Even homemade smoothie in a pitcher. Shaking my head, I grab a bottle of water. "Do the partners have certain team-building activities planned?"

He snorts, following me to the kitchen area and leaning on the breakfast bar. "It's not that kind of retreat. It's more of a 'We brought you here to judge you and see how you negotiate in the shark-infested waters of your direct competition' getaway."

"Ohh. Fun," I drawl.

"In the meantime . . ." He rounds the breakfast bar, approaches me, and backs me against the counter. After pushing aside the coffee maker, he hoists me up. "She did say we should relax after traveling."

"Actually, she said *freshen up*."

He shrugs, slipping his hands under the shoulders of my jacket and sliding it off. Dragging his lips up my neck and over my jaw, he whispers in my ear, "I could've sworn I heard another f-word."

I throw my head back, laughing, but that soon turns into a lot of groaning as he shows me exactly which f-word.

🕯

"You must be Zora."

I turn around from the exquisite view of the unspoiled natural beauty of the western Colorado plateau, glass of Moscato in hand. Irritation dances within my chest, and I try to cover it with my customary polite smile. Still, I escaped to the shadow-draped stone balcony after dinner for a little privacy. I'm used to working with all manner of people and being "on," but it can be exhausting. And I've spent all day and evening engaged in small talk and smiling. I'm just . . . tired.

Yet I'm here for Cyrus. And as I turn around and greet the gorgeous redhead who, if I recall correctly, is married to a handsome, gregarious, and complete douche of a guy named Derrick, I keep Cyrus uppermost in mind. It wouldn't do to offend any of his coworkers or their wives.

"Guilty."

"I know you've probably had a ton of names thrown at you today. I'm Jill. My husband's Derrick." Jill smiles, and the warmth in it reaches her hazel eyes.

She extends her hand, and I shake it.

"It's a pleasure to meet you."

"You too, Zora. I love your name. And your earrings. Ranjana Khan, right?" She refers to my dangling freshwater-pearl earrings. Before I have a chance to confirm or deny—and I would confirm—she half turns, waving toward the dining room behind her. "I have to admit, we—most of the other wives—are curious about you. They're just too uppity to ask. As if they're above a little gossip." She snickers, her eyes gleaming with humor. "Fortunately, I am not."

Okay, I'm kind of liking her. Her douche husband notwithstanding. I'm a little surprised she's so chatty considering Derrick didn't let her do a lot of talking. At dinner, he tended to speak over her often, even when someone asked her a direct question. Like I said, a douche.

I laugh because she's not only gorgeous and married to an ass—and I feel sorry for her—but she seems nice. Still, I'm not an idiot. Proceed with caution.

"We're all dying to know. How did you and Cyrus meet? I don't mind telling you several of us tried our hand at matchmaking for a long time before he started dating Val. Now, she's gone, and he's immediately started dating you. Which, can I say—as I've spent exactly one hour in your company—is a vast improvement? So we want all the details of how you two came to be a couple."

Cyrus had prepared me for this question, and we'd come up with a story, but it doesn't ease my nerves telling it. Adding yet another lie.

I'm sitting on a mountain of them by now. And I have the tiara to go along with it.

"At a restaurant. I was in the middle of a horrible date, and he intervened, saving me. We ended up having dinner, and the rest, as they say, is history."

Stick as close as possible to the truth; that way we have fewer details to remember.

"Chivalry is not dead." She sighs. "I can so imagine Cyrus doing something like that. He's such a nice, honorable guy." Jill glances behind her, then edges closer. "Can I be honest? I don't know if you've met his ex or if he's told you much about her, but he deserved better. I have no clue if you two will go the distance, but today and tonight, he's smiled more, talked more, relaxed more than I've seen him since he joined the firm. And I can only attribute that to you. Cheers to you, Zora."

She holds up her own glass of wine and taps it to mine, a warm smile curving her lips. Shock whistles through me, and so does something much more fragile and treacherous. I refuse to even name that fledgling and utterly foolish emotion.

"Thank you, Jill. Cyrus does deserve the best. He's a good man." I pause, not sure if I should say anything else, but after a moment, I continue. The truth is in another two months, I won't be here, but she will be. "I'm glad he has you and the other wives looking out for him."

Jill beams, and she reaches out, clasps my hand, and squeezes.

"Always. He can't get rid of us. Even though sometimes I think he wishes he could."

Wow. Does Cyrus realize how many people care about him? For some reason, I got the sense he was a bit of a loner, but these women look out for him, are concerned for him. He's not alone.

A fist of emotion grips my throat, and I have the inane urge to go hunt Cyrus down, throw my arms around him, and bury my face against his chest. Then beg him to take me back to our minihouse and make love to me.

I mean fuck me. Take me back to our minihouse and fuck me.

Damn. That's one hell of a Freudian slip.

Good Lord, where is my head today?

"Jill, are you out here pumping Zora for information?"

Jill spins around as Cyrus steps out onto the balcony, a half smile curling his mouth.

"Of course I am," she unashamedly boasts, gliding up to him and hooking her arm through his. Rising up on the toes of her stilettoes, she smacks a kiss to his cheek. "And she so graciously let me." Crinkling a couple of fingers at me, she says, "It was wonderful talking to you, Zora."

Cyrus looks at me, lifting his beer after Jill blows him a teasing kiss and then walks away, probably to deliver the gossip about me and Cyrus's serendipitous meeting. The sight of that beer has satisfaction stirring in my belly. No fancy Glenlivet or fifty-year Scotch for him just because he's around the law firm partners. It's an IPA for him.

"Did someone have a mild heart attack when you asked for that beer?"

He snorts. "They had to do a little treasure hunt, but they came up with it." He cocks his head, studying me. "You okay?"

I don't need to ask him what he's referring to, and I nod. "Fine. Jill's nice. What's she doing with a guy like her husband?"

He laughs, but it's hard, abrupt. "Damn if I know. They're complete opposites in every way that counts. Though both she and Derrick are from old money, she is a sweet, considerate, generous woman." He moves past me and props his forearms on the balcony. "Derrick joined the firm a year before I did, and from the first he pinpointed me as his rival. Yes, he competes against the other associates—we all do—but with me, it's almost personal. It's definitely vicious. And on several occasions, underhanded."

"But . . . why?" I settle next to him, leaning my hip to the wall. "Other than being an adult bully. And from what I've seen tonight, he's the same way with his wife. And having to be the main attraction in the room."

"I'm not sure. I tried to get along with him like I did everyone. And at first, I thought we were fine, thought he was a good, professional attorney like most of the associates I work with. But then he poached one of my clients. Smiled in my face and then turned around and lied to it. One thing I can't abide is a liar and a thief. And to me, they're one and the same."

Dozens of spider legs creep up and down my spine, contributing to the ill swish of bile in my belly. I glance away from him, from that perfect profile, and train my unfocused gaze on the dining room, where people still congregate in small groups, chatting and laughing.

Part of me wants to make an excuse, any excuse, to run at the mention of the word *liar*. It's like a scarlet *L* on my chest. But the other half . . . that half keeps me glued to the spot, determined to listen, to pay silent penance for a sin he has no idea I'm committing just to be close to him one more day, one more hour, under the guise of this "relationship."

Because somewhere along the line, this arrangement became an excuse. For both of us.

But what do we have? I don't know if I can categorize it under something as convoluted as a fake relationship or as simple and uncomplicated as friendship. My friends don't set off undercurrents of desire so hot, so needy, that it's an alive, breathing thing that consumes. I don't go to sleep at night, arms and body empty of my friend but mind full of him, only to wake up in the morning the same way.

My friends don't inspire me to wish for foolish things.

And foolish is allowing myself to fall for a man I'm lying to and have been from the day we met.

"I'm sorry, Cyrus."

He glances down at me. "Are you now apologizing for Derrick, Zora?" he teases, leaning down and brushing a kiss across my forehead.

Closing my eyes, I savor the softness of the caress. *For show. For his colleagues,* I remind myself. Even though I don't think any of them are paying attention to us. Still, I need that reminder. It keeps me from going down that rabbit hole of . . . hope.

"I'd never do something as silly as apologize for him. Especially since he wouldn't—and most likely still doesn't—see anything wrong with what he did. I'm sorry you were harmed by his actions."

He shakes his head, sighing. "People like him, they rarely see how their behavior affects other people. They don't see lies as harmful because they don't leave bruises or cuts. But the damage is worse because they're longer lasting. I think about my aunts who lied to the social workers about providing a safe, secure home for me just to get a check. Or my cousins who lied to my aunts about me stealing from them so I could be punished. Or my parents who lied to me when they promised they'd never leave me."

His voice trails off, and he shifts his gaze back to the shadowed red rock plateau. A muscle tics along his clenched jaw, and I sense he didn't mean to let that last sentence slip.

"They don't see lies as harmful because they don't leave bruises or cuts. But the damage is worse because they're longer lasting."

Hot, acidic guilt and shame eat away at me.

He's right.

No wrong can be justified away. And I'm wronging him by keeping the truth away from him. He deserves better than that.

He deserves better than that from *me*.

Heart pounding against my rib cage like a hammer against an anvil, I turn to him.

"Cyrus—"

"Excuse me. Cyrus."

I jerk around, and Cyrus pivots, pushing away from the balcony to face Jill, who stands just inside the entrance to the dining room. No longer effervescent and smiling, she's pale, her mouth pressed into a thin line. Somber. That's the word that pops into my head.

Dread curdles like sour milk in my belly, and instinctively I seek Cyrus's hand.

"What's wrong, Jill?" he asks, enclosing my fingers in his and moving toward her.

"I—" She shakes her head, crimson suffusing her face. "This is not—I'm so sorry," she finally whispers, obviously flustered.

Confused, I move forward, her obvious distress upsetting me.

Then I draw up short, as if a wall of ice has sprung up before me. And that cold seeps through me, freezing my breath, the blood in my veins.

Valerie Summers.

Valerie Summers stands behind Jill.

"The fuck?" Cyrus growls.

"Cyrus." Val steps forward, stunning in a blue wrap dress that clings to her beautiful figure. "You are a very difficult man to get in touch with. Luckily, Derrick informed me about the retreat, and I thought this would be the perfect opportunity for us to talk."

"You? You're responsible for this?"

Cyrus swings his attention to Derrick, and for the first time, I notice Jill's husband, who's been standing behind Val all this time. Rage hums in Cyrus's voice, and it's the murderous heat from it that melts my paralysis. One glance at Cyrus's flat blue gaze and the grim set of his mouth, and I slide my hand from his and grasp his elbow, restraining him. Not that I can do much if he goes for this asshole's throat.

Derrick shrugs a shoulder, his grin smug and wide. So he's an idiot as well as an asshole not to sense the threat right in front of him.

"You can thank me later."

Maybe my movement snagged Val's attention, because it shifts to me, and her eyes widen, instant recognition flaring; then they narrow.

"You're kidding me. You *must* be kidding me." She advances on me, but Cyrus shifts, blocking her from me. She looks from me to him and laughs, the sound high and sharp as glass. "Isn't this just perfect? I just handed you over to him, didn't I? How long did it take you to slide in and jump on my leftovers? Although, Cyrus." She tsks. "I'm really surprised. I didn't expect you to be so broken over me you'd rebound to slumming it."

"Stop. Talking," he snaps, his body so rigid the barest of winds could crack him down the middle. "Don't speak to her; don't even look at her if you aren't able to do it with a civil tongue in your mouth. I'm not going to stand here and let you disrespect her. For damn sure not in front of me. She did you a favor with that little breakup errand, and she's done, out. Any loyalty she owes you after that is over. As far as slumming it? What do you call this? Showing up here where you're not wanted? It reeks of desperation, Val."

"Loyalty she owes me? You're damn right she owes me loyalty. I paid a fee and have a contract that clearly lays out that loyalty."

"What the hell are you talking about now?" he demands.

"Cyrus," I whisper, although by now that sinking in my stomach is yawning wide into a dark abyss that I can't crawl my way free of—an abyss of my own creation.

Shock crosses Val's face, chased by utter delight.

"Oh my God." She laughs. "Oh my God, this is too good. He doesn't know, does he?" She smiles at me, and it's so cold another shiver ripples over me. "Cyrus, I paid Zora Nelson to break up with you for me. That's what she does. She breaks up with people for a living. And you were just a number. A case. And you call me desperate?" She arches an eyebrow at me. "Tell me, Ms. Nelson, how desperate does it make a person to scavenge their clients' leftovers? Is this a common practice for you? Or is Cyrus just special?"

Derrick chuckles. "Wait a minute, wait a minute." He holds out his hands, a grin splitting his face, and it's ugly, mean. "You mean to tell me Val broke up with you by proxy? And you turned around and brought that woman here to fob her off as your girlfriend?" He laughs again, loud. "Just wait until Donald and everyone else hears about this. I knew something was up with you two, but I couldn't place it."

"What's wrong is he brought an imposter who doesn't belong here," Val murmurs, her glacial gaze on me.

"Cyrus," I try again, laying my hand on his arm. "Please, if you'll let me explain." Although I have no idea what I can say.

What Val said . . . it was ugly and spiteful, but it was all true. I violated Val's trust. I did lie to him about my identity. I had an opportunity—plenty of them—to confess the truth, and I didn't. And even though I justified why with reasons, when it comes down to it, those reasons weren't enough.

Not when he's staring at me with betrayal and anger in his eyes.

"Is it true?" he softly asks.

"Can we—"

"Is it true?" he interrupts.

Please let me explain. Please let me tell you why you were worth the risk. Just . . . please.

"Yes," I whisper.

"You should go back to our bungalow. You can stay there tonight, and I'll arrange for a flight out for you tomorrow."

Pain blasts through me, and I don't understand how I'm standing. How I'm breathing. None of the panic from the conflict assaults me because I don't care. Not when I'm losing Cyrus from my life. I can feel him physically slipping away from me, and I want to scream, fall to my knees, beg him to listen, to not do this, to . . . not hurt me like this.

But one look in those cold, shuttered eyes, and there's no point. I've lost him.

Every worry, every fear, every nightmare is colliding like a catastrophic pileup. And there's nothing I can do to stop it.

And I've no one to blame but myself.

"Goodbye, Cyrus."

I step away from him; it's agony for me. Forcing my feet forward, I walk away from him, past Jill, who gives me a sympathetic look; her smirking asshole husband; and finally Val.

My former client reaches out and grasps my elbow, halting me.

Bending down, she whispers, "Next time, you'll learn to stay in your place. And don't think I'm not going to share exactly how you use your clients' information. I'm going to ruin you and your little business."

Anger surges out of the depths of my pain, swirling and hot. Yes, I betrayed her trust. But I am not less of a person or beneath her. And I'm through allowing her to treat or speak to me that way simply because of the zip code where she lays her head every night.

"My place is wherever I decide it to be. And you, or anyone else, don't get a say in that. And you can come for me all you want; I deserve it because, woman to woman, I owe you an apology, and I'm sorry. But, Ms. Valerie Summers, the day you decide to come for my business, which belongs to my family, all bets are off. And I'll come right back for you."

Her lips curl in a sneer. "Didn't take long for that Five Points to come out of you, did it?"

"Hold on, Zora," Cyrus says from just behind me.

I stiffen.

"Val, you can go too. You don't have any business here."

She straightens, blue eyes glittering. "I was invited here."

"You allowed yourself to be used by an insecure, manipulative, malicious bitch. That's not my fault. And I would feel sorry for you if you didn't have your own agenda for being here. You cheated on me with another man behind my back, and when that fell through, you thought I was stupid enough to take you back. Sorry to break it to you. I'm not. I don't want you. That's why I haven't been answering your phone calls and texts. If you are too self-absorbed to get that, then traveling all the way here is your fault, not mine."

She gasps, whipping around on me again. "You told him. That was told to you in strict confidence."

Cyrus laughs, and Val turns back to him at the dark sound. "Oh no, Val. She didn't tell me anything. You did. But I guarantee you this. You go after Zora's business, I'll make sure everyone knows. And then after you were dumped, how you chased me up here? Do you think your pristine reputation can suffer that hit? Me? I really don't give a fuck. But you? With your committees and foundations . . ."

"You wouldn't," Val snarls. "Over *her*."

"Do you want to test me? Go home," he repeats. Then his gaze flicks to me. "Both of you."

Val sputters in outrage, but I don't wait to hear her tirade.

I go as he requested while I can under my own power.

While I can with my head held high.

While I can before I collapse and give in to the pain threatening to tear me apart.

CHAPTER SEVENTEEN

ZORA

The door to my office flies open, and it bangs against the wall, making me jump in my desk chair.

Shit.

Miriam poses in the doorway like a Black Charlie's Angel, a grocery bag dangling above her head and a hand clasping the edge of the doorframe.

Despite the emptiness that has dogged me for a week, I snicker. The woman coined the term *extra*.

"Oh for . . ." Levi lifts her arm and steps over her stretched-out leg, entering the office and tugging on the hem of his vest.

It's after seven thirty in the evening, and my brother is still impeccably dressed in a three-piece blue-and-gray pinstripe suit, as if it's seven thirty in the morning. I don't know how he does it. It's a little unsettling, and if we hadn't shared a womb, I'd check his back for a battery panel.

"You have no flair for the dramatic, Leviticus. Your soul is going to shrivel and perish without watering it with the arts."

"I'll survive," he drawls. "And you took one semester of theater in high school where you played Dancer Number fucking Three on *The Corny Collins Show* in *Hairspray*. That does not make you a thespian."

Miriam jabs a finger at the back of his head as he sprawls into the chair in front of my desk. I think he rendered her speechless. Levi has that effect on people. That and stirring homicidal urges.

"You're the first person going when they enact the purge, guy," she mutters, stalking to my desk and plopping her grocery bag on the top. "Here. I made a promise, and I'm here to fulfill it."

With that announcement she takes the chair next to Levi.

"Should I even ask what you two are doing here?" I ask, reaching for the bag.

It's late, and everyone is gone no later than six. Me included. But I can't stand being at the house that used to be my haven. Now, it's become the opposite. I can't even enter without seeing Cyrus and myself against the wall next to my front door. Or remembering us on my couch. I even swear I can catch his scent on my sheets from one of the nights we spent together in my bed, and I've washed those sheets at least three times.

Work keeps my days busy, occupies my mind. And this office has become my sanctuary in the evenings until I tire myself out to the point that I can't think about Cyrus.

It hasn't worked so far, but I'm no quitter.

"What's this?" I pull out a container of strawberry-cheesecake ice cream, a family-size bag of sour-cream-and-onion chips, and three plastic spoons.

"You don't remember?" Miriam holds out her hands. "I told you when the shit hit the fan I would bring all that and binge with you. 'Cause that's what sisters do."

"Then what am I doing here?" Levi asks.

"Learning empathy. I thought tinmen wanted hearts."

"Filthy rumor."

I chuckle and, shit, hate the sting of tears springing to my eyes. Pushing the carton and bag toward them, I shake my head.

"Thanks, but I'm good."

"What the *fuck*?" Levi slowly leans forward, his voice dropping to a low, menacing growl. "Are you fucking crying?"

An ice storm coalesces in my chest, slicking through my veins. I blink, glancing at Miriam, who appears just as shocked at our brother's reaction.

"Uhh . . . no?"

"Don't lie to me," he snaps. "Yes, you are. Your eyes are wet. Who the hell made you cry? Name." An unholy smile spreads across his face. "Address."

"Oh *shit*," Miriam whispers.

"Zora." Levi slaps his hand on the desktop. "What's his name? Because I'm assuming it's a man. And I don't need the details—matter of fact, I prefer not to have the details—but if someone fucked with my sister, he's going to get fucked with right back."

"Cyrus Hart."

I jerk my head to my sister. "Miriam!"

She shrugs. "What? I like this thug-a-licious version of Levi. And Cyrus needs his ass beat for breaking your heart," she says, her expression and voice suddenly devoid of humor.

"He didn't break my heart."

She cocks her head. "Didn't he, though? Why else are you working yourself to the point of exhaustion since you came back from that retreat? If he didn't hurt you, if you didn't do the most foolish thing in the world and fall in love with that man, then you wouldn't have slept in your office these past two nights so you didn't have to go home."

I've said it before, and I'll say it again. Sometimes I hate having a genius for a sister.

"What happened?" she gently demands.

As if her question unlocks the tightly sealed door inside me, it squeaks open, and the events of the retreat pour out. I don't leave anything out, and Levi and Miriam sit and quietly listen through it all. By the time I finish, I'm exhausted. And tears trail down my cheeks.

And about ten pounds have lifted off my soul.

"This is my fault," Levi flatly states in the silence.

"What?" I frown. Where in the hell did that come from? "Levi, what—"

"It is." He meets my gaze, and his eyes are solemn and heavy with his usual seriousness, but there's a weariness and regret there that I've never witnessed on him. In him. "I'm your older brother. Both of you. It's my job to protect you, not the other way around. But I didn't. Not from Mom and Dad. Not from those assholes you dated. And not even from yourself."

"Levi . . ."

"No, Zora." He leans forward, his elbows on his knees, pinning me with his dark eyes. "I checked out, and I did it young because of Dad. But I abandoned you and Miriam. I let you be our go-between because you were good at it, but at what cost? From what you just told us about this Cyrus, even though I still want to fuck him up, you didn't trust him to see and accept the real you. And that's because the very people who should see and accept the real you because it's in their fucking job description don't. How could you believe he would accept BURNED when our parents ridicule it? I'm not making excuses for you, because you didn't even really give this man a fair shot. You never trusted him. Not really. But hell, I get why."

He bends his head, stares at his balled fist.

"Still, you can't let them rob you of a future with him if that's what you want. The question is—is that what you want?"

"It doesn't matter what I want," I murmur. "I betrayed Cyrus. There are some things he can't forgive."

Miriam snorts. "That's bullshit. And you didn't answer the question. A future with him. Is that what you want?"

Is it?

Levi's words resonate deep inside me, and I close my eyes. I did self-sabotage my relationship with Cyrus. Not intentionally, but subconsciously? As a way of protecting myself from any more rejection, criticism, and pain? Yes. Because if I'd truly trusted he would love me—the real me—then I wouldn't have hidden from him. I wouldn't have lied.

So many regrets. God, I'm sinking in them like quicksand, and I don't know if my head will ever break the surface again.

And yet . . .

Yet I would turn back the hands of time to have another chance.

To be honest.

To start over on solid ground.

To have a future with him.

Because I love him.

"Yes," I whisper. "I want that."

"Well then, heffa." She slaps her hands on her thighs and shoots up from her seat. "Why are we still sitting here? What're we going to do to get your man back?"

"Nothing."

She slaps her hands on her hips and glares down at me.

"What the hell you mean, *nothing*?" she demands.

I shake my head. "I stole his choice for weeks by lying to him. Every day I spent with him and withheld the truth, I stole from him."

"One thing I can't abide is a liar and a thief. And to me, they're one and the same."

"I'm going to send him a letter apologizing and explaining my actions. But if he decides not to forgive me, that's his decision. And I'll have to respect it."

Miriam drops back into her chair, loosing a sound of disgust.

"That noble shit is for the birds." Glaring at me, she snatches one of the spoons off my desk and grabs the ice cream. "We're still eating this, though." She cuts a look at Levi. "You too, lil Levi."

I laugh, picking up my own spoon.

Out of all of this, at least I have my family.

They will always have my back.

And if all else fails, that's enough.

CHAPTER EIGHTEEN

CYRUS

"Bruh, you know I love you like the brother my father had with his side chick, but—and I mean this with my whole chest—you are a raging dick."

I stand up from the couch in my den, sighing, facing Jordan.

"Give me my key," I grind out through gritted teeth, holding out my hand.

Jordan snorts. "It's an emergency set, right? Well, bruh, when you see your boy fucking up, it's a motherfucking emergency."

I lower my arm to my side, curling my hand into a fist.

"Miriam."

"Hell yeah, Miriam." He nods, crossing his arms over his chest. His gaze narrows on me. "But what I don't get is it's been a week. Why is the first time I'm hearing about all of this from Miriam instead of you?"

"Because there's nothing to say."

Yeah, the more I keep telling myself that, eventually it might become true. I stalk over to the bar and pull out a beer. I don't bother offering one to him because he doesn't drink during training or the season.

After twisting off the top, I ignore his frown and tip the bottle to my mouth, downing the cold brew. But like the last few days, all the alcohol does is serve as a distraction; it doesn't make me forget her.

Doesn't bring me oblivion. Doesn't offer me a reprieve from the sight of the pain on her face as all of her deceptions were revealed. Doesn't make her less of a liar and a betrayer. Doesn't make me feel less used or like less of a fool.

Doesn't evict her from my fucking head.

"Oh, this is productive," Jordan says. Sarcasm duly noted. Heaving a sigh, Jordan leans back against the pillar. "Look, Cyrus, I know she—"

"I don't want to talk about it. I don't want to talk about *her*," I snap.

"Tough shit. You're going to," he snaps back. "Miriam said Zora sent you an email; have you read it?"

"No."

I saw it come through. And God, the urge to read it had been so strong I'd had to physically throw my damn phone across the room. But what can she say to me? She made a fool of me. Val fucking paid her to break up with me. Instead of coming clean with me the first time we met afterward, she let me go on and on, making assumptions. And she'd never corrected me. Through all the time we'd spent together, she'd had plenty of time to tell me the truth, but she hadn't.

Not true.

"You don't need to tell me anything. And I don't want to hear it or know it."

The night we had sex the first time, she'd tried to tell me about her job, but I'd cut her off. I shake my head at that whispered admonishment. I'm still not buying it. Even afterward, Zora had opportunities to come clean, and she'd chosen to remain silent.

No matter what's in that email, how could I ever trust her again? No matter how my whole goddamn body hurts like an open wound because all of me misses her?

I blame her for that too.

"You know, martyr isn't your color."

I jerk my head toward Jordan, and if glaring a hole through someone was possible, I would be staring at my gaming station through his chest.

"What?"

"When I say Miriam told me everything, I mean she told me *everything*." He arches an eyebrow. "Yeah, you're the most injured party in this, but, bruh. You and your stupid-as-fuck fake-relationship arrangement along with the 'Don't ever lie to me' stipulation. And you didn't outright say you'd tell Val about Zora but didn't deny you wouldn't. You basically cultivated a 'Don't ask, don't tell' environment with Zora where she didn't feel she could be honest with you. Her brother and sister own two-thirds of her business. She was protecting them with her silence. Which you would know if you read the damn email."

Guilt slams into me.

After downing the rest of my beer, I throw the empty bottle in the trash. "Yeah, maybe that wasn't my brightest idea. And yeah, I own some of this, but at some point, shouldn't she have known I wouldn't have hurt her? Shouldn't she have trusted me?"

"I'll give you that you trusted Zora more than you do most people you meet. But, Cyrus, don't kid yourself. You were only willing to give her so much of yourself. As long as she remained in the box you carved out for her and didn't interfere with that damn plan of yours, you were willing to give her that trust. As long as you could remain in control. But she threatened both, didn't she? You were already discovering you couldn't fit Zora in your five-year plan. That she was screwing with it. So whether Val showed up or not, whether you discovered Zora's secret or not, you were going to do just what you did—find a reason to cut bait and run."

I stare at Jordan, robbed of speech. My very body wants to reject his words. A dense silence falls between us, but inside my head? It's a cacophonous circus of thoughts, objections, and screams. I can't even hear my heartbeat underneath the noise, although I'm sure it's there. I'm still standing, still breathing, after all.

"Which one of you two is Cyrus Hart?"

Both Jordan and I whip around toward the staircase that leads to the upper level. A tall wide-shouldered Black man dressed in a slim-fitting black wool suit stands at the foot of the stairs. Even though he is a stranger—although he seems familiar—he doesn't seem the least bit uncomfortable about being in my house. Uninvited.

"Who the hell are you?" I growl.

He arches both of his eyebrows, sliding his hands into the front pockets of his dress pants. "I'm going to assume you're Cyrus, then. Good." He glances at Jordan. "No offense. But if I have to kick someone's ass, I know I can't take you. You're a goddamn giant. I have a fighting chance with him." He jerks his head toward me.

I pull my phone from my pocket. "I'm calling the police now."

"Yes, do that." He waves a hand toward me. "When I drove over here, I was prepared to go to jail for my sister." A smile slowly spreads across his face, and it's unnerving as hell. "I'm looking forward to the why."

My sister.

Holy shit.

"Levi?" I hesitantly ask.

He nods.

Jordan strides forward, his hand extended. "Hey, bruh. It's good to finally meet you. Miriam talks about you all the time. Jordan Ransom."

Levi shakes Jordan's hand, scanning him up and down. "Are you and Miriam sleeping together? Or am I supposed to pretend not to know about it?"

"Nah, we're just friends."

Levi snorts. "Okay." He returns his attention to me. "You really should lock your front door. I was expecting having to either push or con my way in, but walking right in? That must be rich-white-people shit, huh?"

Jordan snickers, and the deadpan delivery of that has me choking back a laugh too.

"No, just questionable choice in friends."

"Low blow, man," Jordan mumbles.

"Well, as nice as this is," Levi says—and if not for my imminent ass beating that I glimpse in his gaze, I might actually like him—"I have some words for you before I fuck you up for making my sister cry."

"Ooh, Levi, bruh," Jordan pseudo whispers. "Never tell the other guy that he made a woman cry. Breaks the sister-brother code."

Levi looks at Jordan and in all seriousness says, "There's no manual to this shit. There really needs to be."

Jordan shrugs. "I have tons of female cousins. I know these things."

Turning back to me, Levi crosses his arms. "Ignore that part about the crying. But getting back to what I have to say . . . Zora fucked up. She knows she did. And she's beating herself up over it. She's willing to step back from you and sacrifice her own happiness; that's how much she cares about you and is willing to make this right. Which you'd know if you'd read the damn email." His lips curl in a derisive smile. "Yeah, I heard that part. But as much as she messed up, so did all of us. And I do mean *all* of us. We failed her. I didn't stand in the gap for her with our parents. Miriam has allowed Zora to protect her for too long. You didn't offer her a safe space to be honest. And you can come up with as many reasons as you want to vilify her, but you didn't provide that for Zora. Own it, just as I'm owning my shit. If you care for her even a little bit, love her, then you'll decide that forgiving her and loving her is more important than being mad and alone. Now." He slides out of his suit jacket, almost lovingly folds it, and lays it over the arm of a chair. "Let's get this over with."

Oh yeah, I definitely like him.

I snag open the refrigerator door and pull out another beer. And hold it out to him.

"Would you like a beer first?"

Levi stares at the beer, and if possible, his lips curl into a deeper sneer.

"Please. Do you have Macallan?"

"Of course."

"Double. Neat."

Jordan laughs. "Holy *shit*. Is it me, or does anyone else feel a bromance growing?"

Levi eyes me as I pour his drink.

"That depends. What're you going to do about my sister?"

I replace the stopper on the decanter of whiskey and hand him the tumbler.

"I love Zora."

To me that explains everything.

Somewhere between Jordan's come-to-Jesus talk and Levi yanking a knot in my ass, I'd already admitted to myself that I loved her. This past week without her—not hearing her voice, not seeing her smile, not inhaling her scent, not feeling her curves against my body, not being inside her—has been hell. But I've been too caught up in my hurt feelings to see her side of this. To understand her fear. To view my part in it.

And in the end, none of it matters. Not one fucking bit of it. Because it comes down to one thing.

I'd rather have her than my plan.

All these years, I've been working to fulfill this vision, this future, that my parents would be proud of, that they deserved. When all they would've wanted for me was what they had—happiness, family, and love.

They would've wanted Zora for me, of this I have zero doubts.

I don't need to read her email.

I forgive her unconditionally, no strings.

And I love her more.

"I guess that means I won't be kicking your ass." Levi sniffs his whiskey and nods. "Good. Because it's hell getting blood out of these suits. And friends with good whiskey is better any day."

Jordan laughs and throws an arm around Levi's shoulders, and though the other man stiffens, he doesn't shake it off.

Oh yeah, bromance in the making.

But first, I have a woman to win back.

If I'm not too late.

CHAPTER NINETEEN

ZORA

I stare at my inbox.

And stare. As if willing it to give up its secrets. Or just one of them. And that's if Cyrus has read and replied to my email. But, of course, I know the answer.

No and no.

Anger flashes inside me like a struck match. He didn't even bother to read my email yet. Sure, he could be very busy at work and hasn't had the opportunity yet . . . and that's bullshit. Cyrus just doesn't want to have anything to do with me. Not even in email form.

"Too soon," I whisper, shuffling the pen on my desk from one side of the keyboard to the other. Needing to give my hands *anything* to do. "It's just too soon for him to hear from me."

If he ever wants to hear from me. That's possible. And if it is true, I'll have to be okay with it.

No, I *will* be okay.

If all of this has taught me anything, it's I have work to do—on myself. As Levi pointed out, I do have trust issues that stem from an emotionally chaotic childhood. Whether it's Cyrus or someone else, I will enter my next relationship healthy and from a place of strength. I've already scheduled my first appointment with a counselor.

And I've resigned my position of family peacemaker.

I inhale a deep breath, flattening my hands on top of my pants-covered thighs.

Yes, I'm going to be more than okay. I will be fine.

A quick rap on my office door is the only warning I receive before Miriam opens the door and sticks her head in the opening.

"You ready? Our client is here."

I roll away from my desk and stand. After grabbing my suit jacket off the back of my chair, I slip it on.

"I'm ready. But I still don't understand why both of us have to sit in on this meeting. You could've handled it just fine."

Miriam shrugs a shoulder. "Don't I know it. Especially since I came up with this new package I'm dying to try out. Picture this. You know how they have the kiss cam at games? Why not the breakup cam?"

She spreads jazz hands out in front of her, grinning.

I cross my arms. "So basically broadcast the breakup with thousands of their nearest and dearest closest friends?"

Miriam drops her arms and purses her mouth. "The idea could use a little tinkering."

Snorting, I move past her into the hall. "Just a little."

We walk toward the lobby, and just before we reach the end of the hallway, Miriam reaches out and captures my hand. Startled, I stutter-step, glancing down at our clasped hands, then looking at her.

Concerned, I frown. "Are you okay?"

She squeezes my fingers.

"Yes." She smiles at me. "I love you, and you deserve all the good things."

"I love you too," I say, returning the smile but confused. "And thanks. What's going on?"

"Nothing. And everything." She grins wide and strides out into the lobby.

Shaking my head, I follow . . . and draw up short.

Shock takes a sledgehammer to my chest and slams the air from my lungs. The power of the blow ricochets through every one of my limbs, rendering me motionless. But anger, fear, joy—those emotions stream through me unchecked and so violent that my head lightens.

No.

Hell no, you will not faint.

I lock my knees and fist my hands, the bite of nail into soft flesh grounding me.

And I need to be grounded, to be present, when facing the man who broke my heart.

"Hello, Zora," Cyrus says, standing in my lobby, as if it's an ordinary weekday and the last time he saw me, he hadn't sent me home alone from a luxury resort.

At least he'd paid for first class on my trip back.

"Cyrus." It's a small thing, but I'm proud that my voice doesn't tremble or, worse, break. "What're you doing here?"

"We were in the neighborhood," Jordan chimes in.

Wow. I'd been so absorbed with Cyrus that I hadn't noticed the basketball player behind him. And that's saying something since his head damn near grazes the ceiling.

"Hi, Jordan," I greet him, and my confusion grows.

Why is Cyrus, much less his best friend, here? What is going on?

To my left, I catch a whispered, "Is that Jordan Ransom?"

Oh great. Miriam neglected to tell me we have *real* clients in the lobby. I turn to Miriam to ask if she can show our clients to her office when Levi strolls into the lobby. Panic screams inside my head like a tornado siren. *Oh shit.* He can't know Cyrus's identity. I mean, he'd threatened the man. I have to get Cyrus out of here—

"It's about time you got here. You're an attorney. Isn't it your job to be places on time?" Levi drawls.

Cyrus dips his head in Jordan's direction. "His fault. He insisted on tagging along. And on me picking him up."

Levi sighs. "If neediness is going to be part of this bromance, I might have to rethink—"

"What in. The actual. *Hell*. Is going on here?" I grind out.

I've entered the fucking twilight zone. It's the only explanation for why Cyrus is in my place of business, clients are fangirling over Jordan, and Levi is apparently besties with the enemy.

Cyrus smiles at me. And it's a full, honest-to-God smile, not just one of those lip quirks or smirks.

It doesn't ease the dread eddying inside me at all. If anything, it sets it swirling and banging against my bones, rattling them.

"I received your email," he says.

Oh. That explains his presence here. Certainly not everything else, but at least one thing. I inhale, my shoulders relaxing a fraction.

"So you read it."

"No, I didn't."

Okay, I'm back to *what the actual hell*.

"Cyrus." I pinch the bridge of my nose. "What are you doing here?" I ask again, and this time, I don't even try to keep the weariness from my voice.

After not seeing him for over a week, being with him for just these few minutes is almost too overwhelming. I want to run to him, throw my arms around his waist, and hold him. I want to be held by him. I want to kiss him, taste him. I just . . . want. So much.

And I can't have any of that. So yes, I'm tired and overwhelmed with the intensity and power of him.

It'd be a kindness if he'd say whatever it is he came here to get off his chest and go so I can start the process of getting over him.

Good luck with that, ma'am.

I can't even argue with my bitchy conscience.

"I'm here for you, Zora Nelson. Because I love you. And after finally getting my head out of my ass, I've come to tell you that and am hoping it's not too late."

I blink.

I'm imagining this. It was bound to happen. Craving something so much, I've cracked, and now my mind has created an alternate universe where Cyrus is uttering all the words I've desired to hear. I've officially gone round the bend.

"I think we've lost her," Miriam stage-whispers.

"Do you mind?" I snap over my shoulder at her, although, damn, she's not all the way wrong. But must she point it out?

Returning to Cyrus, I shake my head, clearing it. "Cyrus, I don't know what's going on here, but . . ."

"I know this is surprising."

"Surprising?" I huff out a serrated laugh that abrades my throat, throwing my hands in the air. "Cyrus, I *betrayed* you. You said you can't stand liars or thieves. Because of my lie, I embarrassed you in front of your colleagues and might've cost you a partnership." And then I ask the question I'd been afraid to in the email. The one that has been torturing me with guilt. "Did you lose your chance at the partnership?"

"I don't know. I'm no longer with Ryson, Dare, and Gregerson."

I gasp. Rage propels me forward several steps, and I'm damn near shaking. "Those bastards fired you?" I demand.

His smile—that real, whole smile—makes another appearance. He really needs to quit doing that.

"No, I quit. It was either destroy employee morale by putting my hands on Derrick every time we saw each other in the halls or leave. Not to mention, I had to acknowledge the culture there wasn't one I'd ever been entirely comfortable with. So I'm opening my own firm."

"And I'm his first client," Jordan boasted, grinning. "But not his last. Not once I tell all my boys about how he'll do right by them and to get their asses to his firm."

This seems to be a morning for surprises. Delight for him bubbles up within me.

"I'm happy for you, Cyrus," I say. "I really am."

"It's different from the plan I've always had laid out for myself, but I've discovered lately that change isn't necessarily negative. It can be the best thing that's happened to my life," he murmurs. "You weren't in my plans, Zora. I could've never seen you coming. But I was prepared. My parents prepared me for you. To be your protector when you need it. Your safe place to land. Your friend. As has been pointed out to me recently, I've failed you on those fronts."

"What?" My chin jerks back. "No—"

"Yes, Zora, I have. Let's go ahead and get this out of the way. You lied to me. You had your reasons. I don't give a fuck about those reasons. I forgive you, and that's unconditional, no conditions. In the end, I didn't read your email because your reasons didn't matter. They wouldn't change the fact that I love you and forgive you. And I ask the same of you. Please forgive me for not being there for you like you needed me. I promise to do everything in my power to earn your trust in the future. Because, baby, I want a future with you. I'm throwing out my plans and asking you to write new ones with me. Because if they don't include you, they're not worth having. Not worth building."

Someone pinch me. No, don't pinch me! If this is a dream, I don't want to wake up.

But then, Cyrus is reaching out, he's cupping my face, and I'm turning into his palm, kissing it. And his singular cedar-and-leather flavor hits my lips.

No, this isn't a dream. It's real. And it's mine.

He's mine.

"Out of all the deals I've made in my life, the one with you was the most important, the one that mattered the most. Because it gave me you. I love you, Zora."

Blue fire leaps in his eyes at his declaration. Desire, yes, but love. Pure love. And joy.

"There's nothing to forgive," I continue. "But if you need the words, then yes. I forgive you too, and you're still one of the best men I know. And just so you know, I have to say 'one of' because Levi's standing behind me."

"That's fucked up," my brother drawls.

Laughing, Cyrus tugs me into his arms, and I fly into them. They're where I've wanted to be since entering the lobby. He lowers his head, finally, *finally* taking my mouth, and dimly, I'm aware of cheers erupting around us.

He lifts his head, ignoring the pounding to his shoulder. We both ignore the whispered, "Do you think we can get a selfie with Jordan Ransom?"

"Thank you for dumping me by proxy, Zora," he murmurs against my lips.

"Thank you for stepping in and saving me from Richard the Dick."

He arches an eyebrow, laughter gleaming in his beautiful blue eyes.

"I thought you didn't need saving."

I shrug. "I see it as us saving each other."

Cradling my face in his big palms, he tips my head back and brushes an almost reverent kiss over my lips.

"I wouldn't have it any other way. Forever."

ACKNOWLEDGMENTS

Thank you to my Heavenly Father, who continues to bless me with creativity, words, and stories. I couldn't do any of this without you. But more importantly, I wouldn't want to.

To Gary. Thank you for being my rock and for always believing that I'm great. Shoot, you believed it when I had a hard time seeing it myself. I love you, and I wouldn't want to walk this journey with anyone else but you.

To Dahlia Rose, my writing partner in crime. Thank you for pushing me, writing with me, encouraging me, and being one helluva friend. There were times I didn't know if I would see the end of another book, and you wouldn't hear of it. You got in the trenches with me and dragged words out of me. Thank you, woman, and I love you!

To Alexa Martin. Thank you for not just being a wonderful writer but for schooling me on the city of Denver. You didn't have to offer your time to me, but you did, so graciously and patiently answering my questions. You're a shining example of why the romance community is special.

To Lauren Plude. Thank you for taking me on as an author and for being as excited about my book as I am! You've helped make my story stronger and more solid, and I don't have the words to express my gratefulness. Also, I want to thank you for your patience and compassion.

You didn't have to give that to me, but you did, and that means a ton to me.

A huge thank-you to my fabulous agent, Rachel Brooks. You've taken my dreams and vision, mapped out a path, and then set my feet on that road to accomplish them. Sometimes this business can be a solitary one, but I know you've always had my back as my champion and advocate. Thank you for being the best. As the Rev says, "We have God, and we have Rachel!" LOL!

ABOUT THE AUTHOR

Photo © 2019 Poetic Images Photography / Avery Carter

Published since 2009, *USA Today* bestselling author Naima Simone loves writing sizzling romances with heart, a touch of humor, and snark. Her books have been featured in the *Washington Post* and *Entertainment Weekly* and have been described as balancing "crackling, electric love scenes with exquisitely rendered characters caught in emotional turmoil."

She is wife to Superman—or his non-Kryptonian, less-bulletproof equivalent—and mother to the most awesome kids ever. They all live in perfect, sometimes domestically challenged bliss in the southern United States.